# Conquest

# By

# Concept

# Books By Duncan Smith

The Vortex Winder

The Maelstrom Ascendant

Cultown

The Tightarse Tuesday Book Club

The Vast and the Spurious

Hammer and Heat

# Music Albums

Waves Upon Waves

Vortex Winder

The Maelstrom Ascendant

Cultown

**Website – www.vortexwinder.com**

# Conquest By Concept

**Duncan Smith**

Alfadex Books

Published by Alfadex Books, Sydney, 2020.


A CIP catalogue record for this book is available from the
National Library of Australia.
ISBN 978-0-9872228-8-6

1. Fiction 2. Politics 3. Culture War.

Alfadex Books orders and information
email: matthew.alfadex@gmail.com

www.vortexwinder.com

# Introduction

Trump, Brexit, Antifa, Black Lives Matter, the far-right, far-left, refugees, fake news, feminism, men's rights, trans rights, race riots, climate change.

We live in times of anger and strife. This is bad for society but good for a novelist. Conflict makes good drama. This is a novel about the 'culture war,' the bitter fight between the political left and right.

The book takes on some controversial topics. It would be a waste of time if it didn't. One of the topics is race and racism. A decade ago it didn't interest me, but now it's impossible to read the news without hearing about it. That's even more so now, in late 2020, than when I began writing this book last year. At the time of writing, there have been three months of race riots in some American cities.

While this and other culture war topics are serious, there's still time to have a few laughs along the way. I once tried to write a fully serious book, with no jokes. Five minutes later, I gave up and went back to my normal style.


Duncan Smith
October, 2020.

# 1
# Meditation Made Me a Fascist

If you want to conquer evil, you have to understand it. To understand it, you may need to become it. When you become it, you may learn that evil was something different all along.

So, to the tale of how I became a 'fascist.' That's a joke, by the way. I'm not a fascist, even if that's what the Antifa called me when he tried to knock me out. Everyone seems to have gone mad these days. It's now normal for complete strangers to attack each other in the street. I'm going to explain how we reached this point, or at least my own part in it.

For me, it all began that night I went to meditation class. It was a last minute decision to even show up. I hadn't been to the Bronte Buddhist Centre for months. Too busy with work, study, and trying to live in harmony with Angie. That's why a little inner peace was so badly needed. 'You haven't got time to meditate? You haven't got time *not* to meditate.' That's what Dipak, the head Buddhist, used to say. Not that I was a Buddhist myself, I just liked to hang out with them sometimes.

So what started my turn to the dark side? It happened like this. I had dinner with Angie, drove to the centre, and parked my car. Then I meditated, came home, and went to bed. And if that lurid tale doesn't lay bare the slippery slope to evil, nothing will.

Actually it was what happened the next day that did it. I got home mid-afternoon, slumped onto the couch, and heard my phone ring. It was Dipak - and he sounded weird.

'John, we need to, uh, have a chat. Can you drop over for a few minutes?'

'I just got home. What's up?'

'It's a... um... a delicate matter.'

'I can't go out again now. Just tell me over the phone.'

'It's a bit awkward, to be honest.'

Dipak was starting to worry me. Clearly something was a big deal, but I wasn't going to play guessing games. By the way, despite the fancy name, Dipak was a white Australian guy like me. His real name was Steve, but he changed it to Dipak when he became a Buddhist.

I sighed.

'Look,' I said, 'whatever you've got to say, lay it on me.'

'Alright. Is there something you'd like to tell me about... what happened last night?'

'What do you mean?'

'Something you did that may have upset someone?'

Alarmed by his tone, I cast my mind back over the events of the night before, yet with no clue what he was on about. Then again, maybe I *had* done something offensive without realising. It wouldn't be the first time.

'Sorry, I've got no idea what you mean. Just tell me.'

'OK then. Someone at the meeting last night...'

There was a long pause.

'Yes?' I prompted.

'Someone said they saw you... exposing yourself last night during the meditation.'

'I'm sorry. What?'

'Exposing yourself. During the meditation.'

The words finally registered.

'Huh? What the hell are you talking about?'

I'm going to omit the next part of the conversation, as it would be in poor taste to start this story with a stream of profanities. Faced with such a bizarre accusation, you can't really blame me. Still, it can be left out of the current account. Here's a cleaned up version of what was said, and I'll skip forward a bit.

'I can't believe you're taking this seriously, Dipak. Do you really think someone's going to go to the Buddhist centre, sit around in a circle with everyone else, and pull out his penis during the meditation? Do you realise how crazy that sounds?'

'I know.'

'Who would make such an absurd claim anyway?'

'I'm not going to say who it was.'

'So some nut job is allowed to destroy my reputation, and you're going to protect *her*. It *was* a her, wasn't it?'

'I'm not going to reveal her gender.'

'You just did. Jesus Christ!'

'It's a serious allegation and I've a duty of care to protect the victim.'

'*I'm* the victim! I can't believe we're having this conversation. How can you possibly take this seriously?'

'It is odd, John, I'll admit. But why would she make such a story up? What would be her motivation?'

'I don't know. I'm not a psychiatrist. It must be this Me Too mania. I mean, of course I support the fight against sexual harassment. Who wouldn't? But if this is what it's come to, it's turned into a damned witch hunt - and I ain't no witch.'

'I believe you, John. At least I want to. Look, can you think of anything that might have caused this person to make a mistake? Something she may have misinterpreted?'

The events of the previous night flashed before my eyes, like in one of those near-death-experiences you hear about. There I was hurrying to finish dinner with Ange. Then I pulled a pair of long trousers out of the wardrobe, squeezed into them, and drove to the centre.

I like to meditate sitting up, and I remembered putting a chair in the circle, moving one of the red yoga mats aside to make room. Soon after, a young woman I didn't know came back from the bathroom and sat down on the mat I'd moved. She'd seemed to frown a little, which seemed of no account at the time.

As Dipak began leading the meditation, we tried to get comfortable so we could sit still for forty-five minutes. I'd found it harder than usual, realising as I struggled that I'd put on a couple of kilos since last year and the trousers were a bit snug. It's harder to lose weight in your thirties. In search of a comfortable posture, I'd undone the top button and loosened the zipper... by about one centimetre. Two at most.

No. Surely it can't have been that. Then again, what else could it be?

The flashback continued. The aftermath when Dipak went round the circle 'checking in' with everyone about how their meditation was. I'd said mine was fine! Then the girl who'd given me the stink eye when I moved her mat had declined to comment. There was a sort of weird vibe when she said it. Yes - it was definitely her who made the complaint.

I returned to the phone call.

'Look, Dipak. I think I know what happened. I haven't been in for a few months, right? You might have noticed I've put on a little weight.'

'Well... er... maybe a little.'

'So my pants were a bit tight and I undid the button and put the zipper down a centimetre. But how did this nut job turn that into me *exposing myself*? What the fuck, man!'

I would never normally have sworn while talking to a spiritual man like Dipak, but I was rattled.

'I know who it was too,' I said.

'I'm not going to say who it was,' Dipak replied.

'It was the girl on my left.'

'All I know is she was extremely upset. She came up to me after the meditation almost in tears.'

'Call me heartless,' I said, 'but I don't feel a great deal of sympathy. I mean, I go in there for a little peace of mind and this happens! It's outrageous.'

'Look, John, leave it with me. I'm going to have a word to the person who made the complaint. See if she might agree she could have been mistaken.'

'Sure, Dipak. You do that.'

I hung up and swore loudly. Then I texted Angie, 'You won't BELIEVE what just happened!' Still seething in righteous indignation, I was about to call her.

Then stopped.

My mind flew back to our conversation from last month during the Ford-Kavanaugh sexual assault case in America.

Some judge named Brett Kavanaugh had been chosen to head the US Supreme Court. Then a woman, Christine Blasey Ford, made an accusation he'd assaulted her at a party thirty years before, when they were both teenagers. Kavanaugh was President Trump's pick for the Supreme Court, and some said Blasey Ford's action was a political stunt to get at Trump. Others said it was a scandal that a possible rapist could be given the highest legal job in America. So, was Kavanaugh guilty? There was no real evidence either way. It was just another he-said-she-said.

The case was a big deal, especially with the recent Me Too craze about women being sexually assaulted by men in power. Even here in Australia it was all over the news. Angie and I were sitting there watching it on TV one night. Blasey Ford, a middle-aged blonde academic, was in the witness stand wearing her fragile, brave survivor look. Later it was Kavanaugh's turn, his dignified features tarnished by anger under cross examination. I had my hand in the small of Angie's back, and felt her body tense up when Kavanaugh appeared.

'Look at that jerk,' said Angie. 'Sorry, frat boy. You don't get to be supreme justice if you abuse women.'

Angie is Australian but has picked up American terms like 'frat boy.'

'You think he's guilty?' I said.

'Look at him. He's just the type.'

I stared at the TV and saw a middle aged white man. He could have been my dad - and I mean that in the same way Obama said Trayvon Martin could have been his son.

'What about Ford?' I said. 'What's her type?'

'She's one of us. All of us,' said Angie. She raised her voice and addressed the TV directly. 'We believe you, Chrissie!'

Angie stood up, as if roused to action. Even angry, she was still gorgeous. Petite, pretty, with short dark hair. She turned to look at me, waggling her finger like an enraged pixie who'd caught me stealing her brownies.

'Why is this case still going? He's guilty!'

I hesitated.

'It's probably just the lack of evidence.'

'You can't expect evidence after thirty-five years!'

'I suppose they just want to make sure.'

She stared at me with sudden intensity. 'You believe her, don't you, John?'

As she stood looking down at me, I was overwhelmed by her elfin beauty. I wanted nothing more than to pull her down to simultaneously comfort and ravish her. Yet it was hardly the appropriate time for that.

'Of course!' I replied. 'As a feminist, as a male ally, I believe her. But what if she's made a mistake? Or... or remembers things different to what really happened?'

'Why would Christine make up something like that?'

'I'm not doubting her for a second, but I heard she's a professor at a top university, and she wore a pussy hat in the women's march against Trump.'

'Fuck Trump,' Angie said automatically, in the way some people say 'Bless you' after a sneeze.

'Fuck Trump,' I quickly echoed. 'But maybe there's some agenda there. You know, to get at Trump through Kavanaugh.'

'There's an agenda alright,' Angie said darkly. 'To push back women's rights and ban abortion and contraceptives. They want to send us back to the fifties. Kavanaugh's a Christian, you know.'

'I see.'

'Only a small number of rapes get reported, John. You know why? Because the victims have to go through another ordeal in the courts. It's like a second rape. No woman should have to do that, and it's about time we started believing survivors instead of violating them all over again.'

'Sure. I've got no problem with that. We should always believe women - and any man who's done nothing wrong has got nothing to worry about.'


I jolted back to the present. After this meditation incident, maybe I was Kavanaugh now. Instead of phoning Ange, I went to my laptop and Googled 'false accusations.' The search results were too general, so I tried 'false sex accusations.' This brought up quite a few cases.

I then searched for 'why we should believe women,' which brought up a lot of feminist blogs, yet also a video, which turned out to be some kind of satire about the Ford-Kavanaugh case. To my surprise, it seemed to be mocking women in general, and Ford in particular. As a male ally to feminism, this seemed jarringly misogynistic. Yet after the shock of Dipak's phone call, a part of me was newly receptive to seeing women treated as less than saintly, infallible beings.

A couple of lines in the video stand out, both of them voiced by women. 'Because my inability to get over a two second ass grab from thirty years ago makes me a strong woman,' was one. The other was, 'Because a man's right to due process is far less important than me showing I don't like rape, like, at all.' This was said in a foolish, vacuous tone of voice meant to represent people on social media. I laughed, then looked around guiltily in case anyone had heard me.

My phone beeped. *What's up?* Angie texted.

I was about to text her back when the phone rang. It was Dipak and he sounded relieved.

'John, I've had a chat to the person who made the complaint.'

'Did you tell her what I said?'

'She does allow for the possibility she may have made a mistake.'

'She's not a complete nut job then.'

'You've got to understand, John. Buddhism attracts some people who are deeply troubled, one way or another. Whatever happened last night to trigger this person has got nothing to do with you.'

I felt my anger rise.

'It bloody nearly *did* have something to do with me, though, didn't it? People have had their lives ruined by this sort of thing. I've nearly finished my teacher training. Before you can even teach in schools, you need a police check to prove you can work with children. This rubbish could have ruined my whole career before it even started.'

'I know it's not fair.'

'I mean, look at you, Dipak. You've known me for years, but you were ready to believe her.'

'She was extremely convincing. She seemed so sure.'

'I take it back then - she *is* a complete nut. Anyone who thinks a guy is going to sit around in a meditation circle and pull out his penis needs her head read.'

'We should really try to sympathise. This person has no doubt been abused in the past.'

'What's that got to do with me? Sorry, but I'm not going to be collateral damage to whatever trauma she's been through. Don't expect to see me at meditation for a while. I'm going to stay as far away from this person as possible.'

'I want you to feel welcome back anytime. We want it to be a safe space.'

'If you keep people like her away, it might be.'

After our chat finished, I texted Angie.

*Forget it. Just a mix up. See you when you get home.*

I shuddered and sank back onto the couch, hoping that would be the end of it - and in one way it was, and in another way, it was only the beginning.

# 2
# Angela's Antifa

I got home the next afternoon to find a posse in the living room. For a second I thought they were there for me, but it was just Angie and a few of her student pals.

As usual, I had a sense of being the 'older guy,' barely visible, but given some substance as Angie's boyfriend. I was thirty-five, for Christ's sake. Resisting the urge to greet them with a facetious 'hello fellow kids,' I sat down in an armchair. Some of them were wearing black masks, slipping them on and off their faces as if trying them on for size.

'Why didn't you tell me it was fancy dress?' I said.

The remark drew no response. There was a strangely solemn air to the little gathering.

'Why the long faces?' I persisted. 'Seems more like a wake than a party.'

'Tonight's the Nazi rally,' said Angie. 'I told you ten times already.'

That explained the masks. Angie's Antifa comrades were suiting up for combat. Antifa, the anti-fascist group dedicated to fighting the new wave of right wing extremism.

'Oh yeah - the rally.' I raised a fist. 'Bash the fash.'

Angie gave me a terse look. My jokey tone was only meant to cover social awkwardness, but perhaps it was coming off as mockery. I quickly moved the conversation on.

'Who is it again?'

A young guy in a Che Guevara t-shirt answered. Leon, I think his name was.

'See for yourself,' he said, pointing at the flyers on the coffee table.

I picked up a flyer. It showed a bald, middle aged white man and a beautiful young blonde girl. The words 'Hate Speech is not Free Speech' were printed across the top.

'Stefan Molyneux,' I read out loud. 'And Lauren Southern.'

Angie cast a hateful glance at the images.

'Give me five minutes alone with that Nazi bitch. That's all I ask.'

'Me too!' I nearly said, but remembered just in time the lecture on 'rape culture' Angie hit me with last month. Those sort of old school innuendo jokes were on the nose these days.

Leon took the opportunity to showboat in front of my girlfriend.

'You get her, Ange, and I'll take Molyneux. If only the pussies didn't hide behind security. They wouldn't even say where their rally was 'til an hour ago.'

'Then how can people attend? I asked.

'They keep the venue a secret 'til the last minute,' Leon replied. 'Shows how tough they are.'

'What are they afraid of?' I said, rather surprised.

'Us,' said a blue haired waif, who looked about sixteen. 'They want to deny us our free speech to protest their event. Typical fascists.'

I hesitated to reply. The girl, Nina, was one of Angie's best friends. She was tougher than she looked and had a fiery temper.

'I suppose they've got a point,' I said slowly, 'if you're trying to shut them down.'

'They shouldn't be here in the first place,' Nina snapped. 'New Zealand kicked them out, why can't we? If only we had a strong leader like Jacinda Ardern instead of the pathetic racist government we've got here.'

I picked up the flyer and scrutinized it.

'So they're Nazis, are they?' I said. 'What have these people done?'

Angie snorted.

'What *haven't* they done? They're Islamophobic, misogynist, racist. Did you see what Lauren Southern was wearing when she got off the plane? An *It's OK to be white* t-shirt. Disgusting.'

I stared at her blankly for a moment.

'Er... yeah. So what are you guys gonna do?'

'We'll meet up in town with everyone else, then stalk the venue and call out the lowlifes going inside. A few of us have got tickets to get in so we can really fuck those guys up. Anyhow, you're coming, aren't you?'

Angie stared at me with those big brown eyes. I looked away.

'I would but I've got that assignment due Monday.'

'Do it tomorrow. This is important.'

I paused. Staying in good with Ange was always a priority. I was still dreading the thought of her hearing about what happened at meditation, even though I was innocent. Better not push my luck. Besides, there was no way I could knock her back in front of her Antifa pals.

'Alright, I'll go.'

Angie took my hand.

'Maybe you can do the movie with Leon.'

'What movie?' I asked.

Angie gave the flyer a withering look.

'The bitch has made some propaganda film about South Africa. Probably wants to bring back apartheid. Can you believe it?'

'How can they?' I said. 'South Africa's majority POC, isn't it?'

POC means *people of colour*, if you don't know.

'Like it always was,' said Angie. 'That's imperialism for you. Ten percent of the population and they think they can run the country. We've got two tickets to the film, so someone has to go in and disrupt it.'

'What do they have to do?'

'Fuck them up, one way or another. Yell out. Get into the projection booth and smash the equipment. Whatever resistance you can come up with.'

I frowned.

'Geez, I don't think I can smash the equipment. Bit extreme, isn't it?'

Angie rolled her eyes.

'Yeah, like apartheid isn't extreme or anything.'

'If I get arrested, that means a criminal record. It might stop me working in schools.'

'For stopping Nazis? That should get you *more* work not less. You *should* be teaching kids to oppose fascism.'

'If I heckle and boo, will that do?'

Angie turned away with a disappointed look. 'You up for it, Leon?'

'Hell yeah. I'm a-gonna punch me some Nazis!'

'There's two tickets so someone has to go with you.'

She looked around the group. A young Somali woman raised her hand.

'Not you, Bilan,' said Angie. 'I don't expect a woman of colour to sit through that white supremacist filth.'

She looked round the room once more, until her eyes settled on me.

'Looks like you're it, John.'

I raised my hands in surrender.

'Fine - but what will the rest of you do?'

'We'll be outside confronting the scum going into the show.'

'Won't they be at the movie?'

'No, that's just a warm up. The main event is Southern and Molyneux giving a lecture about their racist crap. As soon as the film's finished, come and meet us outside and we'll try and stop people going in.'

We picked up the train at Bondi Junction. Angie spent most of the trip texting, probably liaising with other members of Antifa heading to the rally. I spent the trip staring at Ange. It was kind of pathetic, really. I was like one of those teenage girls who writes her boyfriend's name in her diary. *John Gilbert plus Angela Gardiner*. Not that I ever called her Angela, although I might on our wedding day, if that ever happened. Certainly never Angel. She might have punched me. But definitely Ange or Angie, as the mood took me. As she tapped messages into her phone, I sat by her side, staring at her impossibly cute features and dreamy creamy complexion, dark brown hair in a pixie cut, and cherry red lips. Yes, I was definitely one of those pathetic teenage girls.

She caught me, and laughed.

'What are you staring at, you old perve?'

I laughed too, a little too loud. Yes, I was ten years older. So what? It was perfectly normal for a guy to date a younger woman. Ten years was nothing. When she turned forty, I'd only be fifty, and our kids would be in school.

I checked out my own reflection in the train window. Not bad, not bad at all. Not totally tall, dark, and handsome, but at least tallish, darkish, and handsome-ish. Conventional good looks - nothing wrong with that. I'd thought of getting a tattoo, but nah. It would look try-hard. I was a solid 7.5. Good enough. Yeah, Ange was a 9, but so what? It would even out over time. I gazed at our combined reflection. We looked good together, dammit. A handsome couple. Anyone would have thought so.

The sign for Town Hall station appeared.

'Come on, John,' said Ange. 'Let's go.'

We walked the few blocks to Darling Harbour. The first surprise was the size of the venue. The Convention Centre was no shady dive, but a modern glass-fronted building in the centre of town, and on the harbour to boot. Whoever was coming to this meeting, it looked like we weren't dealing with the back street fascists.

'Who knew there were so many Nazis in 2018?' I said to Ange, walking beside me.

The second surprise was the number of cops. There must have been thirty or forty of them spread out around the entrance to the Convention Centre. There were also quite a few Antifa keeping an eye on the joint, clustered in groups a little further back. As for the people attending the event, those who were here for the propaganda film had already begun filing into the venue. Some had their heads down, aware they were under scrutiny. Others strode ahead, wilfully defiant.

Angie's crew had already masked up, but as my brief was to infiltrate the movie, that didn't apply to me. Angie came up and slipped the film ticket into my hand. She gave me a kiss on the lips, and with the romantic exhortation to 'Fuck them up, babe,' sent me on my way.

I joined the back of the line and began walking towards the entrance. As the line progressed, I was suddenly aware that to the watching Antifa, I must now look like one of the enemy. There were many more Antifa present than the handful we'd travelled in with, and most of them didn't know me. Realising this, I turned to the crowd with a cheeky wink as if to tip them off about my true allegiance. When this seemed to inspire a low rumble of anger, I put my head down and hastened through the glass doors and into the venue.

Once inside, I checked out my fellow filmgoers. They were mostly white and male, but with a scattering of women too. We took the escalator up a level to the main auditorium, a spacious arena which could have easily seated a few thousand.

There were only a few hundred here now, although numbers would swell for the speeches to be held after the film.

Leon and I went to opposite sides of the auditorium, working on the theory that yells from each side would create the illusion of a bigger protest. We agreed that half an hour or so into the film, Leon would start chanting slogans, and I would immediately join in from my side, possibly also making an assault on the projection room itself with the hope of stopping the screening. Yet as I settled back in my seat, I decided projector smashing was out of the question. Some loud yelling should be enough to show Ange I'd 'done my bit' to stop the march of white supremacy, after which I'd beat a hasty retreat and rejoin the comrades outside.

The film began and my eye was drawn to the evil Lauren Southern herself. *What a doll*, I thought, before quelling the shameful sexual objectification from my mind. Still, there was no denying her beauty. How could it be that a maiden so fair was infected by the curse of fascism?

Southern started by giving a brief history of South Africa. In truth, she was less arrogant than I'd imagined. I'd expected a smug supremacist. Then again, this was a propaganda film, and no doubt she'd been told to tone it down so as to draw in the gullible.

As for the film itself, it was mainly Southern interviewing local South Africans, mostly whites, and a few token people of colour. Again, I was a little surprised. I'd always had an image of white South Africans as aloof imperialists, yet these people seemed like decent folks. Given that most of them were farmers, this wasn't really a representative sample. And, to be honest, the tale they told *was* a little harrowing.

Southern's film, *Farmlands*, was about the plight of white South African farmers. The claim was that since Nelson Mandela's ANC party came to power in the 1990s, conditions had declined for the white population. Now, with Mandela's relatively benign influence gone since his death, hostility to whites had escalated. Land owned by whites was being reclaimed by force, and even the black government itself seemed on the point of making this legal. More shockingly, there had been several - perhaps many - cases of white South Africans being murdered on their own farms by blacks out to avenge the apartheid years and reclaim the land in the name of justice. Or so the film claimed.

Southern did one interview with a blonde lady farmer who described, in graphic detail, how her own father had been viciously murdered by intruders in the very living room where they were now speaking. All the while I was trying to manage my surprise, telling myself this was nothing but propaganda. Yet the woman seemed authentic. Shortly after, there was another interview, this time with a black government official who said land repossession would soon be a legal right.

I was speculating that Southern had paid some poor wretch from Soweto a few dollars to perform this fictional scene, when there was a commotion on the other side of the theatre. My comrade, Leon, no doubt thinking along the same lines as myself, had risen to his feet and was creating a ruckus with a chant of defiance.

> Fascists, go away
>
> Come again no other day
>
> Hate speech, spreading fear
>
> Nazis are not welcome here

I was about to join in, but was stalled by the chorus of boos from the crowd on Leon's side of the room. Truth be told, I was reluctant to go up against a roomful of racists on my own.

I could make out Leon scuffling with a couple of attendees, and it wasn't long before security seized him and evicted him from the theatre. To his credit, he continued to chant as he was dragged away.

I opened my mouth to take up where he'd left off, then stopped. After what had happened to Leon, what would be the point? Perhaps I could do more good as an observer, assessing the propaganda film and reporting back to Ange later that night. I settled back in my chair.

The rest of the film was a grim tale of a country in danger of falling into civil war. When Mandela had come to power twenty years before, we'd heard talk of a rainbow nation and a new age of racial harmony. If you believed this film, it was nothing of the sort. The white South Africans seemed to hide behind walls, in the city or on their farms, and the murder rate was as high as anywhere in the world. What had happened to Mandela's rainbow nation?

I walked out of the theatre in a pensive mood, intending to meet up with Ange and the rest of the crew. I joined the other filmgoers and began filing out of the building. As we got near the glass exit doors, it was clear the size of the crowd had swelled considerably. People who had showed up to hear Southern and Molyneux speak were milling around near the entrance, and the numbers of Antifa had also risen. The mutual hostility was palpable.

I once read a book called *Legends of the Firm*, about football hooligans. It was a bunch of interviews with members of the 'firms,' as they called their gangs, of which there was one for each football club. Apparently, violence was some kind of bizarre hobby for them. Standard procedure was rival firms setting up some kind of 'gentlemen's agreement' whereby they'd meet up before or after games to beat the crap out of each other. These clashes could be between rogue units of five or ten thugs from each firm, right up to full scale battles with hundreds on either side.

That's what it was like tonight. Antifa was on one side, most of them wearing their anonymous black masks, and the fascists here to attend the meeting were on the other. It seemed about to boil over at any minute.

And it did. Just as I cleared the glass exit doors, fighting broke out some twenty metres to my left, the very direction in which we were moving. I resolved to press on, hoping to meet up with Ange and her crew somewhere among the throng. As it happened, there was little choice due to a surge in the crowd behind me. In a few seconds, I found myself spat out of the line into a little laneway with about five of my fellow filmgoers. As bad luck would have it, the space was filled with ten or fifteen masked Antifa, who immediately set their sights on us.

'There they are!' one of them yelled.

Realizing my predicament, I raised both my hands and my voice.

'Wait! I'm one of you guys!'

A burly, masked Antifa laughed at me.

'Bullshit. I saw you go inside. Let's see you wink now, you fucking Nazi!'

'What! I'm Angie's boyfriend, you fool. She's high up in Antifa. Give me a second and I'll phone her.'

I pulled out my phone and tried to dial Ange, but the Antifa guy knocked it out of my hands with a violent swipe.

'What the hell's wrong with you?' I said, now more angry than afraid. To which he replied - and I'll never forget this -

'What's wrong with *you*, you white cunt?'

On impulse, I reached out and grabbed his mask, ripping it away from his face. He was whiter than an albino's ghost. I looked round the group and saw the skin showing, up above their masks. They all were.

Then it was on. The Antifa dude threw a right hook at me, which I just managed to avoid. The rest of his masked mates joined in, fighting the half dozen filmgoers who'd been spat out of the line with me. The next minute was a chaotic mess of punches, kicks, oaths, and cries of pain. I'm no brawler but was surprised to find that cometh the hour, cometh a capacity for self defence previously unknown. I landed a blow on the face of my assailant, who went down hard. Yet just as I was standing over him in an uneasy haze of triumph, disgust, and adrenaline, I felt a surge of pain from a blow to the back of the head, and my consciousness went out like a light.

# 3
# RP 4a WC

I woke up with a headache and two guys standing over me. There was a tall, gangly fellow, and a thickset stocky one. I made a weak attempt to snap back into fight mode, then realised I was no longer in the street. It looked like some kind of cheap hotel room. I was lying on a tatty old couch at the side of the room.

'Take it easy,' the taller guy said. 'Don't try to get up.'

'What happened?' I said.

'Fucking Antifa,' the stocky one replied. 'Lucky for you our hotel was only a couple of blocks away. You can crash with us, but you'd better stay here. We're going back to the show.'

Realisation dawned.

'So you guys are from the Nazi rally.'

The tall guy laughed.

'The Nazi rally? Yeah, just like you, mate. Are you OK? You were out cold.'

I tried to stand up and winced. The guy put his hand on my shoulder and pushed me gently back down on the couch.

'You'd better sit this one out, old boy.'

A thought occurred to him.

'Hey, give us your ticket. I know someone who needs one. May as well use it.'

I felt a rise of panic. When they found out I had no ticket to the event, my cover could be quickly blown. I sat up and went through the motions of searching my pockets.

'Oh no. I must have dropped it in the fight.'

'Never mind,' he said. 'Come on, Davo, let's go.' He gave me a backwards glance. 'See you later.'

I lay on the couch for a few minutes. When the two Nazis didn't return, I got up and made a cautious inspection of the room. Despite its cheap look, it was quite spacious, almost like a living room. Two single beds on one side; the couch on the other, and a table and chairs in the middle near the door.

The room itself was on the second floor above street level. I looked down and saw traffic and a few pedestrians. I tried the door, half expecting my new friends to have locked it from the outside, but it opened easily onto a hallway and a flight of stairs leading back to the street. I was about to make a hasty exit when it occurred to me I'd have to head back to the rally to meet Ange. Having been knocked out once, going back to a riot wasn't an appealing prospect.

What then - go home? It would look a bit weak if Ange came back and found me home in bed, having bailed out of the fight. Maybe I should stay where I was. Hell, this might even be a happy accident. I'd managed to infiltrate the enemy's camp without even trying. What if I stayed for a while, got talking to them, and found out their plans? Acting as a double agent, I could eavesdrop on their white supremacist talk and win big points with Ange when I reported back to her with the lurid details. If nothing else, it would make a great war story and put Leon's film arrest in the shade.

Then again, facing up to these fascists wasn't very appealing either. If I gave myself away somehow, they could murder me in this room and no one would ever know. To make matters worse, my head was still aching from the blow. I decided to lie down for a few minutes and think it over.

I sank back onto the couch and closed my eyes. I must have dozed off because the next thing I heard was the sound of a key in the door, as the two white supremacists came inside. The taller guy led the way, followed by the stocky one holding a carton of beer. As soon as they were inside, he placed the carton on the floor, relieved at laying his burden down. He tore open the top of the box, took a bottle for himself and handed one to his colleague. Then, catching sight of me, he gave me a bottle too. Not knowing what to do, I sat up and accepted the beer, then took a big swig to settle my nerves.

'How you doing, mate?' said the taller one. 'On the mend?'

'Not bad,' I replied. 'Still got a bit of a headache.'

'I've got some painkillers in my kit.'

He rummaged round in his backpack and pulled out a small plastic bottle. Removing the cap, he tipped a few red pills onto the coffee table. I eyed them suspiciously and took another swig of the beer.

'I shouldn't mix those with alcohol,' I said. 'Could be dangerous.'

'I've done it myself and never had a problem.'

'You sure?' I put my hand to my aching head.

'You'll be fine.'

I sat down at the table with them. Hesitantly, I reached out and took one of the red pills. It was bitter to the taste so I took a big gulp of beer to wash it down. Gradually the room came into sharper focus. I looked at my 'captors' for the first time. The tall gangly fellow seemed to find it hard to fit his body into the table and chairs. He had to twist his limbs slightly to fit. He was pale skinned, dark haired, and a short, straggly beard gave him an unruly look. I guessed his age to be in the mid-forties.

The stocky one was younger, early-thirties, and your classic Aryan blond. Muscled and coarsely handsome, he would have fitted right in at tonight's event.

The tall fellow stretched out his hand.

'I'm Ed. Edward Hall.' He turned to the stocky one. 'And that's Davo.'

'John,' I said. I shook hands with them both, then accepted another beer. They were on the other side of the table; Hall to my left, and Davo on my right, between me and the door.

'Was there any more agro?' I asked.

'Not really,' said Hall. 'A bit of push and shove on the way in, but it had all fizzled out by the time we left.'

I wondered when Angie had gone home and if she was worried about me.

'So how was the... show?'

'Brilliant,' said Davo. 'It's one thing seeing their videos but live was another level. Met him and all.'

He got out his phone to show me a selfie taken with Molyneux.

'Cool!' I said, bunging on the enthusiasm. 'You and Steven, eh.'

Davo looked at me quizzically. 'What?'

'You and Steven Molyneux. Awesome!'

'Steven? What the - ?'

'Stefan. I meant Stefan.' I glanced towards the door, then back to the fascists. 'Sorry. It must be the bang on the head!'

They laughed, but a look passed between them.

'So what did he talk about?' I said, trying to move the discussion forward.

'Oh the usual sort of stuff,' said Hall. 'You know.'

'Of course,' I replied.

'Why do you like him, John?' said Hall. 'What first attracted you to his philosophy?'

'Me?'

I felt my face flushing and hoped it wasn't obvious.

'Yeah, you,' said Davo.

'What attracted *me* to his philosophy?' I said. 'Well, that's pretty obvious.'

'So what was it?' said Hall.

'Probably the same as everyone else, I suppose?'

'But what specifically?'

I took another long drink of beer.

'Well, gee... uh... the white power, I guess. The hatred for political correctness and people of colour. The PC and the POC!'

I laughed a bit too loud. Davo looked sideways at Hall.

'White power?'

Suspecting I'd made some fatal blunder, but having no idea what it was, I tried to change the subject.

'I'm more into Lauren really,' I said. 'That film! I never even knew about South Africa. Who'd have thought the black people of colour were killing the white farmers?'

Hall raised an eyebrow.

'You're an odd one, John. Who the hell says black people of colour?'

'Well, I...'

'Big fan of Lauren Southern, are you?'

'Hell yeah.'

'And Stefan Molyneux.'

'Sure. Who isn't?'

Hall sniggered.

'Our friends in Antifa, for a start. So tell me, John. Apart from Lauren and Stef, what other YouTube speakers do you like?'

'What do you mean?'

'What other rebel philosophers are you into with the same sort of views?'

I readied myself to bolt for the door. I'd have to burst past Davo though, so it might be worth trying to bluff it out one more time.

'Look guys, I'll come clean. I'm a bit of a noob. Stef and Lauren are the only ones I really know. Why don't you give me some tips though? Who else is good?'

Hall sat facing me, arms folded in front.

'Big fan of Lauren are you, John?'

'Fuck yeah!'

'Then answer me this. What do you think of Lauren's plan to round up all non-white illegal immigrants, put them in concentration camps, and gas them if they can't speak English? You agree with that?'

'That's not for me to say,' I parried. 'I'll leave that up to the proper authorities.'

'But do you *agree* with it?' said Hall. 'That's all I want to know.'

I looked over at Davo, in mute appeal.

'Answer the question,' he said calmly.

'Well,' I said. 'If you're going to put me on the spot, I do agree with it. If those boat people come here illegally, it's their own fault if they get gassed.'

'So you agree with Lauren's video on the topic? The one that came out last week that everyone's talking about.'

'Yes, of course. That one I definitely did see.'

Hall looked at Davo.

'That's weird, cos there ain't no such video. Lauren would never say something as ridiculous as that.'

I jumped up and ran for the door. Davo stuck out a leg and tripped me. I went down, skittling a pile of the empty beer bottles stacked on the floor. By the time I regained my feet, Hall was blocking the exit. I tensed my arms and prepared for my second fight of the night.

'Look, you guys,' I said. 'If you want to be Nazis, fine. It's none of my business. Just let me go, alright?'

Hall looked at Davo and laughed.

'You believe this dude? He really thinks we're going to murder him.'

Davo laughed as well, then seemed to recall something.

'Hey, remember what happened just before the fight? John here told the Antifa he was one of them.'

'Is that right?' said Hall. He fixed me with a stern look. 'Sit down, old boy. Better come clean.'

I sat back down at the table.

'Alright, alright. Here's the truth. I'm not really that political. I've never heard of Stefan Molyneux or Lauren Southern before today. I only came because my damn girlfriend is in Antifa.'

'Really?' said Hall. 'Guess she's a feminist then too.'

'Sure.'

'I suppose that makes you a male ally?'

'I support equal rights, if that's what you mean.'

Hall raised his eyebrows.

'I support equal rights too. That doesn't mean I'm a feminist.'

'That's what feminism is all about - equality.'

'That's like saying diversity is our strength.'

'Well, it is, isn't it?'

'So I keep hearing. What's your girl's name?'

I hesitated.

'Angela.'

'Right. So Angela's in Antifa and she's a feminist. So, just a stab in the dark here, John, but does Angela also love globalism, refugees, and thinks Trump is literally Hitler.'

'Well, not *literally*.'

'But close enough. So, is she beautiful too?'

'Beautiful and intelligent.'

Hall was about to reply, but changed his mind. He turned to his friend.

'For Christ's sake get John another beer. Bring the whole six pack!'

I was by now feeling the effects of the alcohol, with the pill having some impact as well. As it seemed the Nazis weren't going to actually kill me, I decided to go with the flow. Hall gave me an appraising look.

'So you're not in Antifa yourself, but you'll go to a protest just to stay in Angela's good books?'

'Well, you know what they say. Happy wife, happy life.'

'You're married?'

'Not yet.'

'Then there's still time. So, to please her, you'll go out and protest something you know nothing about. What do you really think of her politics? Assuming you think at all, that is.'

'Give me some credit,' I replied. 'Anyway, I do agree with her. I was born and raised on the left and voted Labor all my life.'

'And you support her Antifa antics - fighting Nazis and fascists?'

'Well... in principle. If that's what she wants to do.'

Davo spoke up.

'Who are the real Nazis here, John? We just wanted to have a meeting. It was none of your business but you showed up anyway to abuse and attack us. We don't go to left wing meetings and do that. So which of us are the fascists?'

'But you guys are racists. White supremacists.'

'Says who? Your girlfriend? Your dumb Antifa pals? They'll call Lauren and Stefan Nazis, but they'll call *anyone* Nazis. It's ludicrous. And look at you - you don't even know what you're protesting.'

'So you're not racists?'

'No. At least, no more than anyone else.'

'Look John,' said Hall, 'just because you question if diversity is our strength doesn't make you a concist.'

'What are you getting at?'

'Let me ask you this. Multiculturalism was supposed to lead to a social Utopia, right? Everyone living together in perfect harmony. Is that's how it's turned out?'

I paused, unsure how to respond.

'Not yet,' I said at last. 'We just need to give it more time.'

'How long - another few decades? A century? Put it another way: if multiculturalism is such a great idea, why is it all we ever hear about now is race and racism?'

I answered a little recklessly.

'Because of people like you who hate foreigners.'

Hall snorted.

'There you go again with your assumptions. We don't hate anyone.'

'You guys want to stop immigration, don't you?'

'It wouldn't hurt to stop for a while. At least until everyone makes up their minds if we're supposed to be in the post-racial age or not. You can't go a single day without people banging on about racism. That's not how it's supposed to work.'

I remembered what happened earlier that night.

'I've got to admit things are getting weird. Like when I went up against that Antifa.'

Davo laughed.

'I heard what he called you,' he said. 'Another self-hating white person. These kids go to uni and get brainwashed into hating their own kind and the culture they grew up in. How's that going to work out for us long term?'

'Haven't you noticed anything else?' said Hall. 'Something that doesn't add up?'

I paused, then was apparently drunk enough to spill the beans to these extremists.

'Yesterday I got falsely accused... of a sex crime.'

Hall raised his eyebrows.

'Go on,' he said.

'All I did was go to Buddhist meditation.'

'Ah Buddhism, the religion of peace,' said Hall. 'The real one. They don't eat animals.'

'Anyhow, I showed up to meditate. Next thing I know, some nut job's accused me of exposing myself during the meditation.'

'And did you?'

'Of course not!'

'What did Angela say?' asked Davo.

'She never found out. I convinced the Buddhist guy it was a mistake and they dropped the charges.'

I went into further details of the sordid event. At the end of my tale, Hall shook his head.

'Oh dear, that could have been very nasty for you, old boy. You nearly got caught up in this whole Me Too witch hunt.'

'That's what *I* said.'

'I read a blog last week and it said there are three kinds of women making these Me Too claims. First you've got the real victims, which is fair enough. Then you've got the ones who try to turn some trivial incident into something bigger. Finally, there's the kind who use it to get back at men they don't like, or bring them down out of spite.'

'Is there a fourth category?' I said. 'Women who are mentally disturbed and imagine ridiculous things that never happened?'

'Clearly there are, as you now know. Don't forget twenty years ago we had the repressed memories craze. Some psychologists led their patients into thinking they'd been molested as kids and buried the memories. Trouble is, some of the cases were complete fabrications.'

'Is that right?'

There was a pause. Hall seemed lost in thought. He turned to me with a conspiratorial air.

'Well, Johnny, seeing as you've been straight with me, I'm going to be straight with you. Truth is, I used to be just like you. Good hearted, idealistic, a bit naive. Never had an Antifa girlfriend, but not far off. Finally, I wised up, but only by luck. A different fork in the road and I might still be drifting through life a blue pill normie like you. Now seeing as I had help, it's only right I pay it back, and pass on the knowledge to you.'

'What do you mean?'

'Circumstances have brought us together, and you're primed for a change of outlook. In the space of a few days, you've been falsely accused of a sex crime. You've been racially abused by someone as white as yourself. You've gone out to protest an event you know nothing about, and now you're sitting here in casual conversation with so-called Nazis.' Hall laughed. 'If all that ain't enough to prompt a little self questioning, I don't know what is.'

Hall picked up a room service pad from the table, tore off a piece of paper, and handed it to me.

'I'm going to send you some of our alternative media videos.'

'Your fascist propaganda?'

'Just an alternative to the propaganda you get from your usual news sources. So this is your Matrix moment, John. You're going to write down an email address on this piece of paper and give it back to me. If you want to remain a blue pill normie, it's easy. Just write down a false address. But if you want to take the red pill and start to question what you've been told to believe, write your real email address.'

He handed me the paper and looked me in the eye.

'The choice is yours.'

# 4

# Borders and Boarders

'My hero.'

With Angie's arms around me and her cheek against mine, it was easier to give in to her version of events. At first, I'd tried telling the truth - that I'd been assaulted by Antifa and rescued by the 'Nazis' - but it just wasn't getting through.

'I can see how it started,' she said. 'After all, our lot didn't know you were a double agent. But you said you got hit from behind.'

'That was halfway through the fight. I'm not sure which way I was facing.'

'Obviously the Nazis assaulted you and took you back to their base for interrogation.'

She kissed me.

'John, you could have been killed. Are you sure you don't want to go to hospital?'

'It's just a headache.'

'Let me see.'

I sat down on the chair at my desk. Angie stood behind me and caressed the back of my head.

'There's no swelling. How'd you get away? Tell me again.'

'Like I said, they were drinking a lot of beer. After a while, the tall guy nodded off. When the other one went to the toilet, I ran for the door. Lucky they didn't tie those knots too well.'

'Did they interrogate you?'

'Yeah - and tried to make me watch their propaganda videos.'

'Oh God. As if Southern's film wasn't enough! You poor baby. What were they like?'

'Pretty nauseating. White supremacy stuff. I tried to block it out. Tried thinking of you.'

I sighed. Angie's small, strong hand was warm at the back of my neck.

'What you did last night was important, John. Every act of resistance counts, especially with what's happening in America.'

'What is it now?'

I felt Angie's hand tighten a little.

'Trump's putting kids in concentration camps. Innocent families of colour are just trying to cross the border to make a new life and they're getting rounded up by ICE's troops.'

'What's ISIS got to do with it?'

'Not ISIS. ICE. Trump's fascist border security. They're probably *worse* than ISIS. They're separating kids from their parents and locking them up in detention camps.'

'This is the southern border with Mexico, right? The one where he wants to build the wall.'

'Yeah. Those poor refugees from Mexico and South America. All they want is a fresh start but Trump won't let them. Imagine locking kids up.'

'And the parents?'

'They're in camps too. It's obscene. If only there were more like the Red Hen.'

'Huh?'

'It's a restaurant in Virginia. That Nazi whore from the Whitehouse stopped there for dinner. Huckleberry, or whatever her name is. Trump's press secretary. Guess what? When the owner recognised who it was, she came straight out of the kitchen and kicked her out! Entry denied, bitch!'

'Wow.'

'I would've just pissed in her soup or something, but doing it publicly sends Trump a message. Hey, you don't want brown people in the country? We don't want you in our restaurant. No visa for you!'

'You need a visa to go out for dinner now?'

'Oh, you know what I mean. Anyhow, I'm late for class. If you're up when I get home, I'll give you a massage.'

'Don't be late - you're the teacher.'

That was Angie's night job. By day, she was an arts-law student at Sydney University. By night, she was an ESL teacher at a language school. That is, she taught English as a Second Language to immigrants, or 'new Australians' as they used to be called.

After Ange went to work, I sat down to start my own teaching assignment. I was going to be a high school English and History teacher, if I could just get through my last year of training. First I checked my emails, and there it was - a message from Edward Hall. He didn't say much, just posted links to a few of his propaganda videos. Shaking my head at having been dumb enough to give my real email address, I deleted the message at once.

That should have put the matter to bed, yet somehow peace eluded me. Whether it was procrastination against my assignment, or just an itch that needed scratching, I found myself going to my deleted emails list to retrieve the wretched message.

I clicked on the first video he had sent. It was by a woman named Janice Fiamengo discussing a false rape case and the Me Too movement. Clearly Hall thought this would appeal to me after my 'meditation incident.' I did watch the video more closely than I would have a couple of weeks ago.

Even so, the sight of a woman criticising feminism was hard to process, like seeing a Muslim slamming Islam. I'd assumed all women were feminists as a matter of course. To see one voicing not just small doubts - as, say, a clergyman might wonder if the virgin birth was a literal or symbolic truth - but doubting feminism itself, was very odd.

The next video was clearly a piece of racial propaganda, for it seemed to imply doubt about the worth of multiculturalism. *Here we go*, I thought, *here comes the white supremacy.* As everyone knows, the strength of societies lies in their diversity, yet this video was implying it makes them weaker. The speaker even used the racist slogan 'demographics is destiny,' which is the paranoid notion that immigration leads to long term changes in a country's identity.

I would have returned to my assignment, had not a new video followed on automatically. As it featured none other than the comely Lauren Southern, I left it on for purposes of 'research.' Strangely, there was a connection to my past. Southern, as some kind of stunt to stir up Islamophobia, had sought out the most Islamic suburb in Sydney. It was a place called Lakemba - the very suburb where my own father had been born and raised.

I hadn't been to Lakemba in years. Now the memories came back of the simple, depression era house where he'd grown up. His brother - my uncle - had lived in that house his whole life, right up until he was old enough to go into a nursing home.

When I was a boy, our family had visited him in Lakemba from time to time. It's odd how quickly a city can change. On one visit, my uncle had a book with black and white photos of the suburb's past. It showed that Lakemba had begun as an almost rural area on the outskirts of the city, only gradually becoming part of the urban sprawl in the 1950s and 60s. Yet it must have been twenty years ago I'd seen that book. Lakemba had changed again. In today's video, I watched the scantily clad Lauren Southern walking streets that may as well have been from an Islamic city in the Middle East. All this in less than a century.

Somewhat rattled, I went on to the next video Hall had sent. Titled 'White Left' by someone called 'Black Pigeon

Speaks,' the video discussed the *Bái Zuô*, a derisive Chinese term for Westerners on the political left. I was surprised to learn that some Chinese people view white leftists not as noble fighters for justice, but delusional idiots who work against their own interests. I had heard the right wing sneer, 'social justice warriors,' and this *Bái Zuô* must have been the Chinese version.

Strangely, the video did not trigger me to anger as much as a sense of relief, for I found myself in guilty agreement with some of what the chap was saying. After all, when you have to hang out with people like Ange, you get tired of the deadly seriousness with which they take everything, including themselves.

This mood made me receptive to the next video, called 'Dear Virtue Signalling Celebrities,' by Paul Joseph Watson, which slammed mega-rich stars like Lily Allen, George Clooney, and JK Rowling. It seemed they'd made a big song and dance about helping refugees and criticizing those who didn't, while leading lives of luxury themselves. As the speaker pointed out, none of them had taken in any actual refugees. The video was still in my thoughts the next day, as I had breakfast with Ange.

'It's a tough one,' I said over coffee. 'We all want to support the families of colour getting to America, but you still have to house and feed them when they arrive. It must put a strain on the new country.'

Angie sniffed.

'I'm sure America can afford it.'

'As long as there aren't too many at once,' I said. 'Much as I hate Trump, I suppose the border's there to keep it all under control.'

'Borders are racist,' said Angie. 'When we get rid of borders, we'll stop seeing each other as different. When we finally realise we're all the same, there'll be no more fighting.' She paused. 'It'll also save time getting through customs next time we go overseas. We won't even need passports.'

'That's true.'

Angie was global-warming to her theme.

'Borders are about setting up walls between the haves and the have nots. That's why we have wars. Get rid of borders and we'll end war.'

I hesitated, not sure if it was wise to go on.

'I know what you mean about the haves and the have nots,' I said. 'It's like those celebrities who live in gigantic mansions and preach about what *other* people should do for refugees. I heard JK Rowling has seventeen spare bedrooms in one of her mansions. How many refugees did she take in?'

Angie frowned.

'If it was me, I'd definitely take some. I'd buy them a whole house.'

'It's easy for us to say,' I said. 'We'll never be in that position. Maybe we'd be just as much hypocrites as them.'

This seemed to rile Ange.

'I'm no hypocrite,' she said tersely. 'I'm the one teaching them English, right? I'd gladly take in a refugee family.'

I finished my coffee.

'Me too - if only we had somewhere to put them.'

Then, foolishly, I sent Ange the video about the celebrities. What a dud move that was. Not so much because she didn't talk to me for two days - which was bad enough - but for what happened the next time we *did* speak.

She'd gone off to teach her ESL night class as usual. I mooched around at home, wondering when I'd be let out of the doghouse. Sitting in my room, studying, I heard the sound of the key in the lock, then voices. I went to the living room and saw Ange standing with a handsome young Latino guy.

'Ah John,' said Ange. 'This is Mateo.'

I felt a surge of jealous rage at the sight of my girlfriend with another man. I suppressed it and shook hands with him. He smiled and squeezed my hand. He looked about twenty-five, Angie's age. His skin tone was at the lighter end of the spectrum for Latinos, but he still looked South American rather than Nordic European. He had brown hair, thick eyebrows above brown eyes, and a layer of stubble I imagine some women would find attractive.

Sporting an odd expression, Angie explained.

'I owe you an apology.'

That was unexpected. I looked from Ange to Mateo and back again.

'When you sent me that video,' she said, 'I was pissed at first. Like, what have JK Rowling's seventeen spare bedrooms got to do with me?'

'I wasn't having a go at you,' I said. 'I just thought it was funny.'

'But it did get me thinking,' Ange continued. 'The guy had a point. People *should* be doing more for refugees. Not just those celebrities either.'

'Well, *mainly* those celebrities.'

'No - all of us. We've all got white privilege, right? So I'm chatting to Mateo after class and it turns out he's getting evicted and he's got nowhere to go. So I said he can stay here for a bit 'til he finds somewhere better.'

I stared at her blankly for a few seconds.

'Where's he going to sleep?'

'He can crash on the couch. You don't mind, do you, Mateo?'

The recipient of Angie's largesse smiled, showing flashing white teeth.

'And you know the beautiful thing?' Ange continued. 'Mateo's from Chile. At the exact same time Trump's trying to keep people like him out of America, we're opening our doors.'

'Chile!' I said to Mateo. 'You're a long way from home.'

Mateo kept smiling but did not reply.

'What are you doing out here?' I pressed. This caused Ange to step in.

'John, please,' she said. 'This isn't border security. Let the poor guy settle in.'

'I'm just making conversation.'

After Mateo had gone to take a shower, I spoke to Angie alone.

'OK, you're no hypocrite - not that I ever said you were - but how long's he going to stay?'

Angie waved a hand in airy dismissal.

'A few days, a week or two. Just til he finds somewhere else.'

'Have you told Josef and Renata?'

'They're not even on the lease.'

'They might move out.'

'Good - Mateo can take their place.'

I retreated to the sanctuary of my room. Having resolved one fight with Angie, it was hardly wise to immediately start another. It occurred to me the situation would never have arisen if I hadn't gone to the wretched Antifa rally and somehow been duped into giving my email address to the Nazis. I emailed Edward Hall a half-humorous message.

> Thanks for sending me the video about the virtue-signalling celebs. I showed it to my girlfriend. Now she's taken a homeless South American into our home to prove she's not a hypocrite, and to get back at Trump for putting refugee kids into concentration camps. Whatever you do, don't send any more videos!

I put on some music and forgot it, but half an hour later there was a reply in my inbox.

If you mean the insanity of what's happening on the US-Mexico border right now, a few points:

You know those pics the media's been running of Latino kids in 'concentration camps' to prove Trump is Hitler? They're actually from the Obama era. The fake news media didn't mention that, did they?

It's not Trump endangering those kids. If those parents cared, they might keep them at home instead of putting their lives in danger.

All countries should protect their borders. Most of these Mexicans and South Americans aren't refugees, they're 'economic migrants' seeking a better life. But the US can't just let everyone in.

Did you know some of the southern states used to be part of Mexico? The Mexican govt wants to reclaim them, so they encourage their citizens to conquer America one person at a time. None of those people will ever have an allegiance to the US, their first loyalty will always be to Mexico. Let's see how that works out long term.

This rang a bell. I knew there had been tension between the two nations, perhaps even a war. I checked online and found that the American-Mexican war took place in 1846-48. It only lasted three years - but what if the counterattack took place over the next two hundred, so slowly you couldn't see it happening? It sounded like a paranoid right wing conspiracy theory. Then again, it would certainly be a cunning way to get revenge.

Still, that was all academic and happening very far away. There were more practical concerns to face. I walked out to the kitchen for a glass of water. When I turned on the living room light, Mateo was already asleep on the couch. He grimaced and turned his head to see what the intrusion was.

'Sorry,' I said. 'I didn't know you'd gone to bed.'

I turned off the light, retraced my steps, and took a drink from the bathroom tap instead.

# 5
# Diversity is our Stress

We lived in a cosy four bedroom house in Tamarama. That's 'cosy' as a real estate agent would use the word, as a euphemism for small. If it was snug with four, adding a fifth person took it from cosy to cluttered.

Angie had the best room up the front, the one with the ocean view. It was more of an ocean glimpse, really, but better than nothing. Just down the hallway was Renata, a science researcher from Sri Lanka. The living room and kitchen made up the central hub of the house. After that was Josef, an IT guy from the Czech Republic, then finally my own room, which looked out on the back garden. With the four of us, it was all AOK. Putting Mateo in that central communal hub was enough to change the whole vibe.

The trouble was I'd become used to having the place to myself during the day, my studies punctuated by random meal breaks in front of the TV. Now, the peace was disturbed by Mateo on the phone every ten minutes. Or I'd go to the kitchen for lunch and see *him* sprawled in front of the TV. Instead of sitting down, I'd take a sandwich back to my room. After a while, I couldn't help fronting Ange.

'Nothing personal against the guy, but it's been weeks. When's he going?'

'When Trump opens the borders or is impeached.'

I stared at my girlfriend in horror. She held my gaze for a moment, then burst into peals of elfin laughter.

'Oh John, your face!'

'I didn't think you were joking. How long's he really staying?'

'What's the problem?'

I made an effort to control my tone of voice. I looked out

her bedroom window towards the glimpse of ocean.

'It's alright for you,' I said. 'You're out most of the day.'

'So you've got the privilege of staying home. Lucky you.'

'It *used* to be a privilege. Now I've got to share it with the loud Latino.'

'Ooh, racial stereotypes. Nice.'

'I can hear him on the phone from three rooms away, and the TV's on all day.'

'He's allowed to watch TV.'

'I'm trying to study.'

'Have you asked him to turn it down?'

I stopped myself from answering. The implication I was too stupid to have thought of this, or too weak to do it, really pissed me off. Ange seemed to notice.

'Why are you so uptight, John?'

'It's your fault he's here but I'm the one who has to put up with him.'

She paused.

'Why not see it as a training?' she said at last. 'If you want to be a school teacher, you've got to handle all sorts of people. If you can't share a house, how will you go in a crowded classroom?'

This 'helpful' suggestion was a veiled stab at my own insecurities. Then again, she was probably right.

'Maybe that's it,' I replied. 'It's not about him. He's just a reminder I'm not cut out for school teaching in the first place.'

'You can't quit now. You've nearly finished your training.'

'The longer I go, the harder it is to chuck it in. I nearly quit after the first prac.'

The 'prac' was my first placement working at an actual school, for a training period of three weeks. It had been quite the ordeal.

'But you hung in, right?' said Ange.

'I nearly quit after the second prac as well.'

'Why are you doing it if you hate it so much?'

'It's not that I hate it. It's just that, well, it's so much harder than I thought.'

I sighed. Why *was* I doing it? You'd have to go back more than a decade to answer that. I'd left school a starry eyed kid who thought he could make it as an actor. Other people did - why not me? Trouble was, a million other wannabes had the same idea. Many are called, few are chosen. But I had an advantage over the rest, right? I had the music too - playing guitar in an indie rock band. And don't forget the screenwriting. I was going to *write* movies and TV shows, not just act in them. Maybe even direct as well. What better qualifications for being a director than knowing the game from every angle?

Some advantage. It turned out I was one of those jack-of-all-trades. A good actor, writer, and musician, but not good *enough* at any one of them to make a mark. Maybe if I hadn't wasted time on the band I would have been a better actor. If I hadn't bothered with acting, I might have gained the skills and contacts to be a Hollywood screenwriter. Looking back, I'd squandered fifteen years chipping away at all three.

So there I was on my thirty-second birthday, nothing but an also-ran. What did I have but a few small acting roles on my CV, a drawer full of unfilmed screenplays, and a stack of my band's music CDs I might as well use for Frisbees.

That's when a friend talked me into giving school teaching a go. It wouldn't even be fulltime, she said. Once I had the certificate, I could pick up three hundred bucks a day filling in as a casual. Couple of days a week and I could still work on screenplays the rest of the time. How hard could it be babysitting a bunch of high school kids? I had to do a three year course to get the quals, but the thought of being a student again myself was quite appealing. I didn't mind study; I enjoyed it.

Who knows? If I took a shine to the job, maybe I'd go fulltime. After all, what more noble subjects can you teach than my chosen fields, history and English? While one dealt with facts, the other fiction, both chronicled the amazing story of our species. Fresh young minds would be swept along with my enthusiasm. In my imagination, I saw eager teens queuing outside the staffroom to seek my views on the finer points of the Victorian age, or the drama of Ancient Rome. Budding authors would write stories for my perusal. No matter how flawed their work, I'd treat them with kindly indulgence, encouraging but never condescending. Years later, those students would look back fondly on their beloved mentor. *Good old Mr Gilbert*, they'd say. *He changed my life.*

Once I started my first prac, the reality was very different. History classes full of bored students indifferent to anything that happened before last week. Tech-addicted kids who rarely read anything longer than a text message.

Then there was the behaviour. Rather than quiet kids hanging on my every word, I found a bunch of rowdy teens who couldn't go two straight minutes without opening their mouths. I spent half my time keeping classroom noise down to a dull roar.

If only I'd had the balls to quit after the first prac. I *would* have quit after the second, but by then I'd fallen in love with Ange. My 'showbiz past' may have impressed her in courtship, but it was useless for any long term prospects. I'd need some reliable income for that. So it was heads down, back to the books, and telling myself there was a future in this teaching caper. It turned out Angie's father was also a history teacher, albeit at university level. In my semi-rational, lovelorn state, I took that as a good omen.

The trouble was there was so much more to the job than the job itself. I'd thought it was just a matter of knowing your subject, showing up to teach, then marking a few exams. Wrong. Turned out there was a huge amount of theory of teaching - *pedagogy*, they call it - which I had to absorb. It was all about how best to teach, learn, plan lessons, give grades, and a hundred other points of theory - and all in excruciating detail. There was no end to the stuff.

Then there are the politics. The 'DIE principles' - Diversity, Inclusion, and Equity - have seeped into education at all levels. This stuff is well meant. Take equity. All children are to be given equal opportunity, no matter their background or ability. It's a fine ideal, and better than the old *work 'em hard and the devil take the hindmost* approach - but putting it into practice isn't easy.

The idea that all children are somehow equal has some odd effects. For example, you can't talk about IQ anymore. Everyone knows some kids are smarter than others, but you can't say that because it implies some are dumber. A guy named Gardner (no relation to Ange) came up with the theory of 'multi-intelligences,' which is the idea that there are different ways of being smart. So there is 'spatial intelligence,' 'musical intelligence,' and so on. A cynic might think this is just a fancy way of saying people are good at different things. You know, some kids are good at sports or woodwork or whatever. But we have to go through the charade of saying everyone is smart, just in different ways.

As for 'diversity' and 'inclusion' this is largely a response to multiculturalism. Whatever one's view of the great modern social experiment, there are practical side effects. There's little doubt it would be easier to teach in a monoculture like, say, Japan - or European nations a few decades ago - where most students share a common background. With Australia now made up of many ethnic groups, schools have to make all cultures feel included. Teachers are obliged to acknowledge them all, as well as avoiding offense.

This does open up a wider range of material, which I like, in the same way that going to the International Film Festival gives you the chance to see films from every continent. But it makes it harder to create a unified school culture and curriculum.

All this 'diversity' is supposed to make up one big happy family. It's great in theory, but it doesn't make teaching easier. Is it a melting pot, a glorious stew, or a dog's breakfast? Who knows? It looked like politicians and social reformers created this experiment from afar for their own reasons, but teachers are the ones left to make it all work.

I turned back to Angie.

'You're right. Teachers do need to learn to get along with people. Being inclusive is something I have to do for work - but why do I have to do it at home as well? Mateo's not even paying rent.'

Ange crossed her arms.

'OK - I'll drop a couple of hints and see if there's any housing prospects.'

'Why not just ask him?'

'I'm not going to offend the poor guy. He's been through a lot.'

'Who hasn't? We've all got problems.'

'Don't compare yourself to a POC. First world problems aren't the same as third world problems.'

'And somehow they've become our problems. What is it they say? Import the third world, become the third world.'

Angie gave me a hard look.

'What's got into you lately? That's a real fascist thing to say.'

'I didn't mean it like that.'

'Well *you* said it.'

'For Christ's sake, I just want to go back to the way things were.'

'Talk's fine, John, but if we do nothing to back it up it doesn't mean a thing! So there's a few inconveniences having Mateo here. That's a small price to pay for helping a POC have a better life. It's the least we can do after what we've done to them.'

'What have I ever done to Mateo?'

'Not you, John. It's what white people have done to his country. We only colonised them, took their resources, and enslaved half of them for our own convenience.'

'Who's *we* - the English? I don't think the British empire made it to Chile. More likely the Spanish, don't you think?'

'Well, they're European.'

'So, because some damn Spaniards went to South America hundreds of years ago, I have to let Mateo stay here rent free?'

Angie frowned.

'You've changed, John. You never used to answer me back.'

'Not until Mateo was here. Look what he's done to us.'

'He hasn't *done* anything.'

'He doesn't have to.'

'It's not for much longer. You might as well make an effort.

I went back to my room and sank into the post-fight hangover that followed our occasional quarrels. It was a sickly sense of having fallen from grace, the fear of being dumped, and a wish to regain the comfortable equilibrium of before.

I decided to try to get on with Mateo. Over the next week or so, I'd smile, offer him a beer or a coffee, and sit down for a chat. It worked. I began to feel more warmly towards the guy. One night I cooked Mexican food and invited him to partake. That could have been a mistake. I was serving it up when Ange walked in. From the look on her face, I'd made some kind of appalling *faux pas*. She ushered me out of the room.

'What do you think you're doing?' she said.

'Trying to be nice,' I replied. 'Isn't that what you wanted?'

'With Mexican food? For one thing, it's cultural appropriation, and for another, it's not even his culture. He's from Chile, not Mexico.'

'So what?'

'Chilean cuisine is different to Mexican.'

'It's still South American. Sort of.'

'No, it isn't! Besides, there's all sorts of diversity in South America, but you're treating them like they're all the same. Mateo might see it as racist.'

'Doesn't seem to bother him. He's tucking in. Why don't you?'

Ange loosened up when she saw Mateo's smiling face. We all had a couple of drinks and a good night. Indeed Mateo introduced us to a *terremoto*, a Chilean cocktail made of some kind of fermented wine, pineapple ice cream, and a red cocktail syrup named grenadine. A few of those and we were on the way to being best friends for life.

For a brief time we lived in some kind of harmony. For me, it lasted all of three days, until I came home from uni and found Mateo sitting in front of the TV with a beautiful young Latina, who was rocking a baby on her lap.

The glassy smile I'd adopted as my default threatened to crack.

'Ah, Johnny. This is my wife, Liana.'

She smiled up at me sweetly.

'Oh... er, hi,' I mumbled. 'Are you staying too?'

'Not long,' said Mateo. 'Don't worry about it.'

I retreated to my room, wondering what Ange would have to say about this. Later that night, I heard her return from ESL class. She was chatting away with Mateo and Liana for what seemed like ages. Looks like she was finally giving Mateo his marching orders. Thank God. Eventually, there was a soft knock on the door. Ange came and sat on the side of the bed.

'Hey, John, I'm proud of you for being so chill lately. It's awesome the way you've been so inclusive.'

'I'm a teacher. That's my job.'

Angie put a silky hand on my leg.

'See how much better we all get along? It doesn't take much.'

'You were right. It was my own selfishness made the problem worse than it really was.'

Angie squeezed my thigh and smiled.

'It doesn't matter anyway,' I continued. 'At least now his wife and kid are here, they'll *have* to get their own place.'

'That would be great,' she said, taking off her jacket.

'Obviously they can't stay here.'

'Not for long,' she said. 'Mateo's applied for government housing.'

'I wouldn't rely on that. It could take months.'

'Those places come up all the time.'

Angie peeled off to her bra. Her breasts were quite large for such a short girl.

'There's a long waiting list,' I said. 'You surely don't think the three of them are going to crash out on the couch until they get public housing.'

'John, of course not.'

'Good,' I said. 'For a second I thought that's what you meant.'

Angie looked a little sheepish, then made a show of defiance.

'They can have my room,' she said.

I was silent for a moment.

'Don't tell me *you're* going to sleep on the couch.'

'No, silly. I'll move in with you for a bit.'

She tried to kiss me, but I stood up and walked to my desk.

'This is another one of your jokes, right?'

'It'll be fun.'

'Look in the wardrobe. I can barely fit into this room myself.'

Angie sighed.

'I'm hardly about to turn a young couple with a baby out on the streets. Is that what you want?'

There was no right answer to this question, so I stalled.

'It's too late to discuss it now,' I said. 'We'll sort it out in the morning.'

Although it was a double bed, I spent an uncomfortable night. We both went to bed angry, for a start. Apart from that, I'm a poor sleeper, even poorer when I have to share a bed. I woke the next day, dog-tired and grumpy.

'Sorry,' I said over coffee, 'but they've got to go. My last school placement's coming up and I'll need every minute of sleep I can get.'

This cut no ice with Ange.

'They'll be gone by then,' she said.

'Let's not risk it. I want them out now.'

'Who do you think you are - Trump?'

'Look, Ange, you didn't even have the courtesy to ask if this guy could stay here. What about Josef and Renata? Did you ask them?'

'I will tonight. I'm calling a house meeting. Let's put it to the vote.'

'Fine. See you there.'

At 7pm, I walked into the kitchen and they were all sitting round the table. Ange, Renata, Josef... and Mateo. Taken aback that he had the audacity to be there, I spoke to him with exaggerated calm.

'Will you excuse us a moment? This meeting is for residents only.'

Mateo looked to Angie, who averted her eyes. After a long, passive-aggressive pause, he stood up and shuffled off to the living room.

That left the four of us sitting round the table. Josef and Renata either side of me, Ange dead ahead.

'Look guys,' Ange said. 'Does anyone have a problem with Mateo and Liana staying here a bit longer?'

'And the baby,' I added.

'It doesn't bother me,' she said, 'but apparently some people do have a problem.' She gave me a haughty look. 'So we're going to put it to a vote. All those who want to be kind and inclusive, raise your hands.'

'Wait,' I said. 'You can't shame people like that and expect them to vote honestly. Better make it a secret ballot.'

'There's only four of us,' said Josef.

'Even so.'

Josef shrugged. Renata sat there in silence, a reluctant presence. Ange looked at me.

'Oh for God's sake,' she said. 'We know which way you're voting.'

I took a shopping list pad and tore off four sheets, then handed one to each voter.

'So, here we are,' I said. 'The great Mexit vote. It's a simple question. If you want Mateo and his family to keep living here, vote R for Remain. If you want him out, write L for Leave.'

There was only one pen so we took turns marking the ballots, before folding and dropping them into an empty tea cup. I reached out my hand to take it, but Ange got there first. With a black look at me, she pulled out the first slip of paper and laid it face up on the table. It was my own vote, with a letter L scrawled in large letters. Mateo leaves. 1-0.

Next there was an R for Mateo remains (1-1) and then another, which I recognized as Angie's handwriting (1-2).

Apparently some people enjoyed a noisy, crowded environment full of freeloaders. If the next vote came up R I'd be stuck with them.

Thank God it was an L - Mateo leaves. Angie cast an accusing look at Josef and Renata to see whose vote it was. Judging from her guilty expression, Renata was the only other rational member of the household.

'Anyone want a recount?' I said.

'There's only one solution,' said Ange. 'We need a tiebreaker.'

She looked toward the door and called out, 'Mateo, get in here.' She turned back to us with a sly smile.

'One vote to break the deadlock. Might as well be Mateo.'

I laughed.

'Good one, Ange. One of your jokes that's actually funny.'

Her face was entirely mirthless.

'Why shouldn't Mateo have a say in it?' she said, pouting like a teenager. 'After all, this vote is about him in the first place.'

'Yeah - that's why. Mateo doesn't get a vote because, first of all, there's a direct conflict of interest. And second, he doesn't get voting rights because he doesn't bloody live here!'

Angie was unmoved by this. As, apparently, would be Mateo.

'Actually, he *does* live here,' she said. 'He's been here more than a month. That should get him squatter's rights if nothing else.'

'Squatter's rights? Gee, why not give Liana a vote too? And I suppose wee Alonso is an anchor baby!'

An 'anchor baby' is a child born to illegal immigrants in the new country, in the hope it will help the parents get citizenship. Angie was unimpressed.

'If you're that selfish, John, why don't *you* move out?'

'You're the one who wants to give up your room,' I said. 'If you're selfless enough to do that, why not move out entirely? Problem solved.'

Angie's eyes flashed.

'You jerk! I offer to move into your room and this is how you thank me.'

'For God's sake,' I said. 'I just need some space so I can finish my teaching degree and start earning a living. Somebody has to pay the rent on this place, and it's certainly not bloody Mateo. I may as well start a college fund for Alonso while I'm at it.'

'You know what, John? Now you've shown just how selfish you are, maybe I *will* move out.'

'Oh, come on. This is crazy.'

'Crazy now, am I?'

'You're breaking up our house over some random guy you never even knew until a few weeks ago. And all to prove some ridiculous political point. You're nuts.'

'Fine. I'll go. Don't try to contact me.'

With that, Angie stood up and stormed out of the room. I went after her, and as I hurried through the living room, there was no mistaking the smug smile on Mateo's face.

I followed her up the hallway and right up to her room, but she slammed the door in my face. Twenty minutes later, an Uber pulled up outside. Angie slung a suitcase in the boot, climbed into the back seat, and they drove away.

# 6
# Hall at the Door

When Angie still hadn't come back after a few days, I went into bachelor mode - staying up late, drinking beer, and binge watching videos on YouTube. It was in this state of mind I invited Edward Hall to stay. Whether it was late night drunken bonhomie or the wish to get back at Ange, when Hall emailed that he was coming to town, I told him to save the hotel bill and come crash on the couch. With Mateo and Liana having moved into Angie's room, Hall might as well take their place.

I regretted it the next day and hoped he wouldn't show. Yet when the doorbell rang mid-afternoon, I opened the door and there he was, all long limbs and straggly beard, leaning up against the porch wall.

I had little choice but to invite the fellow in. Angie's room door was shut, but I could hear Mateo's voice from inside. I ushered Hall down the passage, through the living room, and into my own, where I brought him up to speed on recent events. Hall stood there gazing out my window into the garden, and listened patiently to my tale of woe. He shrugged.

'So your girlfriend's left you because you don't like being squeezed out of your home by illegal aliens. Just another skirmish in the culture war.'

'What's war got to do with it?' I replied.

'Not literally. I mean the battle of ideas.'

'I'm a pacifist,' I said. 'I want no part in war.'

Hall raised his eyebrows.

'The horse has bolted, old boy. As a wise man once said, you may not be interested in the culture war, but the culture war's very interested in you.'

'What are you on about?'

'I'm talking about the defining struggle of our time. The battle for the soul of the Western world.'

I stared at him blankly. Hall gave me a stern look, then came to a decision.

'Sit down, Johnny. Looks like you need a sprint through history.'

I sat at my desk. Across from me, Hall sprawled his long frame into an armchair and half closed his eyes.

'The culture war is the bitter fight between left and right, progressives and conservatives. It's been raging for a while now. I'm gonna take you back a few decades to the 1950s. Things were looking up. Sure, Europe was still cleaning up the rubble of World War Two, but they were slowly getting back on the upswing. Meanwhile, America was the greatest country in the world, as long as you went along with their God fearing apple pie values to some acceptable degree.

By the time the sixties came around, there was a revolution brewing. Not just the sex, drugs, and rock n roll, a bunch of other stuff too. Civil rights. Gay and women's liberation. Alternative lifestyles. It was anything goes, and on for young and old. Well, mainly the young, I suppose.'

'Everyone knows about the sixties,' I said. 'I didn't know it was called the culture war.'

'It wasn't. That's just a name someone gave it in hindsight. Anyhow, that was only phase one, and you know, it was probably the revolution we had to have. Because America wasn't great for everyone.'

'So you approve of all that?'

'I was too young to live through it, more's the pity. But yeah, I would have been right in the thick of it. Not just the sex and drugs, but the street marches, the riots and all. Anything to mess with the uptight conservatives. The squares, as they used to call them.'

'You'd have been a leftist?'

'Hell yeah. All the women's rights, gay rights, anti-racism. Justice and liberty for all, and pass that joint while you're at it.'

'Then what's with these right wing videos you've been sending me?'

'Well, you see, Johnny, the culture war today's a very different beast. It looks the same on the surface, but underneath it's chalk and cheese. I guess you think the left side of politics is still about fighting for justice.'

'So I'm told.'

'Still fighting for freedom, equality, women's rights? Fighting The Man?'

'That's what Ange thinks.'

'Of course she does. Then let me red-pill you on that delusion, old boy, cos the left now is a bizarre mutation of what it was in the sixties. Feminism turned from a just cause into a religion. PC hysteria, blatant anti-white racism, the suicide of Western nations, universities brainwashing kids to all think the same. The left has turned into a goddamn cult. I was onboard with 'em for their first revolution. Ain't no way I'm going along with this one.'

Hall stretched, then sighed.

'There's two parts to it,' he said. 'First, their behaviour, then their crazy beliefs. The sixties radicals wanted to stick it to The Man. They fought censorship and control. Well, look at 'em now. It ain't conservatives shutting down public meetings, or kicking people off Facebook and Twitter. It's not the right forcing conformity and policing speech. It ain't the right indoctrinating kids.'

Hall seemed in the mood for a long tirade, so I sat back and let him vent.

'As for their beliefs,' he said, 'half of 'em don't even make sense. I mean, the left are supposed to be 'anti-fascist,' right?

Presumably because they think fascists are authoritarian, anti-gay, and repress women. But the left turns a blind eye to Islam - a system which does all that and more. Now, if you point out to leftists that Islam seems a wee bit 'far-right,' they'll attack *you* for saying it.'

'Surely Muslims aren't all bad. The individuals, I mean.'

'Course they ain't. Most of them are decent folks, no doubt, and if they want to believe in Islam, that's their own affair. I just want to point out the hypocrisy of the left giving them a free pass while demonising the so called far-right.'

'Are you sure Islam is really right wing?'

'It's not hard to make a case - but don't take my word for it. Listen to some of the ex-Muslims, the apostates. Most of them believe it's a misogynistic system. Well, where are our feminists? Dressing up in handmaid outfits and pretending it's white men oppressing them. Meanwhile Islam's spreading in Europe and they don't say boo. Well, if the caliphate ever comes into power, it'll make the far-right look like a walk in the park.'

'So you're an Islamophobe?'

'Yeah, and so should the left be, if they had any logic or foresight. Instead, it's refugees welcome, and open borders, and one day all the halal chickens will come home to roost.'

'Of course people are going to help refugees - especially people of colour - or they'll be accused of racism.'

'You're right. Racism's all we ever hear about these days, isn't it?'

'It's certainly all over the news.'

'Three jeers for multiculturalism,' said Hall. 'Who'd ever have thought putting scores of incompatible cultures together would lead to racial tension? It's almost like they didn't think it through or something.'

'Maybe it just needs more time.'

'Sure. A few more centuries and we'll get to that *Star Trek* future of universal brotherhood. Right now it's more like *Lord of the Rings*.'

'You'd think putting cultures together would lead to more understanding,' I said.

'That's what we were taught in school,' Hall replied. 'And you know, I can see the sense in it. I can see the idealism. All cultures living together in peace and goodwill, like at Christmas. Except you can't have Christmas now cos that might offend someone. Tell you what, though, it might even have worked if they hadn't ruined it with the identity politics.'

I gave Hall another blank look.

'Geez, Johnny, you're a bit behind, aren't you? I mean the obsession with classifying everyone by their race, gender, sexual preference, and the like.'

'That's identity politics, is it?'

'Yeah. It was a big deal in the sixties, culture war phase one. Women's rights, gay rights, black power. Like I said, fair enough to recognise people's struggles and give 'em a fair shot in life. But over time, it's turned into a pathology. Everyone's obsessed with being oppressed, and they've got more axes to grind than an army of Orcs.'

'Well, I suppose they've got a point,' I protested mildly.

'Sure, but look how they went about it. They could have done all the girl power, gay pride, and the rest, but it turned into a revolution. The victims' revolution, as Bruce Bawer called it in his book. And revolution against what? White men and Western civilisation. The universities have got a lot to answer for. They teach kids that men are the enemy, especially white men.'

'What about the white male students?'

'They're supposed to hate themselves. They're meant to hang a shame placard round their necks and let everyone abuse them for their original sin. It's like something out of a socialist purge.'

'Surely you're exaggerating.'

'Not much. Grievance studies are all the rage. A university student these days is supposed to be a good little revolutionary against Western civilisation and white males.'

'That seems pretty pointless.'

'Not to the universities. It's their yellow brick road to a world of pure equality. There's just a couple of wee problems with their revolution. All this blaming the West and whipping up anti-white hate might seem like a plan, but how's it going to help create the multicultural Utopia? The only thing they're creating is civil war. They're targeting white males as the most powerful group, then trying to hobble them in search of their fool's paradise of an equal society. Well, there's plenty of white males have bowed to the pressure, but there's plenty who ain't. Not now they've got an inkling what's really going on.'

'I suppose there's a weird logic to it,' I said. 'Maybe they think if they hammer down on the highest nail, the white men, they'll level everyone down to the same height.'

Hall laughed.

'It's a bed of nails alright. We've made it and now we're gonna have to lie in it. What a disaster. Putting a bunch of different cultures together was a stretch anyway, let alone making the local population fair game for all comers. If you didn't know better, you might think it was all a set up. You know, one of those *conspiracy theories*. Ha!'

Hall shook his head in disgust. For a moment I thought he was going to spit on the floor, right in the middle of my bedroom.

'I tell you what,' he said. 'Multiculturalism *might* have worked if they went about it better. But throw in this hateful identity politics? Forget it. I can even state it as a mathematical formula. MC + IP = HOE.'

'Come again?'

'Multiculturalism plus Identity Politics equals Hell on Earth.'

I paused, not sure how to respond. In truth, there was an odd sense of liberation in letting Hall rant his evil right wing ideas, the mere whiff of which would have got me instant exile from Ange and her crowd. I sat passively by and let Hall vent, absolved by the knowledge I wasn't saying it myself.

'Everyone does seem to be angry most of the time,' I said. 'That's due to your culture war, is it?'

'It's what happens when you divide everyone up into teams and make 'em jostle for scraps. See, people are competing anyway, but if you hammer home the message that we're all class enemies, it's a recipe for civilisational collapse.'

'So you're saying diversity *isn't* our strength?'

'Not if we're all fighting each other. If striving for 'diversity' means endless jostling over racial quotas, then the premise is flawed.'

'And gender quotas,' I added.

'Sure. Don't forget feminism. Like I said, a just cause when it started, but look at it now, indoctrinating young minds about phantom oppressions. They teach women to hate men - and plenty of men are willing to return the favour.'

Hall pulled out a packet of cigarettes.

'Do you mind?' he said.

'I'd rather you didn't. Not in my room.'

As Hall stood up to move to the back yard, it occurred to me the neighbours might overhear his ravings.

'Sit down,' I said. 'I suppose it doesn't matter, just this once.'

Hall spied a small, empty bowl lying on my desk, and decided it was a suitable ashtray. He put it on the side of his armchair, then lit up a smoke.

'What does the left actually want?' said Hall, exhaling. 'What is this Utopian world they're trying to create?'

'A world without rich and poor,' I ventured. 'Where everyone is equal and there's no discrimination. No sexism or racism.'

'Right. They want that golden *Star Trek* future. No more nations fighting each other. Why do you think the left wants open borders? No borders, no nations, no wars.'

'Ange said something like that.'

'And of course dividing up the planet's wealth among all its inhabitants. No doubt if you live in the third world, you'll be all for it. Beats me why the first world would want a bar of it.'

'We are all Africans. That's what Richard Dawkins had on his Twitter heading.'

'We certainly will be.'

'Does it really matter?'

'It does if you want to preserve the culture you grew up in. Anyhow, you can see why immigration is the number one issue these days. Globalism vs Nationalism. The right want to keep national borders so they can protect their culture and run their countries without interference. The left wants to destroy nationalism to create their glorious One World future where everyone's equal.'

'So you're a skeptic?' I said, with a smile.

'It's Utopian nonsense. It'll never work, but they'll ruin the Western world trying.'

'Maybe they'll succeed.'

Hall snorted.

'I'd give them a chance if they were sane, rational people. If they were really loving and tolerant, like they say they are. But they ain't! Look at the way they freaked out when Trump won the election. How did your girlfriend take it? Do you remember?'

# 7
# Doomsday 2016

Did I remember? How could I forget? To be honest, I'd never much cared about US politics. Living in Australia, it was just background noise. But as my new girlfriend, Angie, did care, I found myself following the Trump - Hillary battle of 2016 very closely.

Having been raised in a leftist family, I automatically backed the Democrats - and Hillary Clinton's win seemed assured. All the media experts said it was a sure thing. Hillary thought so too, and just before the election she warned Trump to respect democracy and accept the will of the people when the votes came in.

Ange was therefore in a buoyant mood on November 9th as we turned on the TV to see the election of America's first woman president. With the time difference, it was morning in Australia. Ange and I were a new couple, and she'd spent the night with me at my rented house in Tamarama. We woke early and I brewed a big pot of coffee so we could settle in for the broadcast.

It was still too soon for results. Angie seemed possessed by a pent up, nervous energy. This found a musical outlet, for she had just learnt to play the ukulele - which naturally I found charming at the time. I joined in on guitar and together we sang little songs about Hillary's coming victory, making up the words as we went along. Angie's strumming was manic and her singing erratic, but it was all part of the vibe.

We worked off some more energy by going for a long run around the coast. Ange then surprised me by joining me in the shower. After we'd towelled off and dressed, feeling rather self satisfied, we sat back on the couch to watch history unfold.

Some odd early voting patterns put a dampener on the mood. At first, Ange was merely annoyed Hillary's win would be by a smaller margin than predicted. As the numbers kept growing for Trump, annoyance gave way to anxiety.

'They must have counted all the deplorable states first,' I offered, alluding to Hillary's description of Trump's supporters.

'They shouldn't be allowed to vote in the first place,' said Ange.

'Never mind,' I said. 'There's no way she can lose.'

Angie returned to a state of uncomfortable denial. Her demeanour mirrored that of the political pundits on TV. Yet when the early voting trends did not reverse, cracks appeared in their smug personas. The talking heads were facing a major public embarrassment. First, by the election of Donald Trump, a candidate they despised. Second, in the flagrant failure of their profession to predict the result. It was a nightmare, unfolding live on TV.

It was all too much for Ange.

'This is bullshit!' she screamed, when the shocking result could no longer be ignored.

Of course, *anger* was only stage two in the 'Five Stages of Grief.' We'd spent most of the morning in stage one, *denial*. We were about to move on to stage three, *bargaining*.

'There must have been a mistake,' said Angie. 'There's got to be a re-count. Or a re-vote.'

'They're not allowed to,' I said. 'It's like with Brexit. Once the vote is in, they can't go back on it.'

That was a naive comment, in hindsight, but we weren't to know it at the time. My remark seemed to propel Angie into the fourth stage of grief, *depression*.

'It's not fair,' she wailed, her face crumpling like a child's. Her finger stabbed at the remote control as she turned off the TV. Then she actually lay on the floor, face down, and cried.

I sat on the couch looking down at her, feeling foolish and impotent, for there was nothing I could do to make her feel better. In desperation, I tried to pull her back to stage two by mustering a state of righteous indignation.

'Fuck Trump!' I shouted, rising to my feet. Looking round for a target, I took what was nearest to hand and grabbed the couch, upending it so it lay upside down behind us.

I stormed into the kitchen and saw the two dirty coffee mugs we had used, lying unwashed in the sink. One of them, which bore the logo *I Drink Male Tears*, Ange had chosen to use while watching Trump's defeat speech. The other, inscribed with the words *Male Feminist*, I had received as a gift from her some weeks before. Now, in my state of empathetic rage, I picked up both mugs. With a bellow of faux-despair, I yelled, 'What is the point? The game is rigged!'

With a violent oath, I threw both mugs against the kitchen wall, so they shattered. I made sure, however, to throw them against the base of the wall so the shards did not scatter too far and would be easy to clean up.

My ostentatious display served to rouse Ange, if only from surprise, for she had never seen me given to wild shows of emotion. As a male ally, I felt the gravity of the situation required it. Ange lifted her head up from the floor.

'Just chill, John,' she said in a defeated voice. 'There's no use smashing the place up.'

Then she returned to tears. Her head sank back onto her forearms, and I could see her shoulders shaking as she sobbed. I looked down at her helplessly. Feeling rather foolish, I picked up the overturned couch and restored it to an upright position, before sitting down on it once more. I would just have to wait for Ange to move on to the fifth stage of grief, which is acceptance. She would accept the election result, forget about it, and we could move on with our lives.

It never happened. Not for Ange. Not for the political left in Australia. Not for millions of Democrat supporters in America, or the Democrats who served them. There would never be a move into stage five, merely an endless cycling through the other four stages: denial, anger, bargaining, and depression.

In the coming years, denial would be expressed in the idea that Trump's win was due to Russian collusion. Anger was voiced through an endless torrent of anti-Trump vitriol in social media. Bargaining manifested in the eight-hundred-and-forty-seven Democrat impeachment attempts. And depression was ever present, like the smog-induced grey skies over Beijing.

At last, Angie eased herself up from the floor, her makeup smeared by tears. 'Come on,' she said. 'Let's go to the pub.'

I was about to say *it's barely lunchtime*, but had the sense to button my lip. If ever there was a time to become an alcoholic, it was today.

We caught a taxi to Newtown and walked into the Marlborough Hotel off King street. Angie's friend Nina was already there. She was barely an inch taller than Ange and nearly as pretty, though she seemed to be in rebellion against that too. The blue hair was temporary, the tattoos permanent. Still, she and Ange could have been sisters. I had sensed a muted hostility towards me on the few occasions we'd met. Still, it was up to me to overcome this. Adopting a sombre expression, I approached the table where she was sitting.

'Hi Nina. How are you holding up?'

She stood up and walked past me, embracing Ange with a sisterhood hug. By the time they parted, there was not a dry eye between them.

'I need a drink,' said Nina.

'I need ten,' said Ange.

'Allow me,' I said, taking out my wallet.

The bar TV set was showing the US election. Hillary still hadn't conceded defeat. There was no sign of her, just scenes of roomfuls of her supporters, shell-shocked and tearful.

'Three beers and three straight scotch,' I said to the barman. A grinning Donald Trump appeared on the TV screen. I shook my head and looked back at the barman.

'Better make 'em doubles.'

I plonked the booze down on the table in front of the girls. Although I would never have admitted it to them, I felt thrilled, and faintly surprised, to be sitting down with two such pretty girls. A part of me still couldn't believe Ange was my girlfriend. Looking back, I was completely entranced by her. However, love was the last thing on my companions' minds at the moment.

'I don't get it,' Ange said, with a dazed look. 'All the polls said Hillary was going to win.'

'People lie,' Nina said grimly. 'They say the right thing to the pollsters, but when no one's watching, they'll vote for the white supremacist every time.'

Ange took a sip of her beer.

'It's not fair people are allowed to vote in private,' she grumbled. 'Everyone should vote online on a public website, so we can all see it. Then we'll know who's voting for fascism so we can kick their arses.'

'I know, babe,' said Nina, squeezing Angie's hand. 'Then anyone who voted Trump could be kicked out of uni or have their workplace boycotted. Fascists don't deserve the right to vote.'

I was feeling a little conspicuous. Neither of them had said a word to me, not even to thank me for the drinks. I threw out a little virtue signal.

'I can't believe he got elected after what he said about groping women. Imagine having a pussy grabber in the White House.'

A few days before the election, a private conversation had emerged, taped a decade before. Trump had said something about star-struck women - some would call them groupies - who let celebrities 'grab them by the pussy.' The Democrats had distorted this into Trump saying he was allowed to grab any woman at any time. The remark seemed certain to sink his campaign. Apparently not.

For the first time, Nina was staring at me - but there was fury in her eyes. Maybe I'd said the wrong thing. Nervously, I blundered ahead.

'Mind you, they did have Bill Clinton. I hate to think how many Lewinskies are going to cop it now.'

Angie gave me a sharp look and Nina swore loud enough that a few people glanced over at our table.

'Poor Hillary,' said Nina. 'Whatever did she do to deserve this?'

Angie put a consoling hand on her arm, as if Nina herself had suffered these betrayals.

'I'm so sick of male leaders,' Nina continued. 'It's about time women had a turn.'

Ange nodded. 'They'd do a damn sight better job running the world than men. Don't you think, John?'

'A hundred percent,' I said, nodding decisively to affirm my full and unreserved agreement with this view. 'I mean, just look at Markle. She's doing a wonderful job.'

There was a pause.

'What's Meghan Markle got to do with it?' said Ange with a frown. 'Just because she's hooked up with a prince doesn't give her any political power.'

'I mean in Germany.'

For the first time in hours, Ange smiled. She punched my arm.

'That's Merkel, dummy. Angela Merkel.'

'What did I say?'

Nina drained her beer glass, then sat looking contemplative.

'I wasn't sure about her for a while. A few years ago she said multiculturalism was a failure. A total Nazi thing to say. But she came good in the migrant crisis.'

'What do you mean?' I asked.

'All the refugees that came into Europe last year. Thousands of them. Maybe millions. No other country wanted to take them. It was Merkel who led the way and opened Germany's gates. See? That's why women should be in charge. At least they'll govern with wisdom and compassion, not fascism and white supremacy.'

'We might have to move to Germany too,' said Ange. 'I don't see how people can feel safe anymore now hate has won.'

'Come on,' I said with a smile. 'Surely it won't be that bad.'

That was a mistake. For the first time, Nina addressed me directly. Although accused might be a better word for it.

'It's alright for *you*, John. You're a fucking white male! You're normal. The default.'

'That ain't my fault,' I said. I later learned that 'default' is a term of abuse in some circles. It means you're supposedly the standard for normal against which all other types of people are deviations. As for my protest, Nina was having none of it.

'Zip it, John. Stop talking and listen for once.'

*For once*? I hardly knew the girl.

'Yeah, just shut up!' Nina continued. 'You think you're so special because you were born a man?'

I took a sip of beer.

'Not particularly.'

'You think we want to hear your profound thoughts on the election? You want to explain to us what happened?'

'Hey, what did *I* do wrong? I was going for Hillary!'

'This is not about you, John,' said Angie. 'Stop making it about you.'

'I didn't. Nina did.'

'This is nothing to do with you,' said Nina with a withering look. 'This is about everyone *but* you. It's about the woman of colour working minimum wage illegally cos she can't get citizenship. It's about the trans soldier kicked out of the military. It's about the gay couples who'll get their marriage cancelled now Trump's in.'

'He can't do that,' I said.

'Don't be so bloody naive, John,' snapped Angie. 'Did you see the way Trump mocked that disabled reporter? The Nazis sent disabled people to the gas chambers, you know.'

'I am aware of that,' I said mildly. 'After all, I *am* a history teacher.'

I tried to change the topic.

'Speaking of history, this has all happened before. In the 1950s, the US government deported over a million illegal Mexican workers. They even called it *Operation Wetback*. How racist is that?'

'And look what's happening now,' said Ange. 'They're going to deport all the Muslims.'

'And what about Roe and Wade?' said Nina 'They're going to overturn it and send us back to the 1950s.'

'Oh yeah,' I said - then paused. 'What's that again?'

'The right to abortion, John,' said Nina. 'For fuck's sake, I thought you said you were a history teacher.'

'It's only a matter of time 'til they do the same thing here,' wailed Ange. 'It's going to be impossible to get an abortion soon. I'm going to get pregnant so I can have an abortion while it's still legal. John?'

I took a long sip of my beer.

'Uh, steady on, Ange. Maybe we're all getting a bit carried away. We mustn't overreact.'

'Well, hello!' said Nina, gesticulating at the nearest TV screen, which was once again showing Trump's smiling face.

'Oh Christ,' I said. 'I'm getting some more drinks.'

There was a longer line at the bar this time. By the time I got back to the table with another round of Scotch and beers, the mood had changed. Nina looked slightly less hostile, as if Ange had had a quiet word to her. It looked like she was going through an inner struggle, and Ange had prompted her to some kind of apology.

'Look, John. I didn't mean to take it out on you. It's not your fault.'

'Thanks Nina. Who could blame you on a day like this? I don't take it personally.'

I handed each of them a shot glass - no ice this time - and we upended them. The fiery glow of the Scotch added to our already half-pissed state, and loosened tongues further. Yet I was wrong about Nina's reduced hostility; she was merely redirecting it.

'This is only the beginning,' she said, waving an unsteady finger at me and Ange. 'There's gonna be resistance like you wouldn't believe.'

'I'm going to join Antifa for a start,' said Ange.

'What's that?' I asked.

'Anti-fascism,' said Nina. 'We're going to smash the fash. And the fucking patriarchy.'

'Let's move to America,' said Ange.

I didn't like the sound of that. Perhaps it was just the booze talking.

'I thought you were moving to Germany,' I said.

'Fuck that,' said Ange. 'Let's go right to the source.'

She turned to the nearest TV screen. Bloody Trump's face

was still there. Ange raised a drunken arm towards it and proclaimed loudly.

'And I personally vow to assassinate that there son of a bitch!'

I looked round the room in embarrassment.

'For Christ's sake, keep it down!' I hissed. 'Don't be saying stuff like that.'

'Leave her alone, John,' said Nina. 'You don't own her. If that's what she wants to do, let her. She'll probably win the Nobel peace prize like Obama.'

Angie and Nina gave a little whoo-hoo, and clinked their beer glasses in a toast. Nina was starting to slur her words.

'You go girl! I sholemnly shwear I will support you in court when you get arrested. If your dream is to assassinate Trump, thash cool with me.'

'And I'll visit you in jail,' I said. Angie ignored me and looked at Nina.

'Thanks, babe,' said Angie. 'You know what? You're a beautiful soul. The most beautifullest of all.'

'So are you, girl. You rock! You should definitely win the Nobel peace prize, because peace is your middle name. Angie Peace Gardiner.'

This drunken bollocks seemed to amuse them, for they collapsed into peals of laughter. I sat there, hunched into my beer, waiting for it to peter out. Nina still wasn't done.

'I love you, Ange. And if you really want to know what I think, then...'

Nina froze in mid-sentence, a look of dismay on her face. Angie and I turned in the direction of her stare. A group of youngish guys had entered the pub. They were probably from Sydney University, which was only a couple of blocks away.

'What's wrong?' I said.

The young guys, about twenty metres away at the bar, had their backs to us. From the look on Nina's face, I surmised that one or more of them may have sexually assaulted her in the past.

'Look what he's wearing!' said Nina.

'What?'

'A fucking MAGA hat!'

MAGA hats were the red caps Trump used in his campaign, bearing the slogan *Make America Great Again*. One of the guys at the bar was indeed wearing one.

'He's got a nerve,' said Ange. 'That's like wearing a KKK hood.'

'Just ignore them,' I said. 'Want a game of pool?'

'I can't play pool with people like that around,' said Nina. 'I have a right to feel safe when I go out in public.'

'She's right,' said Ange. 'Do something, John.'

I was silent a moment.

'Do what? Technically, the guy's done nothing wrong.'

'He's wearing a MAGA hat!'

'Come on. It's just a silly little red cap. Why don't we go to another bar?'

'Why should *we* have to leave?' Ange hissed. 'It's up to the hotel to provide a safe and tolerant environment.'

'Look,' I said. 'We're all a bit drunk. Why don't we go home?'

'I'm just getting started,' said Nina. 'And if you're not going to do anything, mate, then I will.'

Nina stood up, all five foot two of her, and walked unsteadily towards the guys at the bar.

'Go after her, John,' Angie ordered.

We were soon within earshot of the five or six young guys. They had our backs to us and were looking up at the election aftermath on TV. The guy in the red cap was the tallest of them.

'I can't believe Trump won,' he was saying.

'Yeah. It's kinda weird,' the guy next to him replied.

'Where's Clinton?' said Red Cap. 'She should have showed up by now.'

This was enough for Nina. She stepped forward and poked him sharply in the back.

'Hillary's not here. But I am.'

The guy turned around. He was a good foot taller than Nina. I saw at once it wasn't a MAGA hat on his head, just some old Sydney University cap that happened to be red. Nina either didn't notice or didn't care.

'Hey, what's your problem?' the guy said.

'What's my problem?' Nina echoed, getting up in the guy's face. She pointed at the TV screen - 'That' - then at the guy's red cap - 'and that. Fuck you and your hate!'

She gave a little drunken hop into the air and tried to grab the guy's red Sydney University cap. He stepped back and stumbled against the bar. This gave Nina time to follow up. She picked up a full glass of beer from a nearby table, and threw the contents in the guy's face. He took off his cap and shook it. Droplets of beer flew in all directions.

'Come on, Nina,' I said. 'Let's go.'

But Nina wasn't leaving. She stepped towards her perceived enemy and tried to shove him. The look on his face was one of bewilderment. Instinctively, he pushed Nina away. Already a little unsteady on her feet, she fell backwards, landing arse-first on the floor. I was reminded of the two second delay you hear between a toddler falling over and the outbreak of loud wailing. While Nina didn't cry, she did yell.

'That's assault. Call the cops!'

Alerted by the sudden noise, all eyes turned in our direction. The two on-duty bar staff were serving customers, so had missed the lead up. Likewise, several patrons only saw the end result, which was Nina on the floor, the Red Cap guy standing over her. This prompted a 'white knight' from the crowd to rush to Nina's aid. *A hero is called.* The would-be saviour looked like he spent hours in the gym and as long in front of the mirror. He jumped to conclusions then into action, grabbing Red Cap by the shirtfront. This was too much for one of Red Cap's mates, a guy in a blue t-shirt.

'Get off, mate' he said. 'He did nothing.'

White Knight looked down at Nina, who still hadn't managed to haul herself off the floor.

'Are you OK? Do you want me to call an ambulance?'

White Knight turned to Blue T-shirt guy and intoned a slogan, as if reciting something he'd learned in school.

'Violence against women is never OK. I won't be a bystander.'

This outraged Mr Blue T-shirt.

'The mad bitch attacked him!'

'Yeah, sure. Look at the size of her.'

White Knight reached a hand towards Nina. She recoiled as if traumatised, and gave a little whimper.

'I'm calling the cops,' said White Knight, as he took out his phone.

The situation was spiralling out of control, so I stepped in.

'Wait a minute, mate. No need for the police.'

The guy turned to look at me.

'Are you involved in this?' He looked at Nina. 'Did this dude assault you?'

The traumatised Nina shook her head and pointed at Red Cap.

'Call the cops!'

I made a face at Nina, trying to penetrate her drunken haze. I reached out a hand and helped her to her feet. This enraged White Knight.

'Touch her again and I'll knock you out.'

I ignored the buffoon.

'Nina,' I said. 'Do you really want to involve the police? If this goes to court, they'll look at the CCTV footage. Everyone will see what happened.'

Nina was still too drunk to think this through, but I could see a glimmer of light dawn in her eyes. Ange, in her wisdom, decided to help her out.

'Fuck the cops, babe,' she said to Nina. 'They're Nazis anyway. Let's take this to a private university hearing. At least then we'll get some justice.'

Ange cast a menacing look at Mr Red Cap, who had remained silent.

'What's your name?' she demanded. 'I want to see ID with your name and student number.'

She got out her phone and started recording. This was the last straw for Red Cap.

'Look, I don't know who the fuck you people are, but like your bro said, it's all gonna be on camera. So go on - call the cops. Screw it, I'll call 'em myself.'

And with that, he shoved White Knight away. Next thing you know, it was on - a bar-room brawl. Red Cap's mates jumped in, as did a few goons in the crowd. I grabbed Ange and Nina and pulled them out of the fray. As I did, I caught a glimpse of Nina's face, a pyromaniac gazing at a fire.

'Come on. Quick,' I said.

I hustled them through the glass doors of the Marlborough Hotel. We ran a few metres up to King street, then joined the flow of pedestrians, melting into the crowd. By the time we reached Newtown train station we were safe. Ange and I caught a train to Bondi and a cab home, while Nina went on her merry way elsewhere.

I flashed back to the present. Edward Hall was scrutinizing me.

'So, how *did* Angie take the election result?' he said. 'Was she upset?'

'Oh no,' I replied. 'Not at all.'

I laughed and told him the story.

# 8

# A Nation of Thugs and Cowards

I shook my head.

'I still don't know how Trump won.'

'It sure was a shock to people like Ange' said Hall. 'The political left still hasn't got over it - but why do they hate him so much in the first place?'

'Was it the pussy grabbing thing?'

'That's just a sideshow. They hate him for a bunch of reasons. For a start, he's a nationalist. Second he's not PC. Third, of course, he's a white male - the number one enemy of the left. I mean, they'll cop someone like Trudeau...'

Hall snickered.

'Trump really crashed the party, didn't he? It was meant to be the glorious progressive moment the first black president handed over to the first woman president. What did we get instead? This vulgar white man who seems to go against everything they believe in. Pussy grabbing ain't the half of it.'

'He was a bit of a comedown from Obama,' I said.

'Sure, he was a smooth operator, Obama. A sharp dressed, handsome, articulate black man. He was the liberals' wet dream when it came to their ideal president. But he was always so PC, with a platitude for every occasion. Compare that to Trump - a loose cannon who'll say anything at any time.'

Hall laughed.

'You want to know the main reason everyone freaked out?' he said. 'Trump's win signalled that the left is no longer winning the culture war. That and Brexit.'

'What's it got to do with Australia?' I said. 'We never used to care that much, did we?'

'We're as caught up in the culture war as anyone else,' Hall replied.

'It doesn't really affect me.'

'Don't be a fool.'

Hall glared at me.

'Look Johnny, let me give you a heads up on Australia today. We're a nation of thugs and cowards.'

He paused for a moment.

'Do you think and speak freely? Do you form your own opinions?'

'About what?'

'Gender, race, right and wrong. All the issues of the culture war.'

'No one's going to tell me what to think,' I said. 'I'll listen to both sides and make up my own mind.'

'But you won't *hear* both sides, and what you hear about the 'wrong' side won't be given fairly. Haven't you noticed there's a constant coercion to think a certain way? To be considered a morally good person, there are certain ideas you have to go along with.'

'Like what?'

Hall looked at his watch.

'Let's break it down to the big four: gender, race, equality, and progress. First, gender. Now, never mind if it's a social construct or how many there are. There are some basic beliefs you have to hold about the gender war between men and women.'

'Gender war? You said it was the culture war.'

'The gender war is a major battle within the culture war.'

'You're confusing me.'

'Then let me dumb it right down for you. The basic idea you have to believe is that men are bad but powerful, and women are good but have been held back, so they must be empowered in all things. Also that feminism is a noble cause and anyone who questions it hates women.'

Hall raised an admonishing finger.

'If you're a good boy, and sensible, you'll be sure to regularly praise women and criticise men. In public. That's rule number one.'

'So what do I have to believe about race?'

'That racism is the worst problem in the world and the biggest sin. That whites are the only racists, and Western nations have a terrible past they have to make up for now. There are other ideas that go along with this. Nationalism is bad and a sure sign of fascism. By extension, nations are bad, and borders suspect.'

'Is that all?'

'You also have to believe all cultures are equal, and multiculturalism is a great idea. This is tied to the idea of globalism - that we should be one world and not separate nations. Multiculturalism is globalism on a small scale.'

Hall looked speculative.

'If you join all those ideas together, you might see a pattern. Now, the next main idea is that inequality is the worst problem in the world, and equality the greatest goal.'

'You said racism is the worst problem.'

'So I did. Scrub that; inequality is the worst. Now, as there's no equality in nature, those who want it are always pushing uphill. Fighting nature means pushing for more government control, and all that goes with it.

Tied in with this, the fourth idea is about progress. Leftists dream of a world of perfect equality. No more rich and poor, no more social classes. But there's also perfect freedom. So, the leftist's ideal world has both perfect equality and perfect freedom – which is impossible, like trying to make a square circle.'

'But that don't bother them,' Hall continued. 'Leftists have a vision, and neither logic nor reality are going to stop them.

And OK, the more reasonable ones will admit it – *we're never gonna reach Utopia, but by God and Karl Marx we'll get as close as we can.* So they settle on the idea of progress, towards this ideal world they have vaguely conceived. A world of peace, tolerance, universal goodwill...'

Hall shook his head.

'It follows that all who believe in this world are progressive and morally good. Those who question it must be evil. Why else would anyone oppose them, except to protect their own power, or out of downright meanness? To leftists, all morally good people are on the left, and only backwards or evil people are on the right.'

Hall lit another cigarette. I grimaced, but as he'd already sullied the air with one, he might as well keep going.

'These ideas, and many more, we are coerced into believing,' said Hall. 'So where does this coercion come from? School and uni, for a start. You're a school teacher, right?'

'Not yet.'

'Let's say you are. Now, suppose you go on Twitter and make a few political tweets.'

'We've got to be careful what we put online. We can get into a lot of trouble.'

Hall waved this away.

'Not if you say the right thing. Say you tweeted *let's fix the gender pay gap*, or *diversity is our strength*, or some such bilge. Would that get you fired?'

'I suppose not.'

'How about posting an anti-Trump meme? Will that get you in trouble?'

'They all hate Trump.'

'What if you tweet *Is diversity really our strength?* Or *let's give the far-right a fair hearing* - how would that go down?'

'That's getting a bit political.'

'No more than the other tweets.'

'Look, I can't say stuff like that online. Not if I want a job.'

'There you go then. Some opinions are allowed, and some aren't even allowed to be considered. And you a school teacher. Schools are supposed to teach children how to think, but they only teach them what to believe.'

Hall raised a forefinger as if chastising me.

'Now, a real thinker, should be able to look at all ideas, calmly and reasonably. *All* ideas including the ones that seem wrong, or even evil, a true intellectual should take on their own terms. But that's not what happens, is it? Only certain ideas are allowed. Say the wrong thing on Twitter and you'll get smashed by the mob and fired from your job. So naturally you never speak up.'

I sat there, somewhat nonplussed.

'I never signed up for any of this when I began my teacher training.'

Hall laughed.

'Oh, but you did, Johnny. You're a small part of the machine now. The education wing. Still, it could be worse. You could have become a journo.'

'I hate the tabloids as much as anyone else.'

Hall shook his head.

'They're repellent in their own way, but never mind them. I mean the ones we were brought up to believe are the good guys. The *Sydney Times Guardian*, or the BBC in England. They're meant to be the ones fighting for truth and justice.'

'At least they're independent.'

Hall snorted.

'They're more biased than anyone. You said you want to hear both sides of an issue and make up your own mind. Take the gender war, for instance, between men and women. Do you hear both sides of that? Well, as your newspaper employs eighty-nine feminists and no MRAs, I reckon that's a no.'

'What's an MRA?'

'Men's Rights Activists. They dispute the feminist idea that women forever get the short end of the stick - but you've never even heard of them. So much for making up your own mind. You'll never hear both sides from that propaganda rag.'

'Or how about hearing from a nationalist?' Hall continued. 'Suppose there was an article called *Multicultural Heaven: Are we there yet?* Think they'd ever print that?'

'That might not fit their editorial policies.'

'There you go then. It's all about controlling the narrative. Tell you what, there's only two types of people work for that mob, and in public life generally - thugs and cowards.'

'What do you mean?'

'The left have been winning the culture war for a long time. They've claimed the high moral ground for their own side, and laid out a set of values everyone has to accept. To be fair, that's what the Christians used to do as well, but now the 'progressives' are in power they're doing the same thing. Whatever the topic, you have to think a certain way.'

'Surely they're allowed to decide their own values.'

'But they want to decide everyone else's too. So you've got your thugs and your cowards. A thug is an aggressive progressive who puts forward his views in a righteous way. He - or she - is smug with a hint of menace. You've got the high profile people - the media figures, the lame arse politicians. Then there are the enforcers lower down the chain, the 'cancel culture' mob. The ones who'll urge a mass boycott if some celebrity says the wrong thing.'

'I *have* heard of cancel culture. Like when Ange said she didn't want me to listen to Morrissey anymore cos he's allegedly right wing.'

'Yeah. Thirty years campaigning for animal rights, but a bit of wrong think elsewhere and they're on him like a school of piranhas. He should write a song about it. 'The Pariah and the Piranhas.' It's all part of their purge. Bunch of thugs, the lot of them.'

Hall stubbed out his cigarette.

'The coward, on the other hand, is someone who says all the right things in capitulation to the thugs. These guys are terrified of saying the wrong thing, so they make big public displays of *right think* - or virtue signalling, as some call it. I'll give you some examples. Do you mind?'

Hall pointed to my desktop computer, then sat down.

'Are you on Twitter?' he asked. 'Oh that's right. It's *verboten* for school teachers. Never mind. I'll log into my own account.'

Hall went online, then began searching Twitter.

'Here's one. Seamus Becks. A textbook coward. Apologetic white man, male feminist, works for leftist media. Let's pull up a few of his tweets.'

Hall scrolled down the screen for a bit.

'Let's see what he's posted: A quote from Saint Obama... an anti-Christian meme... hmm, also a pro-Islam one... something about LGBT pride... a story about a sportswoman's victory over male trolls online... a photo of Greta Thunberg with Angela Merkel. Standard virtue signalling. You could go through this guy's whole feed and predict his views on any topic.'

'Maybe he really believes in all these things.'

'It's a bit try-hard. Look at this post.'

*So sick of toxic behaviour from men's sporting teams. About time our awesome Aussie women took over prime time TV - Go Matildas, Netballers and our girls' cricket team!*

'What's wrong with that?'

Hall sniggered.

'No offence to women's sport, but lavish public displays of praising women are a red flag. Don't you remember rule number one? Praise women, slag off men. And do it in public.'

'Give me another example.'

'Alright, look at this journo, Stephen Collymoor. Bit of an odd case. Pseudo-intellectual and a blowhard progressive. He's also got this blokey, macho shtick, comes across as a tough guy. I wouldn't pick a fight with him. Not in real life - he'd knock me out.'

'So he's a thug?'

'More of a coward, just a different type. I mean, you'd go to war with him and he might not lack for courage in the trenches... maybe. But one thing's for sure - he hasn't got the balls to ever write anything that goes against the values of the *Sydney Times Guardian*.'

Hall scrolled down a bit further.

'Look at this - he's fawning over Jacinda Ardern, the New Zealand PM. Old Colly. He knows what pays his bills. Give me a second, I'll just troll him.'

Hall began typing something.

*Bookies odds.*

*My bus is on time tomorrow 10-1, No anti-Trump media stories this week 100-1, Snow falls in Summer 1000-1, Aliens land 10,000-1, S. Collymoor fails to praise Jacinda Ardern 50,000-1.*

I read this and laughed, then immediately felt guilty.

'You know, Edward. I've gotta say Angie would kill me for hanging out with you. You seem to have a problem with women. Are you some kind of misogynist?'

'It's not about gender. I might say Ardern's your standard woke progressive, but I'll say the same about Justin Trudeau. If there was a strong female leader who stood up to the thuggish left, I'd vote for her. And when it comes to gender studies, my go-to girls are Janice Fiamengo and Karen Straughan.'

Hall paused.

'But that's not the point - which is the nature of these male cowards. These sycophants will never put one foot out of line.'

'Alright - enough with the cowards,' I said. 'What about some thugs?'

'Easy,' Hall replied. 'Like I said, they're the ones who push their *right think* with the smug assurance no one will dare contradict them. Like that piece I saw yesterday.'

Hall went to an online news site and began reading an item aloud.

## Rise of the Right

## by Paul Wittingly

After September 11, there were fears about Islamic extremism. Two decades later, the threat is closer to home with the radicalisation of young white men into far-right beliefs. This is a backlash against social progress. Privileged young men, threatened by the idea of equality, want to wind back the clock to the days when they could lord it over women, gays, and immigrants.

Terrorism expert, Dr. Brigitta Marguerite, has analysed thousands of online comments and charted a huge rise in misogyny, racism, and Islamophobia. 'Any moral person must be alarmed,' she says. 'Hate has become normalised. We're facing the greatest threat since the Nazis killed six million Jews. Online websites are targeting vulnerable young men who feel emasculated by change. Rather than trying to curb toxic masculinity, these websites promote it. The government should step in and shut them down. Only trusted news sources should be allowed a media platform.'

Marguerite's advice is timely, but with the rise of right wing populist governments, hate is going mainstream. Fragile white men have found a voice, and are emboldened to say things they could never have gotten away with ten years ago.

Hall looked up from the screen.

'They're emboldened alright - to stand up to bullies like Wittingly and Marguerite.'

'So these are your thugs?' I said.

'Thugs deluxe,' Hall replied, 'and what a bunch of baloney. Sure, it's based on something real - people turning away from the progressive left, but let's break down their response. First, it's a superficial look at what's going on. There's no real understanding of why people are rejecting them, and they take no responsibility for any part in causing it. I mean, they've been targeting these 'fragile white men' for decades. Now there's a backlash, and they're *surprised*. That says it all.'

Hall lit another cigarette.

'Next they appeal to morality,' he said. 'They give us some fear-mongering and invoke the Holocaust. Then, sure as night follows day, the next step is calls for censorship and a monopoly on information for themselves. It's textbook thuggery, right here in a mainstream newspaper.'

Hall coughed. I could never understand why people smoke.

'For another thug,' said Hall, 'there's someone like Bunty McLeod, star feminist of the progressive press. Let's check out her latest newspaper rant.'

Hall found the article and read it out loud.

# Men's Rights in the Age of Me Too

## By Bunty McLeod

At a time when feminists have launched a worldwide revolt against sexual harassment, men have come to the Me Too party. How so, you ask. By supporting women and believing them unconditionally? Why, no, gentle reader. By the absurd and pitiful whine that men are also oppressed. *You reckon women have it tough*, the man babies complain. *Well, me too.*

Did you get that, citizens? Men are oppressed too. The dreadful violations against them include being 90% of CEOs and world leaders, earning 15% more than women at work, and being called out on their entitlement to rape and abuse women on a daily basis.

Apparently, giving men a few home truths about their toxic behaviour is too much for fragile male egos to bear. When you've been used to dominating women for thousands of years, it must come as a shock when you're finally called out on your bullshit. Let's make a deal, boys. Try to be passably decent humans for a couple more millennia and we'll call it even. How about that, all you 'good blokes'?

But if you... men's rights activists (excuse me while I belly laugh and vomit into the toilet) really want to say 'Me Too,' why not say it when women share heartfelt details of their suffering? When women say how bad they feel about gendered expectations they should shoulder the burden of housework and childcare, or the sexism they face in the workplace, that's when you should be saying 'me too.' If you don't feel bad about the problems women face every day, then frankly you're an appalling human being, and should be named and shamed as a misogynist.

Oh sorry, you were saying something? Something about men's problems, was it? Do go on. Women enjoy a bit of comedy as we go about our endless unpaid chores.

Hall winced.

'Ooh, can you feel the burn, Johnny? I reckon we've just copped a queen size dressing down! Let's tweet her a little appreciation.'

Hall found McLeod on Twitter, where she had posted her own article. He left a comment.

*Gotta love that sledgehammer sarcasm, Bunty. It's your trademark. I haven't heard anything so withering since I tried to tell my teenage daughter about good music. Why not fire up even more for next week?*

'You have a daughter?' I said.

'Nah,' said Hall, 'but so what?'

He laughed.

'So basically, John, you can see Twitter as a battleground in the endless culture war between left and right. It's a good laugh, long as you have a quick tongue and thick skin. Especially since this whole far-right thing ramped up a few years ago and started firing back against the lefties. Oh look. Bunty's sent a reply.'

*Hey dickhead, thanks for the advice. Stylistic tips from white male assholes are exactly why I go on Twitter every day.*

'Ha ha, there you go. Some more sledgehammer sarcasm right there. She can't help herself. Let's 'like' her reply.'

Hall clicked on the little heart shaped icon so that it turned red.

*You're welcome, cupcake*, he replied. *Anything else I can do?*

The reply came instantly.

*Yeah, go fuck yourself, douche-bag.*

Again, Hall 'liked' Bunty's comment.

*OK hon*, he tweeted. *Nice chatting to you.*

I felt I had to step in.

'Look, Edward. You seem to be saying anyone who doesn't agree with your view of the world is a thug or a coward. You're just dismissing half the population.'

'So?'

'Don't you think it's a bit... arrogant?'

'Sure, John, it is. Now, I could be wrong, and I may be delusional - but I call it as I see it and time will be the judge. Besides, not everyone's a thug or a coward. Most of them are NPCs.'

'Huh?'

'Non Player Characters. The blue pilled masses drifting unconscious through the matrix. The normie conformists, who only say things they've been programmed to believe.'

Hall held up his hands in a half-apology.

'And sure, there are plenty of good people on the left. Intelligent, well meaning people, some of them smarter than me. I don't have a beef with them; it's the thugs and cowards I can't stand. Fact is, I used to be a staunch leftist myself, and I've got to confess to a newfound evangelical streak. I'm like the ex-smoker who wants everyone to quit smoking. See I hate the fanatical cult the left has become, which is why I'm so fervent in speaking out against them.'

Coincidentally, Hall lit up a new cigarette.

'I don't know what's worse - the conformity or the cowardice.

Take artists, for instance. They're supposed to be rebels, right? Ha! More like sheep since this whole Trump circus kicked off. As for myself, I never gave two hoots about the man. But after seeing one artist after another frantically rushing to join the anti-Trump celebrity circle jerk, I'm starting to take his side.'

Hall exhaled a puff of smoke.

'Comedians are just as bad. They're supposed to challenge the establishment, not uphold it.'

Hall pointed towards my bookcase.

'See that comedy annual you've got there. It's supposed to be cutting edge satire on current events. Twenty years ago when those guys went to uni, being a leftist may have been subversive. Go to uni now and it's mandatory. If you're not a leftist, better keep your damn mouth shut about it.'

Hall continued.

'Go through that comedy book and you can predict 95% of the targets - Christians, whites, men, racism, Brexit, blah, blah. You'll get maybe 5% attacking their side - feminists, Islam, socialism, and so on. It's about as cutting edge as a big fluffy pillow. Comedians these days are, totally ball-less. That's why you had all those people on YouTube laughing at social justice warriors. They're doing the job comedy's supposed to be doing.

Why do they think the so called far-right emerged in the first place? It's a response to the left's tyranny. They tried to force their values on everyone. Now, it's the former lefties like me who can no longer stand them. And just because you don't bow down to feminism, white guilt, and the like, we get smeared as Nazis. Well, screw these people. They're no longer the resistance, they're the establishment. We're the real rebels now.'

Hall sat up in the swivel chair and slid it out from under the desk.

'Righto, Johnny Gilbert, me old outlaw mate. I've done my bit in the culture war today. Now why don't you have a go?'

**9**

# Culture Warrior

'No way,' I replied. 'As I told you, teachers can't get into this online political stuff.'

'Relax. I'll sign you up under a false name.'

Edward Hall turned back to the screen and whipped up a quick profile.

'Gilberto the Great,' he said. 'How's that for a name?'

'I don't want to be great,' I replied. 'Just average will do.'

Hall gave me a dry look.

'How about Average Anomaly?'

I shrugged.

'So what do you want me to do?'

'Find someone making idiotic comments, and argue with them.'

Hall scanned the Twitter feed and scrolled down the page.

'We'll start with some low hanging fruit. Let's see what Becksy is up to.'

'Who?'

'Seamus Becks.'

Hall perused the page.

'Hmm, something about women tennis players being paid less than the men. Becksy's on the case. Boring. Let's find something more controversial. Right, here's a post where he calls out racism. We'll tell him what happened to you at the Antifa fight.'

*I was assaulted and abused for being white*, Hall typed. *What do you think of that?*

Hall put the finishing touches to my Twitter profile. By the time he was done, Becks had replied.

*Get over it mate. One thing for sure, this trifling event wasn't anchored in centuries of systemic oppression. As a fellow privileged white male, I'm not going to shed any tears, not while women face domestic violence on a daily basis, and refugees are driven here by climate change, then persecuted by white supremacy.*

'Wow. What a suck up,' I said.

'Yeah. The arse kissing is off the scale.'

'Should I post a snarky reply?'

Hall shook his head.

'Tempting as it is to call him out on his gold medal virtue signalling, he might block you so you can't see any more of his tweets. Better to observe the buffoon in his natural habitat a while longer. Find something more subtle.'

Hall scrolled further down the page.

'Here you go. Some private school in Melbourne's in trouble for not wanting to hire gay teachers. Becksy's all over it. Look at this.'

*This repellent homophobia is now enabled by far-right bigots and legitimised by media complicity. Is it 2018 or 1960?*

'Are you anti-gay?' I asked.

Hall shook his head.

'What do I care?

He began typing.

*Plenty of 'right-wing' people have no problem with homosexuality. Gays should be more worried about the spread of Islam, which seems explicitly homophobic. Agree with you, Seamus, that globalist media are guilty of allowing this far-right movement to spread in the West.*

'There - that'll mess with his head. Now you have a go. Let's check in on Trump's stoush with illegal immigrants on the US-Mexican border.'

Thirty seconds later, Hall pointed to the screen with a *can-you-believe-it* look. The message read:

*Literally fuck every white person who's afraid of undocumented people.*

Hall turned to me. I took the keyboard.

*Sounds painful*, I tweeted.

'Good start,' said Hall. 'Now follow up with a question.'

*Do you have walls and a door on your home?* I typed. *Then you believe in borders.*

Hall nodded.

'An analogy to point out their hypocrisy.'

Someone called Tardis-Girl had already replied to my tweet.

*Your people destroyed the indigenous Indians and brought slaves from Africa so you don't get to decide who comes to this country.*

'What does she mean *your people?*' I said. 'Look at her profile pic. She's a white American.'

'She's trying to dissociate from the guilt she's been taught. Indians, slavery…it's only a matter of time before the Holocaust shows up.'

'Should I reply?'

'Sure, but personalise it. Look at her profile. She's named herself after something from *Dr Who*. You know, the science fiction show. Ever watch it?'

'I used to.'

'So what does the Doctor normally do? Prevents alien invasions of Earth, right?'

I took the hint and typed a reply.

*The Doctor protects Earth's borders against illegal aliens. The Doctor is xenophobic and a fascist!*

Hall gave me the thumbs up.

'You're a natural. Now, mind what I said about the Holocaust. I told you it would come up any moment. Check this tweet.'

*A young Mexican girl has been taken at the border by Trump's ICE troops. Remember when they took Anne Frank from the house in Amsterdam? This is the same. Like Anne, this girl is 15 years old.*

'Here we go,' I said. 'Trump is literally Hitler.'

'The woman who posted this - look at her Twitter name,' Hall replied. 'Calls herself Morpheus, like in *The Matrix*, and has the nerve to think she's part of the resistance. She's just about got that arse-backwards. Go on, write a response.'

I took the keyboard like a born again culture warrior.

*I've visited the real Anne Frank House, and you're trivializing the Holocaust with this comparison. Nazis invaded and occupied Amsterdam for 5 years. US govt isn't invading Mexico, they're trying to stop their own nation being 'invaded' illegally. Big difference.*

A reply came quickly: *Hate is hate.*

I followed up with: *It's apples and oranges. To say they are the same is an insult both to Jewish suffering in WW2 and the US govt today.*

My opponent came back with: *The hatred led to violence against Jews.*

I countered: *The Jews were German citizens who'd been living there for generations. They weren't trying to enter Germany and illegally settle there.*

I waited for the reply but it never came.

'Uh oh,' said Hall. 'You're blocked, old boy.'

I looked at the message. *You are blocked from seeing the tweets of Morpheus.*

'Never mind,' said Hall. 'There's plenty more lunatics out there. This one is from a woman who's actually running for congress. A 'woman of colour,' as your girlfriend would say.'

*Fear must never stop progress! White supremacists use conspiracy theories to harm those that challenge their power. Overthrowing white supremacy is #1 priority for a better future.*

'I'll take this one,' said Hall.

*If you actually believe we live under white supremacy and want to overthrow it, then it can hardly be called a conspiracy theory if they see you as a threat.*

'What do they mean by white supremacy?' I asked.

Hall snorted.

'What *don't* they mean by it? I'll tell you what it really means. A white supremacist is someone who believes white people are racially superior to others and wants to rule over them. Do you know anyone who thinks like that?'

'Not personally.'

'You had them in the past,' said Hall. 'The old style empire builders were white supremacists to some degree. They ruled over others. In a way they thought they were helping. They saw it as a moral obligation to help civilise others. The 'white man's burden,' they called it. Funny how times change.'

Hall raised his eyebrows.

'There's not many of those old style supremacists around anymore. Rule over non-whites? No, thank you. They just want to be left alone.'

'Then why is everyone always going on about white supremacy?'

'It's like this, Johnny. First you establish a multicultural society in the optimistic hope everyone is just gonna get along. Then you target the majority group not just by reducing their numbers, but stirring up resentment against them. This is the work of leftist ideologues, whose brilliant plan in a mixed race society is to make everyone totally obsessed with race. This includes banging on endlessly about diversity quotas. Then, having put a large number of incompatible groups together to compete for the same resources, they act amazed if there are any social problems. Now, if the likes of you or me are to query any of this, or remark on what a dog's breakfast it has all become, you know what that makes us?'

'A white supremacist?'

'That's it. Anyhow, if a multicultural society entails endless jostling over racial quotas, maybe the premise is flawed.'

Hall typed in a name.

'Here's Mona Seyit, one of my old sparring partners. She's blocked me, but since we're logged into your account we can reply to her tweets. Like this one.'

*The most idiotic part of being a white Australian is seeing your racial type over-represented on TV and thinking it's normal and not based on racial privilege.*

Hall typed a response.

*The most tedious part of being white in a multicultural society is being forced to see everything in terms of race. They don't have that problem in Japan.*

Seyit replied almost at once.

*When your country was literally created by pure racism, you don't get to choose.*

'What does she mean?' I said.

'The aborigines,' said Hall. 'Our original sin. Let's challenge her.'

*If we're pointing fingers, our country was created from the labour of white male slaves. The convicts were poor English and Irish whites forced to work for seven or more years as punishment for petty crimes.*

To this, there was no reply. After a few minutes, Seyit re-tweeted one of her followers.

*Great news! Far-right hate preacher banned from Australia! White supremacist Gavin McInnes has been denied a visa, forcing the cancellation of his speaking tour. Yassss!!!!!*

'Wait a minute,' I said. 'Gavin McInnes - you sent me a couple of his videos. He's not a white supremacist, is he?'

'No, he's a satirist who picks holes in the leftist worldview. But that's the left for you. They can't beat him in an argument, so they just ban him. They made a petition to keep him out of the country. I'll bet half of those who signed know nothing about him.'

Hall banged out a reply.

*Do you know McInnes is married to an American Indian and has mixed race children? Not much of a white supremacist.*

'For real?' I said.

'Yeah. I doubt we'll get a reply. We could look at another hundred tweets but let's cut to the chase. Martin Luther King wanted us to live in a post-racial society - an ideal which I once believed. Fifty years later, we live in the age of identity politics, which is nothing but *obsessed* with race.

Another tweet popped up onscreen from Mona Seyit.

*Western Civilisation is a dog whistle meaning white supremacy.*

Hall banged out a reply.

*Diversity is a dog whistle for anti-white.*

'To Seyit,' said Hall,' Everything wrong with the world is the fault of white people, and people of colour are the innocent victims.'

'Poor old POC,' I said.

'If POC live in the West,' said Hall, 'they're victims of systemic racism, and if they don't, they want to emigrate here as fast as possible to get their share of it. Meanwhile, the host nations must pay for their past sins.'

'Like what?'

'Colonialism. Slavery. Even climate change.'

'I'm guessing three Hail Marys won't do for a penance.'

'I'll tell you the three Hail Marys they want. First, we should open our borders. Second, we agree to become a minority. Third, we stand aside and give up social power - positions in government, the media, etc. They see this as karma for colonialism. They want Western nations to share their rich resources with the descendents of their historical victims.'

'Do these... leftists really say this sort of thing?'

'Some do - the hardcore types like Seyit. The white moderates are just sleepwalking through without seeing the end result.'

I stopped speaking for a moment. It seemed our conversation was getting into some dangerous waters. I felt some kind of protest was in order.

'Look, Hall, this all sounds pretty far-fetched. I'm sure Angie would say it's a far-right conspiracy theory. But suppose you were right, why would white people go along with it?'

'They've been hammered with the idea of white guilt, and fallen for it like the dupes they are. Seyit's whole spiel is about guilt.'

Hall lit a cigarette.

'See, you're not even supposed to notice any of this. You're not supposed to notice you're moving towards becoming a racial minority, or the rise of anti-white racism. If you notice, you're a white supremacist.'

'So, nothing to do with believing white people are superior or wanting to rule over others?'

'No. There's something very basic about the tribalism of human nature. *All* racial types advance their own interests. All except whites, who are the only ones silly enough to advance the interests of every racial group but their own. And do you think they'll thank us for it? Only as a sadist thanks a masochist, as Douglas Murray said in his book about Europe.'

'I don't even blame the other groups,' Hall continued. 'They're only doing what comes natural, looking after their own interests. I blame the self-hating whites who've fallen for it.'

'Maybe we can all just learn to get along,' I said.

'We might have done in Martin Luther King's post-racial society. I used to believe in it, same as you. But I told you - multiculturalism plus identity politics equals hell on Earth. And you've got to understand - there will be consequences.'

Another tweet popped up on the screen.

*Fuck white people. Your DNA is a violation against humanity.*

Hall shook his head.

'When the day finally comes that whites become a despised minority in their own countries, it ain't gonna end well. If these do-gooder, self-hating whites are expecting gratitude... If they think all the people of colour, Muslims, and the rest, are going to hold hands in a big circle and do a multicultural dance of joy and thanks...'

Hall stubbed out his cigarette with a violent stabbing motion.

'...if they believe that, they're even sillier and more naive than they look.'

Mona Seyit was still tweeting away.

*Dear white people, do something about your racism. Admit to it. Own it. Renounce it.*

'Right,' said Hall. 'Let's post a response. I've got just the thing.'

Hall posted a quote from a book.

*"You need to know that racism is not something invented in the West, or only experienced there. Racism exists in all societies."* Omar Saif Ghobash, *Letters to a Young Muslim*, p109.

'He's a Muslim?'

'Yeah, this guy is cool. He understands human nature. Oh look, a response already.'

And from there, the conversation went like this.

**Seyit**: *There is no doubt racism was invented in the West. This is well established.*

**Hall**: *Humans are tribal. They favour their in-group and distrust outsiders. This was long before the West began, probably going back to the Stone Age. By the way, Asia is outside the West. Any racists among the four billion who live there?*

**Seyit**: *You are projecting your own cultural norms upon non-Western nations. Racist attitudes may have been picked up by others, but you invented it.*

**Hall**: *That's hard to believe. Aren't all people capable of good and evil?*

This received no reply.

**Hall**: *Your theory denigrates the West and over-idealises everyone else. You seem to think white people are the only ones capable of sin.*

**Seyit**: *Whiteness is not a racial type. It is a system of inherited dominance.*

**Hall**: *Like in the Indian caste system that's gone on for thousands of years? I guess that was made up by the British Raj, was it? Sure, the British used it when it suited them, but the system had roots in ancient times.*

**Seyit**: *I am not going to waste my time debating basic points with those who benefit from institutional power.*

**Hall**: *I don't have any power. You're the university professor. I'm a nobody.*

**Seyit**: *I've been the target of abuse from far-right trolls all week. Take your toxic hate elsewhere.*

**Hall**: *All you do is bang on about white supremacy every day. No wonder it draws a backlash. I cop plenty of abuse too, you know.*

**Seyit**: *Don't compare yourself to a woman of colour. Being an edgy shit-lord doesn't take any real courage.*

**Hall**: *Why do you make assumptions about my own struggles and motivations? You use your status as a WOC to silence anyone you* *define as more privileged than you – that is, everyone. You want to be able to speak but no one can answer back.*

**Seyit**: *Do you think I come here for fun? This is not a game for me, it's a battle of life and death. I'm fighting for racial equality. It's not appropriate for you to come here gas-lighting a woman of colour about racism.*

**Hall**: *Gas-lighting? In my day, we used to call it academic debate. I'm just questioning your crazy theory that racism was invented in the West. Even the man I quoted agrees, and he's a Middle Eastern Muslim.*

**Seyit**: *If he's suffering from internalised white supremacy, that's his problem. Now go away and stop wasting my time. One more word and you're blocked.*

Hall immediately typed out another reply, then erased it. He turned to me.

'Well, Johnny, should we give her one more word?'

'How about two?'

'Tell you what, let's give her a thousand. Look up her university listing and see if she's got an email address.'

Hall went to Flinders University and sure enough, an email address popped up.

'That was easy,' said Hall. 'So, if we can only get one more message to Mona, let's make a good one.'

Hall opened a Word document and began to type.

# 10
# One Thing We Did Not Invent

Edward Hall spent the next couple of hours writing. When he was finished, we took a walk round the coast to Bondi for some pizza and beer. It was late by the time we got back. Hall sprawled his long frame over the couch and tried to find a comfortable sleeping position. As his feet stuck over the end, this wasn't easy. With some irritation, I wondered if the socially correct thing was to offer to take his place. Hall seemed to read my thoughts.

'Don't mind me, Johnny. I've seen plenty worse than this. Go to bed. We'll pick up again in the morning.'

Pick up? Pick up what? It occurred to me that Hall seemed to see our discussion as some kind of 'project' - as if I were his student and he my mentor. The thought made me uneasy.

What happened the next morning did little to change my impression. Hall made some edits to his previous day's writing, then printed off a few pages and handed them to me for study.

'What's this?' I said.

'My rebuttal to Mona Seyit,' said Hall, 'and her absurd claims about the origins of racism. Let me know what you think.'

Hall sat down at my desk and went online. I took the armchair and began to read Hall's essay, which he seemed to have addressed to Seyit directly, as a sort of letter.

Dear Mona,

I've been pondering your theory that racism was invented in the West. It's an extraordinary claim. The West has invented many things - cars, planes, telephones, the internet, and penicillin, to name just a few - but one thing we didn't invent was racism.

First, what is meant by 'the West'? Let's say it means the civilisation that came from Europe in roughly the last three thousand years. So, it does not include Asia, Africa, or the Middle East.

This civilisation spread out from Britain and Europe creating 'new nations' like America, Australia, and New Zealand, as well as colonising parts of India and Africa. You may be right that this sort of expansion was a form of racism, in the attitudes towards the natives of those lands. But the idea that racism itself was actually *invented* by the West is a far stranger concept.

Although you no doubt hold a special academic definition of racism, I'll stick with the simple one we were all brought up on. *Racism is prejudiced or hostile thoughts or actions from one person or racial group towards another, based on race.*

To come right to the point, the idea that racism was invented in the West is one of the silliest theories I've ever heard. To believe it, you would have to hold a highly idealistic view of human nature, and at the same time see Westerners as the only exception, the one group with a capacity for evil. It requires you to believe non-Westerners lived in a state of peace and harmony until the West corrupted them.

It seems a basic fact of human nature that people are tribal, show in-group preference, and tend to be hostile to strangers. This applies even within the same broad racial types. There has been conflict, for example, between different American Indian tribes, between Australian aboriginal tribes, and between countless other groups, not least whites themselves - in two world wars, for a start. If there is conflict between similar groups, there will be even more of it between dissimilar groups. For better or worse, that's what humans are like.

This sort of tribalism far pre-dates 'the West,' which has only been around for about three thousand years. We could even go back fifty thousand years to the theorised conflict between Neanderthals and *Homo sapiens*. As this conflict surely had some elements of 'racism' it's hard to see how the West could have been responsible. Although Westerners have invented many technological marvels, time travel is not among them.

You could look even further at the animal kingdom, noting that predation of one species on another is far more common than predation of a species on its own kind, i.e. cannibalism. Is this too 'racism'? Humans, of course, prey upon many animal species themselves. Humans of all races.

All racial groups protect their own interests. In light of your theory, it is ironic that one of the few exceptions are white Westerners. These supposed 'inventors of racism' have embraced immigration, multiculturalism, and other policies that strengthen other racial groups and weaken their own.

White people are also the only ones discouraged from taking pride in their racial identities. This is in contrast to all other ethnic groups, who celebrate their racial identities. This is a poor policy. As the author, Jim Goad, said - 'eventually whites will come to understand that to dismantle and even demonize white racial consciousness while other races cultivate racial consciousness is a fatal form of unilateral disarmament.'

Let's return to your strange theory that racism was invented by the West. Believing this requires you to accept a number of other ideas, all of which are absurd in their own right, let alone when combined as a team.

For example, you have to believe that before the start of the West, racism didn't exist. If there were any mixed race societies, there was no discrimination within them, and when different tribes or countries came into conflict, there was no racism there either.

If there *was* any conflict, it never had anything to do with race, or with a general distrust for people who were not like one's own tribe. So, all people lived as 'noble savages,' at one with nature and their fellow man.

It was only when the West began that white people invented the idea of race as a way to dominate other groups. But, this hostility was all one way. No Asian person has ever had racist thoughts about whites. No Middle Eastern Muslim ever made judgments against any citizen of the West or about Western civilisation. Or if they did, it was only in retaliation to colonisation or foreign-made wars. The taking of white slaves by the Ottoman empire was also nothing to do with race. Neither were the Crusades.

There can also be no racism involved in conflict between non-white groups. For example, the atrocity of the Japanese 'Rape of Nanking' involved no Japanese racism towards the Chinese. Neither has recent Black-Latino conflict in parts of the USA had anything to do with race. Nor did Genghis Khan's empire-building, or early Islamic countries' expansionist wars against their neighbours.

There's also nothing racist in China having isolated itself for long periods - by building walls in ancient times, and self segregation before 1970 - or in Japan choosing to remain an ethnostate to this day.

Perhaps you will try to redefine racism as a system of power structures by which one group dominates another. This too, is pretty old hat. As I mentioned, the Indian caste system, for example, goes back a long time before the British got to India. While the caste system may not be racially based, it shows that power imbalances are everywhere.

The idea that racism is the sole responsibility of the West, or was invented here, is a theory so far-fetched it's hard to see how anyone could take it seriously. Luckily for you, insanity is the new normal in our universities, so your theory will pass muster, especially as there is clear anti-Western bias among many who work there.

Once you venture outside that safe space, you'll find the going harder. Apparently you've been under fire on Twitter from 'trolls.' Well, you do tweet endlessly about 'white supremacy' and the terrible racism of Western nations. It can't be much of a surprise those comments draw a backlash.

As for my own message to you now, I regret its rude tone, but if you're going to pretend that racism is the sole responsibility of the West, I'll call this out as the absurd - and indeed racist - slander that it is.

I quoted a Muslim author who said racism was not invented in the West, and is part of all societies. This very sensible remark was blasphemy to you, whose whole identity is based on the idea of your racial persecution at the hands of Australia and other Western nations.

It is a sign of the generosity and freedom of the West that you are able to make such an argument in the first place, and even publish it in a book. Imagine if I did something like that in one of those wonderfully non-racist countries outside the West. Perhaps I should go to Saudi Arabia or Pakistan and criticise Islam. Maybe I should go to Beijing and lecture the locals about China's human rights record. Or should I tour Africa and harangue my hosts about all the corrupt and violent governments that have plagued the continent since it gained independence from its former imperial masters?

If I were foolhardy enough to slander my host nation, my first hope would be to escape arrest. If I managed that, I would at least expect a bit of a backlash against my views, people getting upset, answering back, and so on.

Here's a simple question: if the whole burden of your martyred existence is caused by being a 'woman of colour' in racist Australia, why not move to a country which is not majority white? Not the war-ravaged land you came from, but any non-majority white nation. I will speculate on the answers to this question.

First, because some of those countries are far less generous than Western nations in taking immigrants. Some of them police their borders and control their internal affairs. Are we the only 'racists' for doing that?

Second, because you wouldn't want to live there. Australia is free and tolerant, compared to some countries. You're lucky to live here, not that you'll ever show any gratitude.

Third, because if you went to another country and started complaining about 'Korean privilege' or 'Nigerian privilege,' like you do here, no one would take you seriously. Mainly because they are not insane.

Fourth, because your whole identity is based on the idea of persecution, and only in the West can you pursue your sad need for martyrdom, even finding an audience willing to indulge you.

The idea that racism was invented by the West is a pretty far-fetched theory. It may be true that your ancestral nation was wronged by white settlers hundreds of years ago, and you may be entitled to feel anger and resentment on that score, on behalf of your country. But that doesn't justify your concept that racism itself is the sole responsibility of the West.

If you choose to believe such a thing privately, that's your own affair, false and slanderous as the idea may be. But to teach it to your students is to inflict this falsehood on others, damaging their innocent minds. The least I can do is try to dissuade people from believing it.

It's worth noting that if I were to make my comments in a university these days, I would be expelled. Fortunately, I exist outside that lunatic asylum and am not bound by its absurdities, so I can say what I like.

regards,
Edward Hall.


I finished reading and put down the printed pages. Hall swivelled his chair around and faced me.

'Well,' he said. 'What do you think?'

I was about to answer, but before I could speak there was a knock at my bedroom door. I sat bolt upright, as if I were about to be arrested.

The door opened abruptly, and Angie walked into the room.

# 11

# Guilty Pleasures

I spun around, with the sense of having been caught red-handed - but Angie's face showed nothing more than mild curiosity at Hall's presence. I floundered for a moment, gawping like a fish tossed onto a boat. Hall came to my rescue. He stood up and extended his hand towards Ange.

'I'm Edward.'

They were an odd couple. My petite, pretty, punk girlfriend, and Hall the gangly, bearded outlaw. They shook hands soberly, while I tried to process the unsought meeting of my two worlds.

'Ed's staying for a couple of days,' I said, apologetically, before remembering that Mateo's stint as a houseguest was now in its second month. I wondered if Ange was returning home or had merely showed up to collect her things. There was no hint in her expression.

'I hope you're free tomorrow,' she said with the air of an order rather than an inquiry. 'I've got us two tickets to Whiteness.'

A wave of relief washed over me. This must mean we were still a couple.

'What's that?' I asked. 'A new band?'

Angie laughed her pixie laugh.

'It's not a night out. It's a workshop in Whiteness Studies at Sydney Uni.'

'Oh,' I said, with a sinking feeling. 'Good.'

Ange looked genuinely enthused. 'It's with Helda McGovern. I've heard she's awesome.'

Hall raised an eyebrow. 'I've heard of her,' he said.

I realised my YouTube was open, showing thumbnails for

political videos of which Ange would not approve. I quickly closed it and did a search for the workshop.

'Whiteness Studies, with Helda McGovern,' I read out loud. 'Learn to see how invisible structures of white privilege harm people of colour, and why white people refuse to discuss it. Er... wow. Sounds pretty cool.'

Hall turned to Angie.

'Mind if I tag along?'

Angie shrugged. 'It's a public workshop.'

'Are you staying tonight?' I asked, trying to keep any note of pleading out of my voice.

She shook her head. 'I'm just here to pick up some clothes. See you there tomorrow night. 7.30, alright?'

She gave me a quick, unexpected kiss on the cheek, then left. I gazed after her. Soon I could hear her banging around in the living room, talking to Mateo like they were best buddies from childhood. Hall gave me a pitying look.

'Well,' he said. 'I can see she's got quite a spell over you.'

I turned my frustration onto Hall. My life would have been a lot simpler if he hadn't shown up in it.

'What do you think you're doing?' I said tersely.

'What do you mean?'

'Coming to the workshop with us.'

'It's too good a chance to miss. Whiteness Studies. There's no doubt it'll be bat-shit crazy. The only question is how much.'

'So why go?'

'It's a chance to study the enemy up close. We can get a direct gauge on the level of madness.'

I bristled.

'Look, Hall, if you're only coming to cause trouble, stay away. The last thing I need is you embarrassing me in front of Ange.'

Hall raised his hands.

'Please. I'm a gentleman. I'm not going to be a jerk and spoil the show, no matter how much I may despise it. Let's leave that sort of thing to our tolerant friends on the left. I'm going purely as an observer. Best behaviour I promise.'

He gave me a rueful smile.

'And I don't want to cause any strife between you and Ange. There's no doubt you two can make enough on your own.'

Hall and I bussed into Sydney University the next night and found the lecture hall - a six hundred seater - nearly full. Ange had saved seats a few rows from the front, pretty much dead centre in line with the podium. I took the chair to her right and Hall followed suit, so I was sitting between them.

Now, in reporting Helda McGovern's speech, I had better make a couple of disclaimers. First, this is not the whole speech, as that would be far too long - but I think I've got the gist of it. Second, I've dumbed it down a little. Helda was addressing a university crowd, and I want to simplify it for those who haven't heard these sort of ideas before. Having said that, I've tried not to distort her meaning. If anyone thinks I've misrepresented her, they should go to the source - that is, to the academic activists who actually preach this sort of stuff. They'll find the same basic concepts, just stated more verbosely.

Helda McGovern walked onstage to a warm round of applause. That is to understate it. There was an extra note to it. I had an odd sense I was at an evangelist rally, or a talk by a New Age motivational speaker.

Helda herself was a white woman of about forty, slim, with straight, sandy hair that fell down to her shoulders. Some thin rimmed spectacles gave her a scholarly look. She wore an earnest expression, which was relieved by the occasional jokey remark during her talk.

She took a long moment to soak in the adulation and the packed house. At last she spoke.

'Thank you, Sydney.'

The audience noise died down to a murmur.

'I'm Helda McGovern. My pronouns are she and her. First let me acknowledge the traditional owners of this site, the Bedegal people of the Eora nation.'

We paused for a moment, as if in prayer, then Helda got down to business.

'Right, let's get into it. You know what? I've got good news and bad news. The good news is there's no such thing as race. The bad news is there's a hell of a lot of racism. Now, I know that's a pretty basic point for a lot of you guys, so bear with me. There's all kinds of folks come to these seminars. Experts, rookies, and everyone in between. You older hands hang tight while I lay some of the real Race 101 points on the table for the newcomers. So, let me repeat, there's no such thing as race.'

I turned around and took a moment to survey the crowd. It was mainly women, many of them white. There were quite a few people of colour - both women and men - while the white male category to which Hall and I belonged had the lowest turnout of all. The people of colour seemed to include Africans, Middle Easterners, and a few Asians, among various others.

'Race,' said McGovern, 'is a fiction. A made-up concept invented by white people. See, when Europeans went on their mission to conquer the world, they had to justify it. So they used euphemisms. They weren't out to *conquer* the world, they wanted to *civilise* it. This was a Christian culture, right? When they took their Christianity to the world, they had serious internal struggles. *Thou shalt not steal* is one of the commandments. How could it be Christian to steal from other people and enslave them? So what did they do? They dehumanised the indigenous people by inventing the concept of race. We are white; you are not. We are human;

you are the Other - so we can do whatever we want because we're better than you. And at the same time, we are going to turn you into us.'

Helda sipped some water from a glass on the lectern.

'See, that's what whiteness is. It's nothing but a made up system of dominating people of colour by defining them as less than human. But the fact is, there is no race. Science has proved it beyond all doubt.'

There was a ripple of applause. Helda soaked it up, then chuckled and took a joust at the crowd.

'See, what's kind of weird is this: if there's no such thing as race, how come there's so many goddamn racists coming to my workshop today?'

There was an uneasy silence. Helda let it stew for a bit.

'Now hang on a minute,' she said. 'I don't mean you people of colour in the audience. I'm talking about all you white folks, right?'

There was a murmur from the crowd and Helda raised her hands.

'Don't take it the wrong way. There's nothing I'm saying about you guys that doesn't also apply to me. See, I'm a racist too. We can't help it. To be born white in America or England or Australia is to be born in a society where white supremacy is so normalised it's invisible. We grew up as a majority and we just took it for granted it's normal to be white. We saw white people on TV, we went to white schools where our teachers were white, we lived in white neighbourhoods. We all grew up like that with a deeply unconscious assumption that white was not only normal but superior to any other way of being.'

I took a glance at Hall on my right. He looked pissed but was trying not to show it.

'But wait,' McGovern continued. 'I know what you're thinking. *Hey, I'm one of the good white people. I'm not racist. I'm a liberal.*'

Helda checked herself.

'Whoa there. I'd better not use that term. Someone told me that here in Australia, liberal doesn't mean progressive like it does back home in the US. Your 'Liberal' party is the conservative party. Wow, I guess this really is the land down under - you guys do everything backwards! I'll try not to say liberal again, but if it does slip out just from habit, I mean progressive. OK?

So let me be clear. When I say we're all racists, I don't mean we go out burning crosses or taunting people of colour. You see, racism is a system. I guess many of you are students here at Sydney University. But how did you get here in the first place? White privilege. You went to majority white schools so you could get good marks, which meant you could get into a majority white university.'

I frowned. Helda mustn't have had a chance to walk around campus. One might well surmise it to be a majority Asian university. There was nothing very surprising in this. It's well known Asians on average are smart, study hard, and come from a culture which demands high academic achievement. Also, the university made most of its income charging high fees to wealthy foreign students. I wondered if Helda was going to say anything about Asian supremacy or Asian privilege.

'And where did this all start?' Helda continued. 'This whole country was founded on an act of racist theft against the indigenous peoples. Look around you - how many Aboriginal people do you see?'

I took the opportunity to survey the crowd again. I didn't see many Aborigines, just a lot of guilty white folks.

'Not that my country is any better,' said Helda. 'If anything, we're worse. First we stole America from the peace loving Native Americans. Then we took slaves from Africa to build it. Some people want to make America great again. How can they when America is probably the worst country in the history of the entire world?'

This pronouncement met with some applause and a few whoops, perhaps in relief at Australia being let off the hook, if only in having been one-upped for evil by America. But Helda was just getting started.

'You see, history is everything. History controls everything we do, and we can never escape its shadow. It's probably hopeless to even try.'

I felt a nudge from Hall on my right.

'If that's true,' he said, 'may as well pack it in and go home.'

I darted a nervous glance towards Ange on my left, but she was gazing at Helda with rapt attention.

'So what are we to do?' asked Helda. 'What can we do when our countries are founded on evil and shame, and when we finally admit to ourselves that all our achievements have been gained by structural racism and white supremacist systems at the expense of people of colour?'

'Commit mass suicide?' Hall said, loud enough for some people in front to look around. I elbowed him in the ribs and gave him a stern look. If they had heard it, neither Helda nor Ange paid the remark any heed.

Helda brought up a slide on the screen at the front of the room. It contained the following checklist.

## The Five Point Plan for Ending Whiteness

1. No More White Wimpiness.
2. De-centre Ourselves
3. Shut up and Listen
4. Do the Work
5. Get Out of the Way

Helda gave us a moment to read the slide, then addressed us in a let's-goddamn-get-this-done tone of voice.

'OK, white people, let's make a plan moving forwards. I'm going to discuss these points one by one. First of all, do you wanna know the biggest problem talking about racism to white people? It's white people.'

A weak, masochistic ripple of laughter went around the room. Helda looked chuffed.

'There's a term I came up with - white wimpiness. See, white people are so touchy about race that the slightest insinuation they might benefit from racism and they get all mad. I've seen it so often it's no longer a surprise. You see, when I talk to white people, I don't sugar coat it. I tell them their countries were founded on racism, that whiteness is inherently evil, and that everything they've achieved is down to white privilege - and for some reason they get mad. I state obvious truths like white people invented racism and only whites can be racist, and they go all red in the face. Geez, guys, stop being so sensitive. Enough with the white wimpiness. Just own up to it. And you want to know who are the biggest wimps of all? This won't come as a shock, but it's white males.'

Helda seemed to look directly towards Hall and myself. We were, after all, only a few rows from the front.

'Sure, you get the white female liberals - I mean progressives - who get upset too, but it's usually tears from them. That's passive aggression, right? *No, don't attack me, I'm an innocent, pure hearted little girl.* But it's generally the white males who want to deny, argue, and answer back. You see they're so used to dominating they take it as a natural entitlement, and their male egos are so frail that instead of listening when me or people of colour tell them they're racist, they argue and complain. That's white wimpiness! Cut it out, guys. It's pathetic.'

Helda looked smug and took another sip of water. I glanced at Hall and saw him checking his watch.

'OK, step number two - Decentre Ourselves. We're so steeped in white supremacy we just assume the whole world revolves around us, like people used to think the sun went round the Earth. We think being white is some kind of universal norm. Enough! It's time for white voices to hush. It's time for white people to get off stage and spend some time in the margins for once. The world does not revolve around us. Let people of colour and indigenous people take centre stage where they belong.'

Helda stared out into the crowd with a look of righteous zeal.

'I'm not speaking metaphorically,' she thundered. 'White people have had their day. It's time we find out what it's like to be a minority. Stop keeping boat people out of this country. You stole this land. Maybe you guys ought to build a boat and sail back to England, right? Or if you can't do that, build some more boats and go pick up as many refugees as possible and bring them back here. Take them into your homes. Then move out. It's the least you can do!'

Helda was in the zone now. Some zone of righteous redemption where we could barely follow.

'Where was I? Number three - Shut Up and Listen. This one builds on the first two. Now, just because there are some people of colour in your tute class or your workplace or your neighbourhood, doesn't mean you're not racist. *Hey, I live in a one hundred apartment block and there's an Asian family in apartment 97. How can I be a racist?*'

There were some more titters, which fired up Helda even more.

'Do you know, there's some white folks believe there's such a thing as anti-white racism? I guess they also believe in fairies or Santa Claus, right? Given that racism can only be done by those who have structural power, it's impossible for a person of colour to ever be racist. So next time a white person complains about racism, just politely let them know they're talking out their ass!'

Helda smiled triumphantly.

'On the other hand, if a person of colour tells you about the racism they've experienced, you must never ever doubt them. One of the most traumatising things you can do to a person of colour is disbelieve them. If a person of colour opens their heart to tell you how you've racialised them, don't answer back, just goddamn shut up and listen. You might learn something.'

Helda took a big sip of water.

'That leads on to step number four - Do The Work. If a person of colour offers you a lesson, do your homework. Now don't give me any crap about being 'colour blind.' Pretending you don't see race is just one big cop out. It's a total insult to the racial pain people of colour experience every minute of every day. If you don't see race, it's about time you opened your baby blue eyes. You'd better start seeing race everywhere you go. How else are we ever going to move beyond racism?'

I heard a little ping from my pocket. Must have forgotten to turn the phone off. Sneaking a glance at Ange, I fished the phone out of my pocket and saw there was a text message. It was from Hall, sitting twelve inches to my right. *FFS is it nearly over?* I turned off the phone and shoved it into my bag. As if on cue, Helda seemed to be nearing the end.

'OK, step five - Get Out Of The Way. Now, I'm running a little over time, so I'm about to take my own advice! Anyhow, let's just say this one's the same as step two, but it's such an important point, it's worth saying twice. Give up the power and get out of the way of people of colour. It's the least we can do for them. So there you go - that's my five point action plan. I've tried to make it clear, simple, and proactive. Even so, it's still going to take years of practice before we can heal ourselves and end white supremacy once and for all. Now, it's just about time to wrap up my talk…'

I saw Hall do a tiny fist pump below Helda's eye level, under cover of the seating.

'… but the good news is I'm only the warm up act. The real headliner is yet to come.'

I heard a thud and turned to see Hall had punched the back of the chair in front of him. The person of colour sitting there looked round in alarm. Hall sighed and held up his right hand in apology. Truth be told, it looked like a *Sieg heil*.

'So give her a warm welcome,' said Helda. 'Yasmin Chemali!'

A woman who'd been sitting in the front row stood up and walked to the stage. She was a thirty-five-ish woman of colour, whose roots I guessed were somewhere in the Middle East. Fit looking, with shoulder length straight black hair, she was rather attractive, though her face was set in a grim expression just now. There's no way in hell I would have told her to smile, not even as a joke.

Helda embraced her and the crowd applauded loudly. But Helda still wasn't done.

'Before I hand over to Yasmin, I just want to check in with her for feedback. I've already admitted I'm a racist - all white people are - but at least I'm trying to get over it. So I want Yasmin to give me some honest criticism. I'm going to ask her directly - Yasmin - have I done anything racist to you today. Or this week?'

'Yes, you have, Helda.'

'Oh no, I'm sorry. Please give me some feedback so I can learn from it.'

'Remember when we were at Melbourne airport yesterday and those women of colour were sitting near us wearing hijabs? I saw you staring, and I could tell you wanted to ask if I ever wore one too and what I thought about them. You assumed it was some big deal for me and you wanted to quiz me on whether I thought it was feminist, or oppressive, or liberating, and blah, blah, blah. Such a white thing to do, OK? You know what, Helda? It's none of your business. It's lucky you never raised the topic, or it would have been a pretty awkward flight. I don't need you getting up in my face with your white curiosity and your hang ups. Know what I'm saying?'

'OK, Yasmin,' said Helda. 'Thanks for your feedback. I totally get that. It was super rude of me, and I now see it's not appropriate to racialise you like that. Thank you for this learning experience, and once again, I am very, very sorry.'

Yasmin Chemali did not acknowledge the apology. She turned to the audience with a dead serious look on her face, like she was getting ready to go into battle. Then she spoke. Her accent was broadly Australian, so if she'd come as an immigrant, it must have been at a young age.

'This is going to be personal,' she said, 'but I won't apologise for that. I never apologise. OK - I want you to think back to your childhoods. What was it like growing up as a Weetbix and Vegemite kid in White Australia?'

Yasmin Chemali glared at the audience.

'Do you have any idea what a privilege it is to think of yourself as normal? Did you ever think what it's like when every face on TV looks like yours? Of course not. Well, did you ever think what it's like when *none* of the faces on TV look like yours? Or your schoolteachers, or your politicians? Did you ever think that maybe people of colour have a life just as important as your own?

When you grow up thinking people like you are the norm, it's deadly for minorities. You believed it so much you tried to make it the norm for everyone else in the world. Your ancestors wanted to make whiteness universal. They went out and spread it everywhere. At the same time, you refused to allow anyone else to be white. You invented the concept of race and used it to Other everyone you didn't perceive as white. So, whiteness became the universal human standard at the same time as you denied whiteness to anyone who wasn't white.'

I glanced sideways at Hall. Was this some kind of racial Zen koan? But Hall was staring straight ahead. Chemali continued speaking.

'So there were whites and there were Others in a vicious binary. Like Helda said, we can never understand the present unless we have a clear understanding of the past. The past makes us what we are. So when your ancestors went out and raped the world, I'm not just speaking metaphorically. I suppose that makes them a bunch of Other-fuckers.'

There was a gasp, then some instinct in the crowd told everyone to laugh hysterically.

Chemali then went into a long spiel, which I'll omit, about the history of wicked white people. It was a deconstruction of history as a some kind of living 'text' full of symbolic meaning. But mainly, it was all about wicked white people. It was a litany of woes: of empires and thefts, rapes and ravages, until I started to believe we were the only race that ever sinned. On top of that, Yasmin had the notion whites were the only race that had never suffered or been oppressed. In her eyes, we were all born kings and queens.

My mind wandered off. Must have been in denial, or maybe I felt I was back in church like when I was a small child. Eventually, I realised Yasmin was still going.

'So I grew up here a refugee kid. My homeland had been colonised, then bombed into a ruin, and Australia was never my home. It was never yours either. You stole it. But I tried to fit in anyway, for years and years - until I finally figured out why I could never get ahead in my career. Even though I was better and smarter than everyone else, the promotion always went to someone dumber and whiter than me. And finally I realised the system was rigged and no matter what I did, there was no chance I could ever succeed.'

I stopped to consider Chemali's last sentence. Yes, that's pretty much how I felt when I was trying to make it in showbiz.

'But look at me now,' said Chemali. 'My book is in all the best bookshops, I'm guesting on ABC TV, and I'm internationally famous. Although it tried its hardest to grind me into the dust, the systems of white supremacy failed to destroy me. So let me put this into some true blue local language for you. Cop that you white Aussie mongrels - fuck you all!'

There was a hysterical round of applause from the audience, and a few whoops from the back.

'Still, I am just one woman,' said Chemali. 'There are hundreds more women of colour in my position. Thousands. Hundreds of thousands. We are fighting a grim battle for our survival. I believe if we can just collectivise as a combined force, we can bring white supremacy to its knees once and for all. We can give this stolen land back to the indigenous people and give it to the people of colour as well. But here's the thing, white people. We need you to become white allies. Use your privilege for good instead of evil. Use your access to institutional power to raise women of colour up instead of grinding us into the dirt.'

I glanced once more at Hall, who seemed to be napping. His eyes were closed, at any rate.

'Finally,' said Chemali. 'I want to give a shout out to my white girl, Helda McGovern. If you white people want a role model, look at her. See, Helda gets it.'

I felt a nudge from Hall. He wasn't napping after all.

'She'll *get it* alright,' he said, 'once she's outlived her use.'

'Yeah,' Chemali continued. 'She gets it - and she's got the common decency and humanity to try and make up for all the dreadful things whites have done in the past. If only we had a million more people like her. She's an angel. Get up here, sister!'

Helda came back onstage, to clamorous applause. She embraced Chemali and the applause went up to a frenzy. The two of them turned to the crowd and raised their fists, one white, one *of colour*, in a supremacist-smashing show of solidarity. Then Helda re-took the microphone and called for questions from the audience. The alarm bells started ringing for me, and my fears were confirmed when Hall stuck his hand up. In light of that, Helda's next words came as a relief.

'We're going to reverse the normal privilege hierarchy, right? I'm going to take questions from women of colour first, then from men of colour. Then all other genders. After that, I'll call on white women, and lastly, if we must, any questions from white men.'

Hall snorted and stood up to leave. I put my hand on his wrist. It must have occurred to him it wouldn't be a good look if he left the room at that point. So, we sat through another twenty minutes of questions, which I won't repeat here - apart from one which stands out because it was so pathetic. A pretty young white girl in the row behind me, a few chairs to my right, raised a quivering hand.

'I want to ask... well, uh, first I just want to say sorry really. I want to apologise to Yasmin for everything she's been through and the racism she faces every day. I feel so embarrassed of my whiteness and my privilege.'

The young girl's voice tailed off. It may have been my imagination, but Chemali seemed to be staring at her with contempt.

'Do you have a question?' she said coldly, after the girl had been silent for a few seconds.

Sensing the hostility, the girl began crying.

'It's just that I feel so bad about whiteness and the awful things we've done. I feel everything's pointless, you know?'

Now I was sure there was disgust in Chemali's face, but at her target or herself I did not know. Sensing an awkward moment, Helda stepped in to answer the question.

'Now look, I don't want to be unkind because I know exactly how you feel, but your tears aren't helping anyone. You're making it all about you. When you cry in public like this, you're sucking energy away from people of colour. You're putting yourself in the centre and POC back in the margins. You're trying to get people to comfort you and say you're a good person. Well I'm sorry, but you've just got to accept the fact that you're white.'

'I'm sorry too,' said the girl, still crying.

'Then pull yourself together. If you really want to help undo some of the harm you've caused, then use your privilege to empower the people who really need it.'

The girl cried even louder, and I turned away from the pathetic and embarrassing spectacle.

Hall kept raising his hand at intervals, and when Helda could no longer ignore him he was at last given the portable microphone to ask his question.

'Thanks for taking my comment,' he said. He was talking more slowly than usual, as if trying to convey humility.

'If there's one thing I get from both your talks,' Hall continued, 'it seems like the biggest problem for people of colour today is whiteness, whites, and structures of white supremacy. If that's true, isn't the smartest thing to get as far away from white people as possible?'

Helda looked coolly at Hall.

'I'm not sure I understand the question,' she said. 'How can people of colour get away from white people when they're surrounded by them?'

'Not that I know how to do it,' Hall replied. 'I'm just saying that if whiteness is the problem, it's best to get away from it.'

'I'm sure people of colour would be glad to have less white people around. But what are you suggesting - some kind of segregation?'

'No, not at all,' said Hall. 'I'm just trying to reason it out with the logic I've been socialised into. I accept Yasmin's point that whiteness is the biggest obstacle for people of colour. That's why I can't understand why so many people of colour are trying to get into majority white countries.'

I was shrinking into my seat. Looks like Hall couldn't control himself after all. But, to his credit, his manner was so earnest he might have been taken for a dim but sincere leftist, rather than the right wing troll I knew him to be. Even Helda and Yasmin weren't sure, though there must have been a spike in their radar.

Yasmin took the mic from Helda.

'You mean the refugees? They have no choice because they're fleeing countries harmed by colonisation and ruined by war. How can they go back when their countries have been wrecked?'

'I understand about the refugees,' said Hall. 'It's the ones coming from Africa or South America I don't get. Why are all those people trying to get into the US? Haven't they been warned about whiteness? It seems like a suicide mission.'

'America stole its wealth from other countries. The poor people of those lands deserve to come and take back some of the wealth that was taken from their ancestors.'

'But how can they, if they're going to be crushed by the

forces of white supremacy as soon as they arrive? You said yourself there's no way you, as a person of colour, can succeed in this system. If that's true, doesn't it make sense to move to a country where there are hardly any white people? An African nation, for example. There are plenty of Africans who have left so there must be a few vacancies for people who want to escape whiteness. For example, I heard of someone...'

At that moment, Hall's microphone cut out. Helga's had no such problem.

'If you really want to help, how about you focus on being a white ally? Use your white male privilege for good instead of evil. Just support people of colour when they speak. Listen and don't argue. It's not hard. Next.'

The event petered out soon after that. Helda McGovern and Yasmin Chemali made their triumphant farewells, and Hall, Ange, and myself began filing out of the lecture hall with everyone else. We walked into the cool night air, refreshing after all the hot air that had been released in that room. There was plenty of traffic noise in the distance. Yet the leafy surrounds of Sydney University were enough to shield us from the urban realities of the wider setting.

Once the three of us had separated from the throng, it was Hall who broke the silence.

'That. Was. Amazing. So, who's up for a beer?'

I felt a sudden panic. What in God's name might Hall say in front of Ange that could get me excommunicated for life? I was already planning my disavowals when Ange put the kibosh on the idea.

'You guys go ahead. I've got classes in the morning.'

My sense of relief was mixed with pain.

'How about tomorrow?' I said. I gave Hall a dismissive glance. 'Just us.'

'I don't know, John. I'm flat out.'

My paranoid, overactive mind even read a sexual innuendo into that. I felt sick. I knew what I said next would mean waving a white flag in our power struggle. I said it anyway.

'Look. Maybe Mateo can stay for a while. And his wife and kid. My only concern was that I've got to pass my school prac next month. Get through that and I'm set for life as a teacher.'

Ange didn't look at me.

'Do you really want me to come back? The two of us in the same room?'

'Yes, of course.'

'Sorry, John. I'm just not sure it's a good idea. I saw a side of you last week I've never seen before.'

'Just give me another chance.'

'Maybe we should stay apart for a while - and maybe you need to prove you can get along with Mateo before we even think about living together again.'

'Oh for God's sake!'

Ange gave me an accusing look.

'There's that temper again. See? That's what I'm talking about.'

'OK, OK. At least let me pay for you to get a taxi home.'

'No need. Daddy lent me the car.'

Angie turned to Hall, who'd been trudging along beside us all the while.

'Nice meeting you... Edward, wasn't it? See you round.'

Hall nodded.

Angie stepped up and embraced me for a second, and gave me a quick kiss on the cheek. Another one. Then she turned and walked away. I stared after her, a lovelorn, deluded fool, as she vanished into the dark.

# 12
# Tale of the Four Animals

At home in Tamarama the next day, I fired up the coffee machine. Ange was back at her parents' house on the other side of town. I handed Hall a cappuccino.

'What did you think of Helda?'

Hall did not reply, and merely gave me a scornful look.

I pressed the point. 'Well, can you refute her?'

Hall snorted.

'All you have to do to refute Helda is watch a few Jared Taylor videos. Or read Jim Goad's book, *Whiteness: the Original Sin*. But if you want to hear my take on it, alright - pull up a chair, Johnny. First, I'm going to tell you a little story. It's something I call the Tale of the Four Animals - the horse, the ant, the elephant, and the frog.'

Hall settled into the armchair in my room.

'First, let me say that a decade ago I had no interest in the topic of race. We were all just human beings. I was prepared to be 'colour blind' in a post-racial world. But that ain't good enough for the likes of Helda and Chemali. They *want* us to see race. They *want* us to be obsessed with race every day, in every way. Alright - let's give them what they want. We'll talk about race until we can't talk no more.'

Hall sipped his coffee.

'Second, I want to disavow any notion of 'white supremacy,' if there even is such a thing these days. In Helda's eyes, of course, white supremacy is the very air we breathe, invisible though it may be. The real meaning of the term is the idea that whites are better than other races and want to rule over them. There aren't many who think like that, so let's put that archaic term out to pasture.'

'At the same time,' he continued, 'in facing this topic, we're not going to be any kind of cringing wimps, like that poor bamboozled lass who asked the question before mine. So where to begin?'

I sat back and listened. At this point, I'm going to give the rest of the chapter to Hall, and not even interrupt with questions. Let him make his case.

Hall began to speak.

'So, I'm going to tell you the tale of the four animals - elephant, ant, horse, and frog - and each of them drawn from well known tales and parables. First we've got the horse - the Trojan horse. If you remember your Homer, the cunning Greeks made a huge wooden horse and gave it to the city of Troy as a peacemaking gift. This was supposed to end the Trojan war, right? Trouble was, the wooden horse was full of Greek soldiers who came out at night and conquered the city from within.

Now, modern Western nations have also accepted a wooden horse, but it's in the form of beliefs. A few examples: Some cultural diversity is good. Women deserve more rights and freedoms than they had before 1960. Western nations did some harm through imperialism and slavery, and should learn from those mistakes.

I agree with each of those ideas at face value, and there are many more you could add to the list. It all looks very pretty on the surface of this beautiful wooden horse - but who'd have thought? The horse is full of parasites. Not soldiers with weapons. Something much slower and harder to see, but equally destructive. The horse is full of ants. White ants, ironically. Also known as termites.

You see, buried beneath the surface of our beautiful wooden horse are some other ideas, most of which never needed to be there in the first place, but for some reason they are.

Some cultural diversity is good? Of course it is. It broadens the mind and makes life more interesting. The hidden white ant is the idea your nation wants so much cultural diversity that it weakens or supplants its *own* culture. Women deserve more rights and freedoms than before 1960? Of course they do. A white ant - one of many - is the idea men should be vindictively punished into the bargain. Western nations did some harm in the past? I won't deny it, but the white ant is the idea those same nations should now harm themselves.

Now, unfortunately, the white ants are so small they're practically invisible. You don't see them for a while unless you look really hard, or until someone else points them out. But they come creeping out of that wooden horse and go crawling all over the city, reproducing and multiplying, and infesting the woodwork and the structures that hold up the civilisation. They get into our institutions - the schools and universities, and into the media, the government. And sadly, they get into the brains of people like Helda and the poor fools who believe her.

Eventually the white ants have done their work and you notice your country has changed. It took you a long time to see it. If I can mix my allegories, it's like the frog in the pot. You've got a frog in a pot of cold water. The water starts to heat up, but it happens so slowly the frog heats up with it and he doesn't notice. By the time the water gets too hot for the frog, it's too late.

So you look around your country. Half the population's gone mad and the other half's asleep. You notice your country's different than it used to be. Some of those white ants have eaten so much of the structure they've grown as big as elephants. You can hardly help seeing them anymore, these 'elephants in the room.' Hell, even the normies start to see them. But for some reason, seeing the elephants is discouraged. People who mention elephants on social media are kicked off it. Elephant spotting is denied, discouraged, and finally made illegal. But they're there alright, walking down the street in plain sight.

So that's my Tale of the Four Animals - the horse and the ants, the elephant and frog - and a grim tale it is indeed.

Let's get back to Helda McGovern. What are we to make of her? First, let's concede that she means well. I don't doubt that for a moment and - who knows? - maybe she does some good along with all the harm. Having said that, I hate to be unkind, but Goddammit I've no choice but to call her out on where she goes wrong. If she's going to vilify our people so harshly, I'm duty bound to defend them. Mind you, there's hundreds more think like her, so I ain't picking on Helda. Think of her as a stand-in for the lot of them.

Second, she's not stupid. Clearly she's intelligent. She can string together words and concepts, and communicate them to others. Trouble is, her mind's full of white ants - a bunch of false ideas infesting her brain. And the worst parasite of all is an emotion - guilt.

You see, Johnny, Helda's like one of them old sinner-man preachers. For her, to be white is to be born with original sin. We're all born guilty because of what some adventurous Europeans did hundreds of years ago. You've probably heard that quote, *the past is a foreign country; they do things differently there*. In that sense, the colonisers did things differently in two foreign countries at once - the literal ones and the metaphorical one. What that's got to do with us in the 21st century, who knows?

Helda's whole trip is about guilt for our supposed wicked, wicked ways from centuries ago. You'd think that would make her feel bad. Well, we both saw her performance last night - she was drunk on her own virtue. If guilt's her thing, she sure gets a kick out of it. It's hard to fathom people like her.

I mean, Chemali's easy enough to figure out. You don't have to be Sherlock Holmes to see what's driving her. It's the three Rs - resentment, rage, and revenge. But what the hell's going on with Helda?

There's no way to sugar coat it. She's mentally disturbed. What you see there is a poisoned cocktail of guilt, virtue, false ideas about the world, and chronic naivety - all bound up in the disastrous impulse to teach.

No doubt she thinks she's doing good, trying to end racism and right the wrongs she never did. But for someone who said there's no such thing as race, she sure has an unholy obsession with white people. Now, don't forget she's white herself, but she doesn't see it as treason to attack her own tribe. She sees it as a holy mission for which she's been personally selected by the goddess Justice.

So where does she actually go wrong? I'll try to break it down.

What you have to realise is Helda's got some very strange ideas. Now, that don't mean she's eccentric. On the contrary, her views are very much the norm among the academic left. There's hundreds more like her. Thousands. But when crazy is the new normal, what chance have you got? So where does she go wrong?

First, she's bought into the cult of equality. That is, she believes in the unattainable goal of an equal world - though if there's any equality in the *natural* world, please point it out to me. Of course, that don't matter to Helda because she doesn't think we're part of nature anyway. She believes everything in human life is a 'social construct.' That means nothing is fixed and everything is fixable, if you'll pardon the pun.

She doesn't believe in race, but she's obsessed with racism. She thinks the idea of race was invented as a tool for domination. So she looks around her own country, America, and sees whites, on average, doing better than blacks. She can't explain it by genetics, and she won't put it down to any failing within black culture. She'll never look at an underperforming school and say it has anything to do with the students, for instance.

She defines 'whiteness' as power, and for an equality cultist that can't be good. How can 'whiteness' be good for people of colour? That's not a term I'll use much, by the way. *People of colour*. It's a mouthful. I'll just say black and white from now on - and remembering that in Helda's belief system, white is bad and black is good.

Don't forget Helda herself is white, so we're not dealing with a shining example of mental health here. Her ideas aren't good for either whites *or* blacks. In her eyes, any white success is tainted as it comes via white privilege and 'structural racism,' whatever that is. At the same time, any black failure or problems are never the fault of blacks, but also the result of white privilege and structural racism. It's lose-lose if I'm not mistook.

To put it simply, she thinks both white success and black failure is the fault of whites. Unfortunately they teach this bollocks as early as school, and how they think this is going to lead to any kind of racial brotherly love, I've no idea. The white kids either turn into grovelling mini-Heldas or incipient alt-righters. Meanwhile the black kids turn into a bunch of Excuse Culture whiners who go polar bear hunting for kicks. And if you don't know, that's a fun game involving the gang-beating of random whites.

So, what's wrong with Helda's system? Where do you start? With history, as she's so obsessed with it. Her first mistake is the idea that the past controls the present. Of course it has an effect, but she exaggerates it to the point where people may as well not get up in the morning - as if what they do today is controlled by what happened to their great grand-daddy two hundred years ago. How that's supposed to be 'empowering' beats me.

Why do the likes of Helda bang on about the past so much? Because that's the scam they're running. Helda's whole spiel is based on guilt and the wicked deeds of white people. Of course, she's American so the Holocaust's not much use to her, but the other two of the big three white sins - colonialism and slavery - that's her bread and butter. Those two sins laid the foundations for white domination and black suffering, as she sees it, their long shadows still in effect and serving to oppress people of colour to this very day.

Now, for starters, let's grant the reality of those two evils. I'm not going to sit here and pretend slavery and imperialism are something to be proud of. But what are you going to do about it? We could sit here and cry about the sins of the fathers and grandfathers, and Helda can self flagellate til the cows come home for all the sins she, you, or I never committed. We can all sit around weeping and wailing and gnashing our teeth - and then we can have a good laugh at the idea white people are the only sinners who ever walked this Earth.

Trouble is, Helda's view of history is mighty partial. There's no doubt history's full of swindles and horrors, but to think this divides neatly along racial lines is just another con. Mind what her offsider, Chemali, said last night - *whites have never suffered, whites have never been oppressed.* Well, hello, try reading some Dickens, for a start.

To refute that drivel, I'd like to call up a few witnesses. Trouble is, they're all dead, but let's hope they're here in spirit. I'll call up a hundred million white ghosts, if you'll forgive the tautology. First - serfs up. Let's have all the wretches who lived under feudalism. Four hundred years of it, and if that system wasn't a fair approximation of slavery, I don't know what is.

Next, we'll have Dickens' hordes of poor from the Industrial age and those 'dark Satanic mills.' Oliver Twist, Nicholas Nickleby, and the rest of the chimney sweepin,' pick-pocketin' undernourished scamps of the streets and poorhouse. They lived and died like rats, and I'm guessing most of them never made it to forty.

Now let's hear it for the thirty million whites who died in World War One, and if trench warfare wasn't one of the outer pits of Hell, then I'm not here. Let's not even mention the sequel, even better than the first, or the millions of Russians killed by Stalin in the meantime. But whites have never been oppressed!

If you want to talk slavery, we Aussies know our colony was founded on the back of convict hard labour. They were slaves in all but name - but here's something I didn't know until Jim Goad mentioned that book, *White Cargo*. Turns out there were plenty of white slaves shipped off to the US too. They called them 'indentured servants' not slaves, but a rose by any other name smells as sweet, and slavery has the same stench whatever it's called. Bit of an eye opener, that book, and it sure puts the lie to any notion blacks had a monopoly on sorrow.

You might say this was all whites enslaving whites. Then what does that tell you? It's not about one race dominating another; it's about the tiny elite class of whatever race dominating the goddamned rest. Look at the African slave trade. You think white Americans went to Africa and picked 'em up from Wal-Mart? Course not - there was a middle man, and he weren't white. Elites in Africa sold them to elites in America and Europe.

And you know the percentage of American whites who owned slaves back in the day? I can't recall if it was two percent or five. A slender minority, at any rate. So how come the entire white population of modern America has to do penance?

Mind you, it wasn't all white on white class warfare, there was the Islamic slave trade as well, which went on for untold years of misery. The white slaves of Barbary - Europeans were the victims that time. There's some believe in reparations. Maybe those guys ought to pay us reparations, then we can pass them on to the POC if that's how business is done.

And Chemali reckons whites have never suffered. Dear God.

Of course, that's not the only problem with Helda's black-good, white-bad view of history. If you believe her, whites have a monopoly on evil. Hasn't she heard of the Aztecs' human sacrifices, Native American tribal wars, or the Japanese rape of Nanking? Here's a little Logic 101 for you: people of colour are human, humans can be good or bad, people of colour can be good or bad. Well, praise the lord for equality.

Now here's another flip side of Helda's scheme - white good. If Helda and the rest of her guilt cult are going to obsess on white wickedness, then how about white goodness and the contributions we've made? You can point to European culture - art, literature, and music. You can cite science and medical advances. You can look at technology and make a case that whites invented the modern world. As Goad said, 'why should whites apologise? For inventing everything and still being spat on by ingrates who appropriate it all without a simple thank you?'

So, bollocks to Helda's view of history. Whites ain't the only villains, and blacks ain't the only victims. Even if Helda's view was true - which it ain't - but supposing it were, what good does it do to see yourself as a pawn to what happened centuries ago? It's a lame arse cop out.

You want to obsess over 'structures of systemic oppression'? Get in line. We're all oppressed, one way or another, and the sooner you lose the delusion it only happens to you and your group, the sooner you stop adding to the sordid whine-fest of modern life.

# 13
# Conquest by Concept

Hall stepped outside for a cigarette. I made him another coffee, and he came back and resumed his spiel.

'Let's get back to the present,' said Hall, 'and see where else Helda goes wrong. First, as to her views on interracial crime stats, don't even go there. But let's look at her attitudes to the cause of some real black social problems in America - the lower levels of education, lower income, higher rates of crime and incarceration, more single parent families - and so on.

Now, those things are facts, and there's a mix of causes, but is Helda going to say blacks play any part in it? Not a chance. Helda's the type loves pointing fingers, but the fingers only ever point one way. In her simple moral universe, none of the black social problems ever have anything to do with them. It's all down to 'white privilege' and 'structural racism' and God knows what else.

Look at this another way and it's a grave insult to people of colour. What she's really telling them is they're so puny nothing they do ever counts. A black conservative like Candace Owens would never say that, but Helda's gonna come in all white saviour and infantilize them as hapless victims too weak to ever rise above the system. For blacks, the likes of Helda are creating an Excuse Culture where nothing's ever their fault and everything's down to whiteness. Beats me how there's any empowerment in that. If I were a POC I'd tell her to get back on the chariot she rode in on and fuck off back to the Department of Victimology.

Now, it's not enough for Helda to be a self-hating white, she also has to idealise blacks to the point of absurdity. For all the talk of equality, she seems to see black and white as two different species. You might wonder how anyone could hold such an odd view of human nature, but Helda's not the first to look through the wrong end of a telescope and see Eden. You can go back to Rousseau in 1750 and his idea of the 'noble savage.' This is the deluded notion that before colonialism, people of colour lived in an idyllic state of love and harmony with nature, before wicked white settlers came along and taught them how to sin.

As for today, Helda imagines that POC live in the same state of innocence, stoically bearing their pain, and the only thing keeping them out of some urban Eden is all that crushing whiteness. If you can believe it, they teach this mental rot in schools. Not surprisingly, there's all sorts of righteous rage aimed at whites as a result. If you teach blacks to hate whites systematically, you also get them to do it individually. So you get your hate crimes and so on, of the type that rarely makes the news, from POC who've been taught to hate whites on the basis of race.

Of course, Helda, in her innocence, can't conceive how blacks could ever be hateful or bigoted towards whites. Don't forget, the greatest sin in her eyes is racism. How is she going to admit POCs could ever be racist to whites, and still believe they are morally pure? So what she and her crew do is actually redefine words.

Helda's god is equality, right? When it comes to who can be racist, the one thing Helda *hates* is equality. See, if we use the basic definition of racism as negative thoughts and actions towards people of other races, then POC have every capacity and every encouragement to do it. Therefore, Helda has to redefine the term 'racism' so it means *prejudice plus power*, with an emphasis on the power. Now, as she contends that white people have 'institutional power' but blacks do not, she has redefined the word so it's impossible for blacks to be racist.

So, for example, even when three black guys beat a white guy named Andrew Quade into a coma for dating a black girl, that's not a racist act. How could it be when it's impossible for anyone but whites to be racist?

In her firm conviction only whites can be evil, there are certain facts about human nature of which Helda is blissfully unaware. Chief among them is that humans are a tribal species and all racial groups favour their own kind. All except self-flagellating white liberals like herself, of course.

In those terms, we are all 'racist.' For all her equality talk, Helda's never going to admit all racial groups can be as bad as each other. So, to maintain the fiction that whites are the only bad 'uns, she has to perform some mental gymnastics.

You may have heard of Alinsky and his *Rules for Radicals*. One rule is 'hold the enemy to his own standards.' Now, Alinsky was a leftist himself - but the whole game plan of the modern left is to *avoid* being held to their own standards. So, to get past the obvious fact that blacks can be racist to whites, these cheats change the definitions. They're not just moving the goalposts, they're actually removing the goalposts from one end of the field so only one team can score.

The left's whole scam is about starting a battle where only one side is armed. In classic Orwellian style, this is done in the name of 'equality.' The whole strategy is to make Group A play by one set of rules, and Group B play by a different set. Like I said, Helda reveres equality as an ideal, but it all goes out the window when it comes to making both groups live up to the same standards.

This is just one of a whole arsenal of dirty tricks Helda's bound to employ. Note how she urged us to always listen reverently whenever a POC feels they've experienced racism, but if any whites complain about racism against themselves, we must laugh it off as imaginary.

Then there's her whole *white wimpiness* shtick. She says any white defensiveness on the topic of racism is 'wimpiness.' So presumably whites who stand by like whipped dogs and let POC berate them are showing strength, while the ones who stand up for themselves are wimpy. Helda wants to tell whites they are uniquely bad, all their achievements come from white privilege, they should be ashamed of their past, and disempower themselves in their present. According to Helda, those who believe this bullshit are strong while those who reject it are weak. This is another Orwellian attempt to reverse the meaning of words. It's a trick only fools fall for - and sadly, many have.

Of course, this is only a shadow of the far bigger trick, which is to persuade white populations to disempower themselves overall. One of the most brazen deceits is to push the idea that we're living under white supremacy, and run around in a moral panic about it. It boggles the mind how they get away with this, when you look at the evidence. Fact is, if we're living under white supremacy, it must be the weakest form of it ever existed in the history of the world!

I mean, what sort of white supremacy is it where 'whiteness,' as Jim Goad said, is used as a synonym for evil? Where critical courses in 'whiteness studies' are openly taught at universities? Where there are pushes for 'diversity' and affirmative action? Where whites are the *only* ethnic group that doesn't do in-group preference, and where whites call each other out for their racism? Where whites are the only racial group you can joke about or criticize? Where immigration from POC countries is constant, and even illegals have a chance at citizenship? My, this must be not only the weakest white supremacist system ever, but the weakest form of nationalism to boot! Imagine a supremacist group so feeble it lets itself lose racial majority status in its own nations by the mid twenty-first century.

As Goad said, we live in 'a logically impossible world where somehow society is rooted in white supremacy, yet this same society's cardinal sin is white supremacy.'

There's no end to the lunacy where these ideologues are concerned. Mind how Helda and Chemali claim whiteness is some kind of universal racial norm for humanity. Beats me where they get that from. Is whiteness a universal norm in China or Japan? In India or in Africa? Granted, the British had an effect in India. But a universal norm? If that theory's not the silliest ever conceived, it's certainly in the top ten.

Mind you, none of those places are masochist enough to commit demographic suicide. Yet you rarely hear about 'Chinese supremacy' or 'Japanese supremacy.' We only hear about whites - a people so supremacist they were twenty-five percent of the world's population in 1950, and will be ten percent by about a century later.

Now, it's not enough for Helda to teach her mad theories in some academic asylum, she has to go on a lecture tour to chastise any resistance as *white wimpiness*. You see, it is actually a *strength* to hate yourself, to allow yourself to be disempowered and displaced. It's really a *weakness* to notice any of the patterns out there and make any objection.

There are many poor souls bamboozled by her spiel. Thankfully, there are some who see through it, and these are what Helda and co would call the 'far-right' - by which she means anyone who has refused to be steamrolled into submission to her leftist agenda. She might call it far-right, or she might call it white wimpiness. I call it having a backbone and some self respect.

This pushback has come as a surprise to both Helda and Chemali. They can't get their heads around the idea of any kind of backlash to the academy's denigration of the West, forced diversity, and the demographic replacement which will in time see whites become a despised minority in their countries. You could say the 'far-right' is a form of identity politics for whites, and this outrages them. Remember, in the game they made up called Equality, there are two teams but only one set of goalposts.

Of course, no one will condemn the far-right more than self-hating Helda. Her brain's riddled with white ants, one of which is the idea that treason to her own kind is noble rather than a betrayal. She thinks her loyalty is to the greater race, of which we are all one. She's like the mother who sends her child out to play with a gang of bullies, not realizing he'll be beaten up as soon as she's out of sight.

And in the end, what will be the consequences of all this racial self-hatred Helda's mob have been preaching for decades? When you teach blacks all their problems are caused by slavery or colonialism from the past, or by white privilege and structural racism in the present, can you expect any other result than the widespread hatred of whites? And if you're foolish enough to allow yourselves to become a racial minority, what do you think is going to happen? Take a look at South Africa for a preview.

Do-gooders like Helda think we're all going to join hands in a multicultural dance as rainbow brothers and sisters. She need only look at dear colleague Chemali for a hint of what will really happen. Sure, Yasmin will tolerate her as a useful idiot for a while, but when the time comes, the only dance Helda will be doing is the one over the cliff. It might not be Helda herself; it'll be her children or grandchildren, if she has any.

You saw Chemali last night. Happy soul, ain't she? She came here as a child refugee - and does she have a scrap of good will for this place? Hell, no. She's not got a shred of gratitude for Australia, just rage and resentment over her professional 'frustrations.' And in the meantime, look at her. Giving talks at uni, publishing books, guesting on the ABC, at the same time moaning about how the system won't let her achieve anything.

She'll whine about growing up as a minority here, and granted it wouldn't be easy. I agree it's hard being a minority - which is why I don't want it to happen to my own tribe. Chemali hates that whites never had to face the consequences of racism, as she sees it. A state of affairs she wants to amend as soon as possible - and she'll do whatever it takes to make it happen.

There's no end to her sermons, whether it's the 'systemic racism' of the present, or the wicked colonial sins of the past. Now we all have to appease her righteous wrath by opening our borders and letting in the third world. Of course, she sees the West as a monolithic whole that must do penance. But as I said, it was the elites in each country who did the damage - whether it was trading slaves, waging foreign wars, and the rest, this has been done by and for elites. The ordinary folk had no say in these dealings. After all, the same elites exploited them as well - whether it was down the coal mines, or using them as cannon fodder in war.

Chemali can get in her pulpit and say the common folk were racist against minorities too, back in the unenlightened past. OK, well some were and some weren't, but that was the past and today's people aren't going to pay for those sins either. And if she's gonna try and say her mob would have behaved any different if the roles were reversed, let's all have a good laugh about that too.

Now, if dear old Yasmin really hates the West so much, let's set aside some special territory for all who agree. They can form their own countries and see if it turns out like Wakanda, or maybe more like Baltimore. Helda can move there and act as her slave if it makes her feel better about herself. Meanwhile, we can get along here just fine without the both of them.

Notice Chemali's obsession with the past. She conflates slavery with her present frustrations, though she was never a slave, and forgetting that vast numbers of poor whites lived in appalling conditions too. She makes the same mistake about the present. Like many such types, she thinks universal problems - like career frustrations, or not feeling loved and appreciated - are specific to her own group. She has no idea that many members of the 'privileged' group feel the same way. Indeed, the very suggestion would outrage her.

Clearly, she is seething with rage, and barely bothers to hide her agenda. Now, remember our Trojan horse. In this case, it takes the form of a very pretty word, *justice*, but inside that horse is a big ugly white ant called *revenge*. You heard Chemali last night. She's got it into her head whiteness is to blame for every world problem, past and present - and all POC must band together to slay this goliath which has crushed them for so long. And to that I say, message received. We get it, Yasmin. You hate us. You blame us for everything. You want to overthrow us and transform our world, and you demand that we help you do it. Thanks for making that so clear. Now fuck off, and take poor deluded Helda with you.

So, kids, the take home message is watch out for all the dirty tricks and double standards you're being sold, especially when it's some pious, self-flagellating white doing the selling. It's conquest by concept, with an emphasis on the con.

And don't forget, it ain't just the whites who should slam the door in her face to tell her they're not buying. People of colour should be slamming it twice as hard. She's selling them a bunch of baloney.'

Hall stood up and fixed on me a look of great intensity.

'I tell you what, Johnny, we've all been had. We've let ourselves be dictated to by fools and cowards far too long. It's time to give that wooden horse a good examination, and track down all those goddamned white ants before it's too late. Or maybe it already is.'

Hall lit up one more cigarette, breathed in, and exhaled a big puff of smoke.

'Time will tell.'

# 14
# Chateau Gardiner

The next day, I phoned Ange and asked her to come home for dinner.

'Why don't you come over here?' she said.

She didn't have to ask twice. I showered and dressed, changing my shirt several times before going back to the first one. Hall saw me putting on aftershave, and raised an eyebrow.

'Hot date?'

'Dinner with Ange and her parents.'

'I see. Do they know about her Antifa activities?'

'Yes. What's more, they approve. They're hard left.'

'Better watch your dinner table conversation.'

'I'm hardly going to bring up any of your theories, if that's what you mean.'

Hall snickered.

'Are you coming back tonight? Or staying over?'

'None of your business.'

'No need to be touchy. Speaking of which, your Brazilian friend's giving me bad vibes.'

'Chile.'

'Pretty icy, alright.'

'I mean he's from Chile.'

'Whatever.'

'Poor old Mateo,' I said. 'Have you taken over his living room? Far as I'm concerned, it's yours, including the TV remote. Feel free to annoy him as much as possible.'

I grabbed my keys and left.

Angie's parents lived in the affluent part of Sydney's inner west. Stanmore was just past the gentrifying but still grimy suburbs like Newtown. You were close to the city, but far enough to avoid the noise. *Chateau Gardiner* was a two storey house, spacious and tastefully furnished. Indeed, I could hardly believe it when Ange had said she wanted to leave it and move in with me. But when you've grown up with something, you always take it for granted.

The Gardiners were high achievers. Her mother, Norma, was a successful lawyer, while her father, Frank, was a big shot in the history department at Sydney Uni. Still, I speculated that those jobs alone wouldn't have paid for a house like this. There was money somewhere in the family background.

Although I was training to teach history, I'd been afraid her father would look down on me as a mere high school teacher. To the old boy's credit, there'd been no hint of condescension. His manner to me was collegial.

I rang the doorbell, expecting to be met by Ange, but it was Frank who let me in. To my surprise, he clapped me on the back and shook my hand. 'We're in the drawing room,' Norma called out. 'Come and have a G and T.'

With Ange having walked out on me a week or so before, I hadn't expected such a cordial reception. Ange herself was smiling, as if we'd had never a cross word.

Frank Gardiner was not a physically imposing man, but had the charisma of the successful academic, and the booming lecturer's voice to go with it. Norma was dark haired and petite like Ange, and forthright in expressing her opinions. From time to time, she seemed to disagree with Frank as a matter of principle, although as far as I could tell they actually shared most of the same views.

After our drink, we sat down to dinner in the formal dining room. At home in Tamarama, Ange and I always ate in front of the TV. Perhaps in twenty years, we'd do it properly like this. I'd been brought up not to discuss religion or politics in company, but Angie's family had no such qualms. Inside ten minutes Ange was giving them a rundown of Helda McGovern's speech. Her parents listened politely. I sat there uncomfortably, all too aware that just the day before, I'd heard Hall's scathing review of the same event.

My unease grew with the next topic of conversation - my 'heroics' at the Antifa rally some weeks before. Ange had clearly told them the story and exaggerated my part in it. Frank and Norma seem to have the idea I'd singlehandedly broken into a den of Nazis, denounced and overpowered them, then fought my way out. Perhaps that explained the subtle rise in respect I'd detected on arriving at the house.

One might think Angie's parents would disapprove of a man who took their beloved daughter to violent political rallies, and would make every effort to stop her going. But no. On the contrary, they saw her Antifa efforts much as a past generation may have viewed a daughter's work with the church benevolent society.

Frank turned to me with a look of pride.

'We've always encouraged Ange to stand up and be counted. Now with the threat of the far-right, it's more vital than ever.'

'I don't know where it's come from,' said Norma. 'These people were in the shadows twenty years ago. What was fringe is now mainstream. It's Trump, of course. Racists have been emboldened to come out of hiding.'

'I don't quite understand the terms,' I said. 'Is the far-right the same as the alt-right?'

Angie answered with a question.

'Were the Nazis in Germany the same as the fascists in Italy?'

'Good point,' said Frank, adjusting his glasses. 'When it comes down to it, much of intellectual life is about examining things that are the same but different. It's the fine distinctions that count.'

'Whatever you call them,' said Norma, 'they're all dreadful.'

Ange's dad turned to me with a jovial look.

'They're not terribly original, these alt-righters,' he said. 'The white race dying out, being swamped. It's all been said before. You only have to go back to Spengler in the early twentieth century. He was peddling the same line a hundred years ago.'

I raised a diffident query.

'If I may play Devil's Advocate, sir, the demographics of Western nations have changed a lot since 1920.'

Frank chuckled.

'Blowing each other to bits in two wars had a part in that. We've made a hash of the world, to be honest, and it's about time someone else had a go.'

After dinner, Angie's mum suggested we watch a film. I agreed at once, not just from good manners, but because the cinema room at *Chateau Gardiner* was a plum part of the house. The recliners were as good as the ones in Gold Class cinema at Bondi.

We all piled into the room, Frank and Norma taking a couch near the front, while Ange and myself took adjoining recliners further back and to their right.

'What are we watching?' I asked, easing the chair into a blissful viewing angle.

'*Human Flow*,' said Frank. 'It's a new documentary on the refugee crisis. Chap in the department recommended it.'

For all our allegiance as history teachers, I stifled a groan. I just wanted to chill out with Ange and watch something fun. Besides, refugees were a hot button issue on the right. It was doubtful Hall would look on the matter very favourably. The film was bound to be confronting viewing. Still, I was hardly going to argue with Angie's father. I sat back and braced myself for a grim couple of hours.

Even so, I was basking in a warm glow that came from the affluence of the house, my acceptance by Angie's parents, the wine we'd drunk at dinner, and the presence of Ange herself. There was another factor - the Gardiners' unquestioned sense of moral rightness and the peace of mind it brought. It was in the very air they breathed. The Gardiners had no doubt they were on Team Good. After the moral ambiguity of Hall's ideas, the sense of assurance came as a comfort. Listening to Hall might give me a nefarious thrill, but the certainty of the Gardiners was, when you came down to it, as comfortable as this cinema room.

Angie's dad turned off the room lights with his remote control. I reached towards the recliner on my left and took Angie's hand in mine.

The film began with a high shot of a small boat crossing a vast expanse of sea. The camera zoomed in to reveal it as a boatload of refugees. We saw them land, probably at one of the countries serving as entry points to Europe. There they would wait to be processed, as part of the long and arduous search for a new home.

The film didn't bother much with story. It was more a montage of some of the millions of refugees trying to get into the Western world. They came from Africa, the Middle East, and God knows where else, some of them fleeing bombed out cities or persecution. They came with a handful of possessions, clinging to children or elderly relatives. If they survived the perilous sea voyage, they might spend weeks or months in refugees camps. Or they would walk hundreds of miles across Europe, coming up against borders and hostility, waiting to find a country to take them in.

It would break your heart if you let it. In one scene a refugee showed a photo of her pet cat from back home. This simple image brought home the truth that underneath, these people were no different to us. At the end of the day, we all just want love and a home.

The warm glow with which I'd begun the film gave way to guilt. Guilt of two kinds. First, there was the irrational distress that comes with seeing people worse off than oneself. This is a strange emotion when you think about it. How is it *my* fault some people on the other side of the world are going through hell? Even so, it was a lousy feeling. I could hardly fail to notice the jarring contrast between the wretched conditions of those on the boats and the first world comfort from which we were watching them.

Perhaps it was this same sense of guilt driving the Gardiners' activism. That's not to doubt their sincerity. Sure, there may have been plenty of Hollywood celebs who'd never lift a finger for refugees except to virtue signal on Twitter, but the Gardiners weren't just going through the motions. They'd follow through to some degree. I felt sure of that.

The second layer of guilt was particular to me. It was the knowledge that in associating with Edward Hall, I was flirting with a different state of mind. Hall was likely to view the refugees with suspicion at best, perhaps even campaigning to keep them out. This might be pragmatic, but could only seem cold-hearted compared to the Gardiners, who would no doubt invite them all in without thought of the consequences.

There was also the sense I had betrayed Angie's family in some manner. Was I now 'far-right' of the very type they saw as so contemptible? What would be their reaction if they knew of my ties with Hall, and the ideas to which he'd introduced me?

This sense of guilt was my silent companion for the rest of the film. When at last it came to an end, Frank flicked on the lights.

'Good God, I need a drink after that. Shocking.'

We adjourned to the drawing room and took our comfort. Norma sighed.

'To think we can sit here drinking sherry while all those poor souls are locked up in the detention centres at Nauru. It makes you ashamed to be Australian.'

'But what can we do?' I said.

'Storm Parliament House and make them watch that film, for a start,' said Ange. 'Then force them to close it down.'

'Parliament House?' I said, stupidly.

'Nauru,' Ange replied. 'It's a disgrace.'

'The trouble is,' said Frank, 'the old refugee act is out of date. It was drafted after World War Two to meet the times, but it's woefully inadequate now. The whole thing needs to be redrawn.'

'Australians are so ignorant,' said Ange. 'They haven't got a clue how privileged they are. Someone should do something about it.'

We all lapsed into silence. Why did we have to watch that film? What was wrong with a little French farce like, say, *The Dinner Game*? That was hilarious.

'Are you staying, John?' asked Norma.

I pretended to be surprised.

'Oh. I hadn't really thought that far ahead.'

'It's too late to go home now,' said Frank. 'Stay in the guest room. You can come in with me in the morning.'

I turned in for the night and was about to nod off when the door opened. Angie snuck into the room and climbed into bed with me. Although she was wearing only a slip, she came for comfort rather than sex. The refugee film had put a dampener on anything else. She did seem comforted as I held her, and was soon asleep. I could hear her soft, childlike breathing.

I could not settle. I tried all sorts of mental tricks, even imagining how unpleasant it would be trying to sleep on a crowded refugee boat, and comparing it to my comfy bed. It was no use. Finally, about midnight, I got up and snuck out of the room, taking care not to wake Ange.

A couple of doors down the passage, I came into a sort of reading room. Frank's study, judging by all the history books on the shelves. I pulled a few out. They were mostly academic works, dry and longwinded. All the better to put me into a state of drowsiness. Just as I was about to dive into one of the turgid tomes, I spied a pile of paperbacks on Frank's desk. Halfway down the pile was one with the provocative title *Rising Out of Hatred*. I took it out and read the back cover. It was the story of some American kid named Derek Black. He'd been raised as a white nationalist but had eventually seen the light and become a leftist progressive.

Was this some kind of omen? Intrigued, but with a sense of foreboding, I began skimming through the book. This was no dry academic work, but a popular page turner. The ironically named Derek Black was born into a white nationalist family. His dad was hardcore, even having his own political radio show. Derek was raised with those values, and groomed as a future leader for the movement.

When Derek went away to university he started mixing with people of colour, Jews, and white liberals. Rather than hiding his identity, Black chose to out himself as a white nationalist, and for a time this made him a social outcast.

In the meantime, he had struck up a friendship and possible romance with a left leaning female student. She seemed to be a hardcore social justice type like Ange. She had the same unwavering, almost smug, conviction as the Gardiners - that she was playing for Team Good against Team Evil. With such uncanny parallels to my own life, I speed-read the book to try to resolve my own predicament.

It's no great spoiler to say that Derek Black recanted his former beliefs and become a leftist, accepting the ideas of globalism, social justice, and the rest of that whole package. He got the girl and the happy ending, and presumably rode off into the sunset to create a better world.

This prompted me to a little self interrogation. Here I was with a brave and beautiful girlfriend from a fine family. I was on the cusp of an honourable career as an English and history teacher, and my whole life was in front of me. What on Earth was I doing letting myself be corrupted by a straggly bearded, smooth talking rebel like Edward Hall? I must have been out of my mind.

Even so, I could hear Hall's voice in my mind, telling me the book was no more than a work of propaganda, right down to its title, *Rising Out of Hatred*. The book equated the globalist, liberal view of the world with love, and a conservative, nationalist view with hate. This, Hall would say, was the sort of crude black and white thinking so typical of the left.

Yet this was no work of fiction. Derek Black was a real person, as far as I could tell. His story had really happened. Perhaps if I'd read the book at home, I may have sided with Hall. But here I was at the Gardiners' house, my psyche having already copped a savage beating from the refugee film. In my weakened, vulnerable state, I realised it was so much easier to give in to conventional morality than to defy it.

It was 4.30am. I returned to bed and fell asleep with my arm around Ange. The next thing I knew she was shaking me awake.

'Quick, get in the shower. Daddy's got to go to work. I'll make you a coffee.'

Half an hour later, I climbed into the passenger side of Frank's Audi. Thankfully, it would be only a short trip to

Sydney University. Frank saw it as the chance to have a private word to me.

'Look, John, I don't want to come across as some kind of chauvinist, but I want to ask you to look after Ange.'

I felt my face flush, but from pleasure rather than any embarrassment.

'Of course, Frank.'

'Obviously, we're proud of her standing up for what's right. Even so, she's very young.'

He paused.

'We're well aware of what you did at that fascist rally. Bravo. I only wish I could have been there with you. Still, I must confess there's an awful patriarchal side of me that wishes Ange would stay away from that sort of situation. Not that I would stop her - wouldn't dream of it. All I'm asking is to show a bit of discretion and watch out for her. She's all we have, really. Never mind the big house and the flash car. At the end of the day, it's family that matters.'

'I understand. You can trust me to look out for her.'

'I hope you don't mind me saying, John. Ange dated a couple of real morons before you. Couldn't stand them. You're different. There's something about you, John - you're rock solid. Maybe I shouldn't say this, but Norma and I have high hopes for you.'

I flushed even more, and hoped Frank wasn't looking at my reflection in the mirror.

'I'm very honoured, Frank. You can rest assured I'll always do my best for Angie. She means the world to me, to be honest.'

Frank didn't reply, but clapped a heavy hand on my right shoulder and squeezed. I was relieved when, shortly after, we pulled into one of the driveways to Sydney Uni. He dropped me off, and I tried not to scramble out the passenger door. In truth, I was thrilled to my core, but didn't want to show it.

I had a class that day but decided not to go. I needed to clear my mind. Home would have been the best place for that - but Hall was there. Instead, I walked around the Sydney University campus and saw students of all colours, creeds, and genders. I saw that underneath the surface appearances, we were really all just the same. We all wanted to be happy, find a home, and take our rightful place in the world.

I caught the bus east all the way to Coogee Beach, bought a takeaway coffee, and sat on the cliff top looking out to the blue expanse of the Pacific. The sea, so vast, so cruel. If I were to set out in a small boat and continue in a straight line, I would eventually come to land. South America, if I wasn't mistaken. What a perilous journey that would be. Perhaps I'd drift off course and land in the Galapagos Islands, famous from Darwin's voyage. It was Darwin who traced evolution back through the aeons - and wasn't it true the whole show started in Africa? Perhaps then it was right they should make the journey again. Who was the human race really, and what rights did we have to deny them to anyone else?

As I gazed out to sea, I imagined, far off in the distance, a tiny speck on the horizon. In my mind, I saw it grow bigger and bigger, until it turned into a boat full of refugees.

I saw a problem, and tossed it over and over in my mind, until at last I reached a decision.

Hall had to go.

# 15

# Back to the Blue Pill

'I want to break up.'

Hall had his back to me. He was sitting at my desk, typing something on his laptop.

'Break up what?'

'I mean, I want out,' I said, 'of this whole far-right thing.'

Hall spun round to look at me.

'Far-right isn't a proper term, you know. It's a label made up by the mainstream fake media. What's got into you? Is it Angie?'

Hall gave me a searching look.

'Or is it her parents?' Hall said.

He nodded, answering his own question. 'Yes, that's it, isn't it. What happened?'

I told Hall about the refugee film. He let me speak uninterrupted.

'So there are refugees,' he said. 'And?'

'Look,' I said. 'This nationalism and race stuff's all very well in theory, but when you see the reality of people's suffering and heartbreak, the theory no longer matters.'

'On the contrary, John, that's when it matters most. So you feel sorry for refugees. I feel sorry for them too. That doesn't mean I'll let my brain turn into a quivering lump of jelly. For one thing...'

I held up my hand.

'Please. No more of your diatribes. When you see someone in trouble, you've got to help them. That's the bottom line.'

'Fine - but what if it's a thousand someones? Or a million? What then?'

'Then all the more so. What would *you* do - turn them all away?'

'Not necessarily. There's a big middle ground between turning them all away and letting them all in - and whatever you do has consequences.'

Hall swivelled on his chair for a moment, choosing his words carefully.

'Don't think me heartless,' he said. 'I can't stand to see suffering myself - and the easiest thing is to let in all the refugees, right? Much easier than turning them away. Your conscience is clear, you feel good about yourself, and you can sleep easy - in the short term. So you let everyone in.

Now, that alone has consequences in this global world. Word gets around what a compassionate Christian host you are, and three weeks later there's another ten thousand on your doorstep. Or maybe a hundred thousand. So do you let them in too, or send them away? Where do you draw the line?

And that's exactly what a border is, ain't it? A line - and it was put there for a reason, due to nature, human nature, and the need to keep order within reasonable bounds. See, whatever's inside the line you've got a hope of controlling. What's outside is chaos. But your do-gooder in-laws want to erase all the lines and let in the chaos.'

'Maybe it's time we did,' I said. 'The days of nationalism are over. It's time we lived as one people and one world, and whatever problems the people over there have got, they're our problems too and by God let's solve them together.'

Hall stared at me soberly, then laughed a sad little laugh.

'I know where you're coming from,' he said, 'but I don't think you know where *they* are coming from. Tell me, have you ever actually been to the third world.'

'I don't care for that term. We are one world.'

'The thing is, Johnny, I've heard that whole One World spiel before, from tender-hearted souls such as yourself, and there's one little flaw in the argument. If we do away with all the borders, some people think the third world is going to magically turn into the first world. In reality, it'll be the first world that becomes a lot more like the third. A hell of a lot more. So eventually, after decades of failure and misery, the same do-gooders who opened the borders might finally admit they were wrong, and wish they could just turn the clock back to the way we were. And by then, old boy, the horse has bolted.'

'Look, Hall, how do you know? Why do you have to be so damned negative?'

Hall shrugged.

'I'm a realist. Misery multiplies if you let it, even if it seems harmless at first. Look at the first fleet that came here and settled Australia. They brought a few rabbits with them. Seemed harmless, right? Then, a hundred years later there's a plague of rabbits wreaking havoc on the natural environment and you've got to invent a brand new poison just to get rid of 'em. So suppose you let in a thousand boat people. It'll be slower, but there'll still be an effect long term.'

'That's pretty insulting. People aren't rabbits.'

Hall shrugged again.

'I like rabbits. In fact, I probably like 'em more than people. Anyway, if you let a few rabbits into Australia it has an effect. So, if Merkel lets a million migrants into Germany, don't you think there'll be an effect there too?'

'They're *refugees*. Not migrants. You think they *wanted* to move to Germany? They had no choice.'

'Don't matter what you *call* them,' said Hall. 'It still has an effect. Want to know who else had no choice emigrating? The convicts on that same first fleet settled this country in 1788. Eleven ships, and of the nearly fifteen hundred souls aboard, at least half were convicts. They came here against their will, seeing as most of them were clapped in irons. Whether you call them refugees, slaves, or victims of bad luck and poverty don't matter. The point is they made a long and horrible sea voyage, like the modern day refugees. And how did that work out for the locals? Were the Aboriginals enriched by all this fresh new diversity coming into their world?'

I opened my mouth to speak, then shut it.

'No,' Hall continued. 'The poor old Aborigines didn't have much choice in the matter, did they? They can call it an invasion if they like, and it's hard to argue the point when you see how it's panned out for them.

So what about the British and Europeans, who are the indigenous people of their own lands? Now all these refugees are 'invading' their homelands, not by choice, but by circumstance, and certainly against their will. But whatever you call them, it will have an effect. So why should the British and Europeans allow it? Is it fascist to shut your borders?'

'Maybe it is,' I said.

'You know what the Dalai Lama said? *Europe is for the Europeans.* I suppose he's a fascist too.'

'You can't turn these people away,' I said, raising my voice. 'Go and watch *Human Flow* yourself, then get back to me with your fancy arguments.'

'Sure. I'll watch it. See, Johnny, I don't mind letting the refugees in for a while. Give them safe haven, food, time to recover. But after a while - a few months, a year or two - they've got to go home.'

'Some of their homes are no longer there!' I said triumphantly. 'They've been blown to smithereens in the wars and the bombing raids.'

'Then send them somewhere else. Don't ask me where. I haven't thought it through.'

'Look, Hall, most of these refugees are just ordinary people like you and me. All they want is some peace and a little help and charity. Most of them are perfectly willing to blend into whatever country will take them. Matter of fact, they'd be so grateful, they'd bend over backwards to repay the kindness of any country that gave them refuge.'

'Are you sure about that?'

'Watch the film. See for yourself.'

Hall's face took on a sad, world weary expression.

'If only it were true. Now look, I don't doubt their sincerity. Not for a moment. Of course, they're so desperate for help they'll promise anything to anyone. Assimilate? Sure. Learn the local language? No problem. Respect the local values? One hundred percent. And they'll give it their best shot, for a while.

But it's human nature that promises made in desperation fade in comfort. As soon as the crisis is past, the horrors of it all start to recede. Then, little by little, our new Europeans are going to want more of what they're used to back home. More chance to speak their own language, preserve their own culture, practice their own values. Like I said, it's human nature - and there'll be no shortage of self-hating Western do-gooders and multicultural fetishists to give them all that and more.

Is that too cynical for you, John? Then we'll be a bit more optimistic. Let's say we let all our refugees stay to become new Europeans, and suppose that first generation honours their promise. Maybe they do remember the horrors of their voyage, and they vow never to forget the kindness of their hosts.

They won't forget it, but their children will. Maybe they weren't even born at the time; they came after. And why should they keep promises they never made themselves? Then these kids come up through our degraded school and university system to get brainwashed by self-hating whites like Helda McGovern. Next thing you know it's all *white privilege this*, and *structural racism that*, and bitter bitches like Yasmin Chemali calling for the overthrow of white supremacy, and whatever other fantastical paranoia is running through her brain.

So this is our refugee stew and a bitter brew it is indeed. And this is not even to mention the ones who come, not from dire necessity, but from the simple desire for a better life. *Economic migrants*, some call them, and really, who can blame them? No doubt, Johnny, if you or I were born in some miserable third world hellhole, we'd be sneaking onto a leaky boat ourselves.'

'Look,' Hall continued, 'no doubt some of them are good people, pure and honourable, who you'd gladly welcome. But plenty aren't! Or even if, all things being equal, they'd be half decent but for the rotten circumstances they've fought through. Uneducated, unemployed, years spent in crappy refugee camps. Hell, you or I would be pissed off and dangerous too.

So some of them go over to Europe and it's all strange and new. Maybe they're from an Islamic country where they've never seen a woman's ankle before. They go to, say, Germany, a country with pretty girls on every street, big breasted Oktoberfest maids, and mixed sex nude saunas as a matter of course. Do we see any culture clash in this powder keg of a scenario? Well, some of them behave, and some don't, and from the ones who don't, you get Cologne and Rotherham.'

'What - those grooming gangs? Rotherham wasn't the fault of refugees. It was long term Pakistani migrants.'

Hall shrugged.

'So you wait a generation or two. It's a mighty risk, that's all I'm saying. So, all these smiling young girls who were holding up their *Refugees Welcome!* signs at the train station; it's a few years later and you've got all the drama, and I wonder what they think of those signs now.'

I was sitting stiffly, arms crossed, looking out the window.

'Have you finished?' I said, when there was a break in Hall's monologue.

'I've only just begun.'

I shrugged impatiently.

'Look, Hall. Maybe you're right, maybe you're wrong, but that isn't my problem. My problem is I cannot sit there and watch *Human Flow* and see people suffering and just do nothing. I especially can't do it in a luxury theatre in a posh bloody home, when I'm sitting with good, moral people like the Gardiners who'd be horrified to know I'm even talking to the likes of you.'

Hall looked taken aback and was silent a long moment. At last he spoke.

'Well, Johnny. I see this isn't just about the refugees. It's about you.'

'It's nothing to do with me.'

'It's about you and Ange and the Gardiners. Are you engaged yet? Or is marriage a dirty word when you're in Antifa?'

'What's that got to do with refugees?'

'You said you want out of this whole 'far-right' thing. That's so you can carry on with Ange, is it? So you don't ruin your prospects as a Gardiner son-in-law.'

I sighed.

'For Christ's sake, I just want to be normal. What's wrong with that?'

'Normal!' Hall exclaimed. 'Is Helda McGovern normal? Is Yasmin Chemali normal? Is it normal to believe your own kind should commit mass suicide? I thought I'd red-pilled you into seeing through all that.'

'I never asked for your damned red pill, Hall. In fact, I'm going to take the blue one again. I'm going to shove it down my throat and wash it down with a bottle of champagne.'

'I see. Like that, is it?'

'And it's about time you left. Go and mentor some other poor fool.'

'Well, well, Johnny Gilbert. You disappoint me.'

'Who do you think you are - my father? I don't have to answer to you. My life's none of your business.'

'You filthy scoundrel, John. I showed you the truth about the insane leftist cult destroying our world. You've sold me out for a pretty girl and a quiet life. I thought you were made of sterner stuff.'

'I'm made of pure marshmallow, I assure you.'

'You really want to turn back into a blue pill normie?'

'One hundred percent. I want to be a blue pill normie. I want a steady job teaching history. I want to marry Ange and have three children, and one day I might even go and live in the Gardiners' house.'

'You mean along with a dozen refugees? You did say it was a big house.'

'Why not? I'm happy to do my bit.'

Hall laughed contemptuously.

'You're so full of bullshit, Johnny. You couldn't even stand a homeless Brazilian sleeping on your couch for a couple of weeks.'

'He's from Chile, you goddamn racist!'

'You blue pilled buffoon! To think I wasted all this time taking you under my wing. All my tutelage, my hard won wisdom, and you're just another clown.'

'Looks like it.'

I felt suddenly free of Hall, and in my liberation, began running around the room doing a silly little dance to mock him.

'I'm a blue pilled fool and I just don't care! A blue pill normie with no underwear!'

Hall gave me a stony look.

'Well, Johnny. You're showing your true colours - and they ain't blue, they're yellow.'

I stopped dancing.

'Look, Hall, I'm done with you. I think you'd better leave.'

'Like that, is it? Turf me out on the street like a refugee, would you?'

'You're no refugee.'

Hall stood up.

'I'm done wasting my time on you. But mark my words, Johnny, you'll be back.'

I snorted. Hall adopted a lofty expression.

'Oh yes,' he said. 'You'll be back. What's seen cannot be unseen. Surround yourself with lunatics like Helda and Ange and the Gardiners and it's only a matter of time. When insane is the new normal, you'll never rest easy. How long 'til the next mad bitch accuses you of pulling out your prick in meditation? How long 'til another Antifa nut punches you out for being white? When you've had enough of crazy, get back to me. Until then, I'll go on with my humble work, and if a more worthy apprentice comes along, I'll tell him the sad tale of lily-livered John Gilbert who sold out his country, his people, and most of all himself.'

'OK, Hall, that's enough. Don't let the door slam your arse on the way out.'

'Why don't you slam it on Mateo's arse, Gilbert? Or are you too spineless to stand up to Angie's compassionate reign of terror? I'd keep an eye on her, son. Mateo's already shown himself to be a cuckoo. He'll make a cuckold out of you and all.'

'Right that's it, Hall. Out!'

'She'll cheat on you, then say it's your own fault. And it will be, you filthy traitor.'

'Out!'

I opened the door of my room and glared at him.

Edward Hall piled a few items into his backpack, then strode out the door. He turned back for one last look.

'You'll be back, Johnny - but I won't take you. You've made your own bed. Now lie in it. Lie in it until it becomes your deathbed.'

With a last contemptuous glance, he turned away and walked out of my life.

# 16

# Plumston Park Prac

With Edward Hall out of the way, my life became a whole lot simpler. No more sneering at the bias in the news. No more the inner critical voice when Ange spouted politics. No more leading a double life, presenting one face to her, another to Hall.

Indeed, just a week after Hall hit the road, Ange moved back into the house. Mateo was still occupying her room, but one of our other housemates, Renata, got a job in Canberra. As soon as she left, Ange took her place.

'Aren't you going to take back your own room?' I asked her. 'What about the ocean view?'

Ange crinkled her pretty little nose.

'Renata's room is too small for a couple with a baby. They can have mine.'

I opened my mouth, then shut it. Why get involved? At least by now Mateo had some part time restaurant work and was paying rent, though I suspected it wasn't the full amount. That meant Ange was still subsidising Mateo, Liana, and their baby son. Or rather, her parents were, whether they knew it or not. Oh well, that was their problem.

With the irritant of Hall removed and domestic harmony restored, I returned to finishing my teacher training. The one last hurdle was my *practicum*, or 'prac' - a five week period of working in an actual school as a teacher. This under the guidance of a mentor, so I was not totally on my own. I would, however, have to stand in front of a class and make a show of doing the job properly.

With my life back on track, I vowed to get it right. In pursuit of this goal, I was able to conjure a certain amnesia about how these pracs had gone in the past. To be frank, I had found them a major trial. I blocked the memory, replacing it with a blind optimism the next one would go swimmingly. If I passed, I'd have my teaching license. I could then get a full time job and marry Ange.

I landed a placement at Plumston Park, a high school in Sydney's south-west. It wasn't a posh school, but hopefully wouldn't be the dregs either. My clientele would be mostly middle class suburban kids, I guessed, with a few of the rougher ones thrown in too.

Preparation would be important. I'd received the course outlines a couple of weeks before, and done due diligence reading them through. That was the easy bit. Sitting in my quiet bedroom writing notes was one thing; fronting up to a roomful of teenagers would be another.

The trouble with school teaching is it's good in theory, lousy in practice. On the surface, it seems like a good idea for a career. I like history and English, so it should be easy enough to teach them to others. Right?

Not so fast. For a start, teaching means standing in front of thirty kids and talking. In other words, 'public speaking,' which some people rate more frightening than death. It would be fine if I had a keen and receptive audience. Yet school teaching is a strange profession. It's one of the few jobs where your clients are trying to stop you delivering the service you're being paid to give them. Your job is to teach these kids. Yet they are obstructing you - by talking, mucking up, passive aggression, and so on.

No one likes to be disrespected. If you're giving a class and some smartarse kid is talking over the top of you, that's disrespect. Some of them actually do that. You're speaking to class, and they're chatting to the kid beside them. It's rude to say the least.

You wouldn't cop it in the real world. If someone disrespects you, you either front up to them or walk away. Neither is an option in schools. You're not even allowed to get angry these days. The teacher training has a whole subject on behaviour management. It's all about strategies for handling annoying kids. Getting angry is not one of the strategies on offer. In other words, kids can give you rubbish and you're expected to take it, deflect it, or pretend not to notice.

Still, these are issues most teachers face, especially early in their careers. I hoped that once I developed a commanding classroom presence, my love of the subjects would enthuse the kids, and any disrespect would fade away. I might even be one of their favourite teachers. *That Mr Gilbert*, they'd say. *He's alright. He's kind of cool, for an adult.*

In the meantime, Ange and I would be bringing up children of our own. But that hypothetical future could only be attained if I got through the current ordeal. As I walked up to the glass doors of Plumston Park, wearing the unfamiliar suit and tie, clutching my briefcase, I was gripped by a sense of dread. What in God's name was I doing here? It was too late to turn back now. Head up and jaw set, I marched into the building. This would be my last battlefield.

I was met at reception by Rebecca Irvine, my mentor. I saw an attractive woman in her early thirties, slim and almost my height. With shoulder length dark hair and glasses, she had a steely, determined look. With shorter hair, she could have passed for Angie's older sister. I fancied she wouldn't take any rubbish in the classroom.

'Rebecca?' I said. 'Nice to meet you.'

'It's Beck,' she replied. 'Or Miss Irvine.'

'Sure,' I said, with a smile. 'Looks like I'll be at your beck and call for the next five weeks.'

I instantly regretted the joke, the more so when it received a stony look from Irvine herself. I put my head down and followed her through to the History and English staffroom. The staff were the usual mix I recognised from past pracs. You had the lifers, the grizzled veterans at one end of the scale, the eager young rookies at the other, with the rest in various stages of transition.

A desk had been set aside for me. Here I placed my briefcase, trying to ignore a chronic sense of imposter syndrome. I looked at the timetable of classes I'd been given to teach. From a distance, I could hear the dull roar, punctuated by random shrieks and yells, of students in the playground. It would soon be my job to stand in front of those savages and hold their attention for an hour.

Still, that was a few days away. First there was the buffer of an 'observation week' when I only had to sit in on my mentor's classes. Here I would pick up on the class vibes, absorb the course content, watch Beck Irvine in action, and ready myself to take the helm in week two.

I flicked through the course outlines Beck had supplied. *Cold War Literature* for Year 12. *Women in History* for Year 11. *Empire and Consequence* for Year 9. They seemed rather political topics. Still, history isn't just about actual wars and conquests, but the battle of ideas, and the way those ideas affect people's lives.

It turned out politics extended to the staffroom. While I tried to keep a low profile and avoid saying anything even mildly controversial, my new colleagues had no such qualms. On just the second day, I sat down to lunch with half a dozen teachers and another prac student like myself. Barely had I unwrapped my sandwiches before a rotund history teacher named Jones was spouting off about Brexit.

'Looks like the xenophobes got their way,' he said. 'Little England will rise again.'

'Disgraceful,' said a tall lady, who came in part time as a reading tutor.

'My Year Eleven girls are traumatised,' said Beck Irvine. 'First Trump, now Brexit. They're very worried about all this right wing stuff coming back. We've only just finished studying the Holocaust.'

Now this was all just so much jibber jabber, and so what? It was the same stuff I heard from Ange and her parents, or on TV. What was striking was their ease in saying it. There were two complete strangers in their midst - myself and the other prac teacher - yet there was this grand assumption that everyone thought like them. No allowance was made for the possibility the newcomers might support Brexit, or have a different take on Trump. It was just assumed the only people who would were grunting Neanderthals who lived off in a cave somewhere.

I realised Hall was right. The left were in the ascendancy and had been for decades, so that their own assumptions were invisible to them. Still, that was Hall's problem now, not mine. It was a relief to have cast off his right wing beliefs and be able to once more blend into the crowd.

On my first morning on prac, the school bell rang at 8.55am. I gathered my briefcase and walked down the corridor with Beck Irvine. We had to merge with the rabble of students, each of them on their own routes. We went up a flight of stairs and found Irvine's room at the end of the building. I took a desk at the back from where I could observe her in action.

'This is Mr Gilbert,' said Irvine, when class had settled down. 'He's going to be with us for the next few weeks.'

Thirty pairs of eyes turned to scrutinise me, then looked back at Irvine.

'Right, Year Seven. Get out your worksheets from yesterday.'

Second period was Year Twelve English Extension class studying Cold War Texts. It was a group of only five students. They were studious types, there by choice not obligation. This was more my idealised notion of teaching. Sober, serious work, and keen scholars who looked at me with respect, not resentment.

I returned to the staffroom at recess in better spirits. This lasted until third period with Year Ten, a roguish band of miscreants who seemed unable to go ten seconds without opening their mouths. Even Irvine seemed to find them a trial. Oh well, I'd just have to do my best with them next week.

It soon became clear there was a political tinge to education, far more than I could recall from my own school days twenty years before. It was in the staffroom banter - Trump this and Brexit that. It was in the course content. It was in my teacher training with its prominent DIE principles - diversity, inclusion, and equity.

It was also in the extracurricular stuff. Part of my internship was to do extras like playground duty at lunch, or school sport on Wednesday afternoons. There was also scheduled, for the Thursday of week two, a workshop called 'Remaking Masculinity.' This came up in conversation with my mentor.

'You can sit in on that,' said Irvine, 'with the other boys.'

'Sure,' I said, eager to please. 'What's it about?'

'Standard issues - consent, respecting women, male privilege. That sort of thing.'

'Oh,' I said. 'That's to do with masculinity, is it?'

Irvine didn't answer. I kept talking in case I'd offended her.

'Great idea, anyway. My fiancée and I often discuss those topics. And what are the girls doing?'

'They've got their own workshop,' said Irvine, 'on leadership.'

'Oh,' I said again. 'The future is female!'

My tone was a little facetious. Irvine glared at me and I stopped smiling. Looked like I'd made another fumble. I scrambled to make amends.

'Well,' I said. 'You've certainly got to admire Jacinda Ardern, don't you? If only Australia had someone like her in charge.'

This seemed to satisfy Irvine. She nodded and dismissed me.

This must be what Hall had mentioned - the feminist influence in education. It was part of a broader leftist slant, which seemed to be mandatory among the staff. If there were any conservative or 'right wing' teachers in that staffroom, they certainly kept their views to themselves. It's a fair bet anyone disagreeing with the prevailing wisdom would be mocked or excluded. And this is odd, because we kept hearing about the virtues of being diverse and inclusive - not to mention the anti-bullying posters that were tacked up around the school.

As for my mentor, Beck Irvine, her views became known to me only by chance. At lunchtime on the second day, I approached her desk to check my duties. Coming up from behind, I saw she was on Twitter. I made a mental note of her Twitter name - Virginia Fox - then cleared my throat and spoke. She shut down the page and snapped back to her professional role to brief me on afternoon class.

That night, I logged onto Twitter using Average Anomaly, the anonymous profile Hall had created for me. I searched for Virginia Fox and 'followed' her. It sounds like stalking, when you put it like that, and to some degree it was. Still Irvine would never know. I was simply curious to get a handle on my mentor's thought processes. Reading through her feed, it was clear she was the type of leftist progressive Hall would have despised. Her opinions were predictable, as were the topics. It was all race, gender, and the rest of the culture war stuff. I made a mental note to watch my words at school.

Despite my efforts to return to being a blue pill normie, it wasn't easy to put Hall's influence out of my mind. This was partly due to the course bias becoming more and more obvious. Year Nine's *Empire and Consequence* had an anti-Western slant. Year Eight's was an indigenous view of Australia's settlement by the British. But it was Year Eleven's *Women in History* course which was the most heavily agenda-based. It was essentially a feminist view of history which pushed the line that men had held all the social power for thousands of years and reduced women to lowly support roles, a pattern which was only now changing thanks to feminism.

This simplistic view of history met with little skepticism from the students. Most of the girls seemed keen to lap it up, and from my observation desk I picked up an odd vibe - a sort of righteous indignation, and gloating triumph at their coming 'revenge' - from some of the girls in the room.

As for the boys, they seemed less engaged in the material - hardly surprising, as their own gender was being cast as the villains of history. Of course, you still had the swots prepared to learn and parrot back anything for the sake of high grades, and a couple of sycophants who seemed almost eager to grovel and apologise for events in which they'd had no part. They were your future male feminists. Several of the other boys, however, seemed apathetic and withdrawn.

One such was a boy named Hunter, a handsome but surly lad who spent most of his class time slouched behind his desk or rocking back on his chair. He wore his hair long, 1970s style, and rarely bothered with school uniform. An articulate lad, he was the only one to raise any dissent against the line being pushed.

'What about the coal miners?' he asked one day.

Miss Irvine was explaining some points she'd written on the whiteboard. She paused in mid-flow and looked around. With obvious distaste, her glance settled on the boy.

'What about them, Hunter?'

'You keep talking about the power of men in history. I just read George Orwell's essay 'Down the Mine' about how hard it was to be a coal miner. I don't see how they had any social power if they had to do that.'

Miss Irvine paused, as if unused to being challenged. I got the sense she actively disliked the boy. His name alone, with its masculine connotations, was probably enough to annoy her.

'What you have to remember,' she said, 'is at least men had the privilege of being able to work outside the home and earn a living.'

Hunter looked down at his desk.

'Not much of a privilege,' he mumbled.

A girly swot at the front of the room shot up her hand.

'Yes, Bianca,' said Irvine.

'Those coalminers' wives had it much worse. They were married at fifteen, pregnant most of the time, had to wash all the clothes by hand, and were beaten when their husbands came home from work.'

Miss Irvine turned to Hunter. It was one of the few times I ever saw her smile. This seemed to irk the boy. He scowled and looked at Bianca.

'How do you know? You weren't there.'

'It's not all their fault,' said Bianca. 'I mean the men. They were socialised into it by patriarchal norms.'

I raised an eyebrow. The girl was headed for straight As and a place at university. But my speculation vanished when Irvine put me in the hot seat.

'What do you think, Mr Gilbert?' she said.

I flushed and tried to summon a coherent answer.

'Oh. Well, er... I think Hunter raises a valid point, but, ah... Bianca makes a sound rejoinder in pointing out the domestic drudgery that was the lot of working class women of that era.'

I hoped that answer would be enough, but blundered on in case it wasn't.

'At the same time, I... ah, feel we should be cautious in viewing the past through the lens of theory and projecting our own ideas onto it. We can certainly speculate and make informed guesses, but without getting carried away.'

I was waffling and seemed unable to stop.

'I must look up that Orwell essay, Hunter. It sounds most interesting. Mind you, Orwell had a few choice words about history, didn't he? "Who controls the past controls the future: who controls the present controls the past." Ominous words!'

I laughed awkwardly and shut up. Beck Irvine was staring at me with an expression I could not place, and did not particularly like. I adopted an earnest look and pretended to type something into my laptop. Irvine turned back to the class.

'Right, everyone. Don't forget to submit your journals. Mr Gilbert and I are going to check them over the weekend.'

This was news to me but Irvine confirmed it in the staffroom that afternoon.

'You don't have to grade them,' she said. 'Just have a read through and write a few comments. It's a way to get you up to speed on the course content as well, ready for your teaching next week.'

I shuddered inside. One more weekend - two short days - then the nightmare would begin.

'What should I focus on?' I asked.

'I'll leave that up to you, as long as you follow the course outlines. It's week six and we're pretty much on track. Here, I'll make it easy for you.'

Miss Irvine slid out a large drawer next to her desk. From there, she pulled out three folders, stuffed full of printed materials. Each folder was over an inch thick.

'Here's a list of resources you can use, and you've also got access to the department's online reserve.'

She turned to me with a breezy smile which I fancied contained a trace of sadism.

'Email me your lesson plans by Sunday lunchtime and I'll have a squiz. Have fun!'

Groaning under the weight of three folders of history, my briefcase, and my laptop, I staggered towards Plumston Park train station. I limped onto the next city bound train, then took a seat, and stared out the window.

By the time I'd transferred to a bus from town and made it back to Tamarama, I was a wreck. I thrust my key into the door, dumped my baggage, and crashed out on the couch.

'Hey teach,' said Angie when she came in from her bedroom. 'Let's go into town tomorrow. I feel like having some fun.'

'You must be joking,' I said from my prone position. '*You* might have a weekend. I've got to read thirty Year Eleven journals and prepare half a dozen lesson plans.'

And that, I discovered, is what teaching is like. It's not a job where you clock off and forget about it. When the end-of-school bell goes, the work has only just begun. Prepping lessons, marking papers, doing your admin. Well, I was too buggered to do any more tonight. I'd turn in early and get stuck into it the next day.

The clock said 5.45 when I crawled out of bed the next morning. I took a cold shower, then made a strong cup of coffee and faced the future. All I had to do was read through four course outlines, prepare a bunch of lessons, and read all the journals. Easy!

As Year Eleven was freshest in my mind, I began with that, deciding to read through the students' journals to orient myself to the themes of *Women In History*. The journals were a series of reflections made by students on the course material. Yet reading them through, I could almost hear Hall reading over my shoulder, snorting and harrumphing, making acerbic remarks. Many of the 'observations' read like letters to *Dear Leader* in some sort of Maoist indoctrination camp. One girl, for instance, said the following about marriage:

> Marriage was a social system designed to subserviate women to men and keep them from power in society. Menial labour and childbearing was the fate of intelligent women who could have risen to prominent stature as leaders and other key positions. This allowed men to keep their privileged status until feminism began in the 1900s and began to question structures of unfairness.

Continuing on the theme of marriage, another student had written much more informally:

> It is mind-blowing to think King Henry murdered his wives whenever he felt like it. Like the first two, Catherine and Anne Boleyn, because they failed the gendered roll of motherhood and given him a male son. Well, hello? Elizabeth was a much better queen anyway, which only proves the idea of male privilege is a phallacy as girls are often smarter.

One of the sycophantic boys had a more formal style and had written:

The frequency of warfare is proof of masculine toxic ideas of domination and competition, which lead to imperialism, which also harmed many women and native cultures. As Hillary Clinton said, the victims of war are mainly women. As they never started the wars, this is unfair. Even in 'peace time' today's women are still paid less than men for the same job, which is a sign of systemic inequality. Women still have a long way to go to achieve equality, as proven by Trump's election which was caused by Russian collusion and the bigotry of white Americans.

I shuddered. One could detect the fledgling, developing minds, and forgive them the *non sequiturs* and occasional clumsy expression. At the same time, you couldn't help notice these same innocent minds had been shaped by an ideology imposed upon them.

I paused to reflect. Although I had returned to accepting leftist progressive values, Hall's influence remained, to the extent that the course bias bothered me. Of course, I would have to go along with it, but perhaps I could inject a cautionary note to balance the ledger.

Yes, that was it. Hall wasn't wrong about everything. Perhaps I could retain just enough of his influence to adopt a more balanced, moderate position. That might be my role as an educator. Pleased, I began to sketch out ideas for next week's lessons. Maybe I could make my own path through this treacherous maze. It wouldn't take long to find out.

# 17
# Mentor, Tormenter

I woke on Monday like a condemned man. After a rotten night's sleep, I needed a cold shower to wake up. At least I'd had the sense to pack my briefcase the night before. It was stuffed full of course notes and lesson plans. I lugged it out the door and began the one hour commute to Plumston Park.

I was off the hook for the first two classes - Year Seven and Nine - as Beck Irvine wanted to take them herself. My initiation would happen first period after recess with Year Eleven. I hoped the lesson plan emailed to Irvine contained enough buzzwords to satisfy her. *In this lesson, class will examine structures of gender inequality at work in post-war Britain.* That was the first sentence of many - but my words would mean nothing unless I could put the lesson plan into action.

As Year Eleven filed in after recess, I was already standing at the teacher's desk, fiddling with my notes. I now had to muster a show of confidence. Gradually, the room fell silent, and with a mounting sense of horror, I felt thirty pairs of eyes zoom in on me. I took a deep breath and began.

'Hello class. I'm Mr Gilbert, as you know, and I'll be with you for the next four weeks helping Miss Irvine.'

I winced internally. It all sounded so lame. I hurried on before they noticed, and tried to adopt a conversational tone.

'I've been reading your diaries over the weekend. Very interesting to read your private thoughts, I must say.'

There was a slight murmur through the room. My pulse racing, I realised my verbal slip.

'Oh dear, not your diaries. My God. That would be embarrassing for both of us. I meant your journals, of course. Your course journals. Your course journals, of course.'

A couple of the students were giving me funny looks. I felt like a fool and shuddered to think what I might say next. *Slow down*, I told myself. *Breathe. Think before you speak.*

'Anyway, I think you guys have got some wonderful ideas about inequality. Some real insights into what life was like in the past, compared to today. And you know what they say about the past. *The past is a foreign country; they do things differently there.* That's a quote. A famous one. Not that I know who said it. Someone from the past, one would suspect, which makes him a foreigner. Or her. It was quite possibly Gertrude Stein, or Virginia Woolf herself. Anyway, the point is, if the past is a foreign country, I suppose that means we're a nation of immigrants. Not that there's anything wrong with that!'

What in God's name was I babbling about? None of this was in the carefully scripted notes I'd prepared the day before.

'Are you alright, Sir?' asked a girl in the front row.

I peered at her.

'Tina, isn't it? You'll have to indulge me a little. This is my first class. I feel a bit like Anne Boleyn the day she had her head cut off. Although before or after it was cut off, I don't know. Probably after, I suspect.'

There was a gasp from the class and a couple of confused laughs. Irvine was staring daggers, and I sensed her weighing up whether or not to intervene and take over the class. To forestall this embarrassment, I suddenly adopted a tone of deadly seriousness.

'And there's one thing I want to make clear. What King Henry did was appalling. He was an actual murderer, far worse even than Donald Trump, and if there was any justice back then, Henry would have been impeached and then executed. What you boys have got to understand is that violence against women is never OK.'

I held up an admonishing finger to the part of the room where most of the boys were sitting. Then I continued my incoherent tirade.

'Mind you, credit where credit's due. Did you know that Henry invented divorce? The pope refused to let him divorce his first wife, so Henry invented his own church and made it legal. I suppose that makes him an early feminist, right? His selfishness enabled something that hundreds of years later empowered women to escape the patriarchal bonds of marriage. The Lord works in mysterious ways. As do I when I teach history.'

I considered grabbing my briefcase and running out of the room. I was sweating heavily and took off my jacket.

'So the point I'm making, and what I want you all to think about, is why do we have inequality in the first place, and is it a gender issue? I mean, we can all agree it's a horrific act of patriarchal violence to behead someone, especially a woman. That's appalling, and I hope you boys realise that and would never do it to your own wives.'

I glared at the boys, rebuking them in advance of any such crimes they might commit.

'But here's the thing,' I continued. 'How many of his wives did Henry execute? Two wasn't it. And how many women in general? Definitely a few. Even so, you can be very sure that however many women were killed by King Henry the Eighth, he probably executed hundreds of times as many men.

They were violent times. Violent and savage. Many people suffered. Women. Men. Children. Go and watch *The Tudors*, if you don't believe me. Not entirely historically accurate, I must say. I mean, the fellow playing him never put on a pound for starters. So yes, we do remember the despicable violence against women but all in all, you had just as many men killed, if not far more.'

I risked a glance at Miss Irvine. She looked grim, and her voice contained a note of menace.

'Thank you, Sir. I believe you have a handout for class and an exercise for them to do.'

'That's right,' I said, feeling the sweat running down my sides. 'Let's hand out the handout.'

I seized the pile of papers I'd carefully laid out on the desk prior to the lesson, and thrust them towards the nearest student. I turned back to the class.

'Take one and pass them on,' I intoned in a pompous, imperious voice.

When they'd been given out, I explained what it was all about.

'I really must give some credit to Hunter for this one.'

The sullen boy looked up from his desk.

'Yes,' I continued. 'That Orwell essay Hunter mentioned. The one about the coal miners. 'Down the Mine,' it's called. I checked it out, and it's a bit of an eye opener in terms of what people went through. So what I want you to do is have a read, then discuss it in small groups of three or four.'

I sat down at the front desk as students formed groups and began reading. I hoped it wasn't too difficult for them. Still, Year Eleven should be advanced enough to handle it. Irvine came up to me as I sat slumped in my chair, completely drained.

'Remember what I said, Sir. Circulate around the room and check in on people.'

Guiltily, I rose to my feet, and began ambling around the room. Most of the class seemed to be getting through the reading, although one of the ruder girls raised an objection.

'This is boring, Sir. What's it got to do with women?'

I darted a look at Irvine on the other side of the room, and hoped she hadn't heard. Then I spoke in hushed tones.

'I wouldn't say that, Donna. The women are... er, implied.'

'But there aren't any. That's sexist.'

'Then that's what I want you to think about. Maybe it is sexist - but who is it sexist against?'

'Women weren't allowed to be coal miners. That's discrimination.'

I flashed another look at Irvine. She was peering at us with a slight frown.

'I agree with you, Donna. Why not write it up in your journal tonight?'

When I could delay no longer, I asked each small group to report to the class with their thoughts. The class swot, Bianca, spoke first.

'Being a coal miner sounds awful,' she said. 'It's terrible that men were socialised into ideas of masculinity that made them have to do jobs like that.'

'You're right,' I said, 'but as the old saying goes, it's a dirty job but someone's got to do it. Those men may have been socialised into being coal miners but, as Orwell said, we might not even have a society in the first place without all that coal. Not as we know it, anyway.'

The class sycophant, Jonathan, raised his hand.

'Women could have been just as good coal miners, if not better, if they were allowed to.'

I raised an eyebrow.

'It sounds like hellish work. I don't think I could do it.'

Jonathan pressed on.

'Women are just as strong as men. After all, they give birth.'

With an effort, I tried not to react to the gold medal arse-kissing on display. I turned it back to the class.

'What do other people think?'

Hunter raised his hand.

'Girls only want some kinds of equality. They want to be equal in the corporate office jobs but not in the coal mine and all the other horrible work.'

Irvine was staring at me with a face of thunder. I tried to close the can of worms I'd opened.

'I know what you mean, Hunter, but we have to remember girls do all kinds of things nowadays they didn't do in Orwell's time - the army, engineering, ah, medicine and science, and... well, all sorts of things. So let's give everyone a chance and not make assumptions.'

The bell rang and my ordeal came to an end. I did have to take Year Seven after lunch, but having got through my first class, that one wasn't quite as intimidating. At the end of the day, however, I was due for a debrief with Irvine. I couldn't help feeling I'd made an awful hash of things, but there was no choice but to front up to the review.

As the last of the Year Seven kids departed the room, I waited anxiously for Irvine to turn her attention to me. I was sitting at one of the desks in the front row, while Irvine remained at the teacher's desk. She left me hanging for a couple of minutes, but at last stopped fiddling on her laptop and turned to me.

'Well, Sir. How do you think it went?'

She had an odd habit of calling me 'Sir' not just in the classroom, but when we spoke in private.

I laughed awkwardly.

'I got through it - tough day! I was quite nervous, to be honest. I don't know if you noticed.'

Miss Irvine stared at me, unsmiling.

'You seemed a bit manic, Sir. You need to relax.'

'Yes, yes. I know. It's much harder than I thought when they're all staring at you.'

'That *is* the job,' said Irvine. She picked up a pen and began doodling on a notepad, before speaking again.

'It's understandable you're nervous. I remember my first class too and I assure you it does get easier. I'm more concerned about your content. You need to have a good read through the course outline and make sure you choose resources that fit the course.'

'You didn't like the Orwell?'

'This course is called *Women in History*, Sir, yet you bring in a text about male coal miners. How is that appropriate?'

'Yes, I see. Point taken. I *was* going to use a book called *Out of the Dollhouse*, which is about the lives of women from low socioeconomic backgrounds. The sort of women who would have been married to the coalminers. That would have been next.'

'Yet you chose to centre the experiences of men. Really, Sir, I have to question your judgment.'

'For the sake of balance, I did want to show that not all men in history were privileged. I apologise, Miss Irvine. What I did was inappropriate. I see that now. It was Hunter really. He mentioned the Orwell last week, and the thing is, he seems rather disengaged with the class, so I thought I'd acknowledge him and include his point of view.'

Irvine put down her pen and gave me a piercing look.

'Mr Gilbert, we have a classroom of bright, articulate young girls in this class, yet for some reason you bypassed them in favour of Hunter. Why?'

'You're right, of course. They're wonderful girls. What it is, you see, is I have no doubt at all they'll do well. They'll all get into uni and do law or engineering or whatever they set their minds to. Hunter, he's bright too, but he's at real risk of dropping out. I'd hate to see him going to drugs or crime, wasting his life, when he could be going to uni with all those bright girls. I mean, what is it now - sixty percent of uni graduates are female? I guess it's the boys who need a little help catching up!'

Irvine sighed.

'Look, Sir, let me speak frankly. The Hunters of the world have had a pretty good run of things for hundreds of years, and it's about time someone else had a turn. Let me assure you I am going to empower as many young girls as possible to take their place at the table. As for Hunter, he's a big boy, and he can take care of himself - and if he chooses to sulk and refuse to engage with the class, that's his problem.'

Irvine picked up her laptop and stood up.

'But this is all irrelevant. Your only concern, Sir, is to get onboard with our program. I advise you in the strongest of terms to think about the sort of material you use for your classes here, and also the way in which you conduct yourself. Don't forget I have to sign off on this prac for you, and I warn you - it's your responsibility to adapt to us, not the other way around. Let's hope I've made that clear.'

I said nothing for a moment. Indeed I was in a state of mild shock, to be honest. It seemed best to make a strategic withdrawal and consider my options.

'I hear you, Miss Irvine. Loud and clear. I'll certainly take what you said very seriously.'

'OK, Sir. You had better work on your lesson plans for tomorrow, and from now on I'd better have a good look at them in advance. Make sure you email them to me by eight o'clock tonight, along with any resources you plan to use.'

'Eight o'clock! I'd better get going then. It takes me an hour just to get home.'

Irvine smiled.

'Better get cracking, Sir. Consider this your baptism of fire. Just make sure you don't get burned.'

What a day. First the classes and now this. But it's not like I could shrug off the day and forget it. No, I had a long journey home, and as soon as I arrived I'd have to go back to bloody work just to finish those lesson plans. Could someone please remind me why I was doing this to myself?

Fortunately, my weekend efforts had been enough to get the lesson plans quite far advanced. My Tuesday classes only need a few tweaks to ensure they didn't contain any more blunders like the Orwell. I finetuned them and emailed Irvine at 8.30pm.

Then I went and stalked her on Twitter.

Now, it may come as no surprise that my political resolve had weakened. My attempt to reject Hall's influence had failed. The fact is, I did not care for Irvine's manner towards me, her indifference to Hunter, or the biased agenda she had barely bothered to hide. Maybe Hall was right after all. These leftists were flawed humans like anyone else, each with their own axes to grind. When it came down to it, Irvine was a right little Nazi. Or perhaps an East German communist might be a better comparison. I felt I was under Stasi surveillance and might be liquidated at any moment for wrong-think. All it would take was Irvine to report me to someone higher up the chain. Or she could simply fail me for the prac, as she had threatened.

What was I doing here? My teaching performance had been nothing short of a farce. Why had I crumbled under pressure? If that was all I could muster, maybe school teaching wasn't for me. Who needs it anyway? Perhaps I was on the wrong path, after all. If so, I had wasted three years of my life on a dead end - and what would I do instead?

I searched for Irvine on Twitter - and there she was under her user name, Virginia Fox. She was once again banging on about Brexit, sexism, and the rest of the usual topics. Like everyone else on the Australian left, she was also singing the praises of New Zealand's charismatic prime minister, Jacinda Ardern.

I decided to reply to one of Irvine's tweets... and the next thing I knew, I found myself engaged in a full blown Twitter skirmish. Myself, posting as Average Anomaly, and Irvine as Virginia Fox.

**Average Anomaly** - I don't quite understand all the gushing over Ardern. What has she actually done to deserve such lavish praise?

**Virginia Fox** - You clearly haven't been paying attention.

**Average Anomaly** - In just a few words, enlighten me on what she's done.

**Virginia Fox** - Her proposed reform of gun laws is admirable. Taking kids out of poverty and fixing climate change. Also, her efforts to ban hate sites on the internet could be very important.

**Average Anomaly** - Thanks for your answer. I don't like guns, or children in poverty. As for so called 'hate sites' there is a disturbing trend towards classifying opinions one doesn't like as 'hate.' I don't see that as admirable in any way.

**Virginia Fox** - She means sites like the ones the Christchurch shooter followed. As you can guess, I'm a diehard lefty so nationalist and white supremacist sites also classify as hate, in my eyes. The "freedom of speech" argument is just rubbish.

**Average Anomaly** – Most of those sites don't endorse violence, and the actions of a rogue terrorist do not justify banning them. I'm sure you don't advocate banning the Quran based on the actions of a few extremists who have carried out acts of terror in its name.

**Virginia Fox** - Seriously? We're going to argue that Islamophobes are fine people? Sounds like Trump's response to Charlottesville. I'd also ban every ridiculous "Right to Life" site about abortion. All religious fundamentalists are repellent. Racists and white supremacists too.

**Average Anomaly** - Since you mentioned the Christchurch shooting, the glaring hypocrisy of the media's response to Christchurch is discussed in this article.

I linked to an article from Spiked Online website. It was called 'New Zealand's Ghoulish Opportunists.' A young white man, apparently driven by far-right viewpoints, had shot forty Muslims in a Christchurch mosque. The article pointed out that after recent Islamic terror attacks in Europe, many media figures had urged calm, kindness, and not to criticise Islam or ordinary Muslims for the acts of a few extremists. The same media figures were using the Christchurch attack to urge panic, condemnation, and censorship of so-called 'far-right' points of view or websites. The article made many excellent points, which is why I recommended it to Irvine. She refused to read it.

**Virginia Fox** - Give me a break. I'm not going to entertain far-right conspiracy theories.

**Average Anomaly** - Are you aware that some of the values of Islam are just as 'far-right' as those of the so-called far-right? Yet you defend one and denounce the other. Why?

This question received no reply.

**Average Anomaly** - Looks like my 'why' question is unanswerable. Must be some sort of Buddhist koan for leftists.

**Virginia Fox** – I oppose fundamentalists from any religion. They spread fear and hate. Even Buddhists have their own extremists.

**Average Anomaly** - Your attempt to write off those 'far-right' values as fundamentalist is an attempt to resolve cognitive dissonance in your belief system. It doesn't work.

**Virginia Fox** - Oh hon, you think I'll be impressed by your use of "cognitive dissonance." You used it wrongly. The English teacher in me is laughing.

**Average Anomaly** - Your posturing isn't fooling anyone. You're a typical lefty holding incompatible beliefs, and you lack the self awareness to realise how silly you look to everyone outside your bubble.

**Virginia Fox** - Bood Bod you lot are thick.

**Average Anomaly** - Bood Bod? Come on English teacher. All the best indoctrinating your students with your morally smug, irrational worldview.

**Virginia Fox** - Whoops. Good God. As for indoctrinating students, give me a break. It's the most ridiculous myth you far-right types believe.

**Average Anomaly** – Well, Virginia, I was on the Left almost all my life until I looked more closely at the issues. Also couldn't stand the arrogance of the modern Left.

**Virginia Fox** - Sure mate - and pigs fly.

**Average Anomaly** - Plenty of ex-lefties have walked away because they feel the same. Why don't you get your students to deconstruct this 'text'? It's a video by an American who can no longer stand the Democrat party.

I linked to a video made by the guy who started the Walkaway movement in America. Brandon Straka was a gay, progressive white man who voted Democrat all his life, but gradually came to dislike them. He made a video giving his reasons, and formed the movement to persuade others who felt the same to abandon the Democrats. Now, Brandon was a gay, white man who still thought of himself as 'progressive.' He just couldn't stand the political left. Again, Irvine refused to look at what I sent her.

**Virginia Fox** - Fuck off. I'm not going to expose my students to the hatred and ignorance of far-right bigots. Your words are full of it. Go away Trumptard.

**Average Anomaly** - I rest my case. Your mind is entirely closed.

This got no reply.

**Average Anomaly** - I wonder how 'tolerant and inclusive' you are if some of your students have different opinions to yours.

**Virginia Fox** - I teach history and English, not politics. It's not only retarded but hateful and ridiculous to suggest that while teaching English literature we have time to brainwash students. Don't expect me to humour your ignorant culture war crap.

**Average Anomaly** - All texts are political to some degree. No doubt your own beliefs and perceptions affect the way you teach them.

**Virginia Fox** - Sure. That you interpret this as lefty teachers (that's almost all of us by the way) indoctrinating students makes your argument absurd. You are an utter moron if you think we have time to sit around plotting to brainwash our kids.

**Average Anomaly** - You've proven my case by refusing to show a perfectly good video to your students. Your bias affects your decisions. You've made up your mind about a video without even watching it.

**Virginia Fox** - I'm teach English, you retard, not politics.

**Average Anomaly** - Yeah, like English texts aren't political. Please...

**Virginia Fox** – Kindly explain why an English teacher should be putting far-right garbage in front of her students. Parents would be horrified, just as they would if I showed them far-left stuff. Your hypocrisy is profound.

**Average Anomaly** - The video I sent you is not 'far-right,' in your terms. It was made by a gay man with liberal values who voted Democrat his whole adult life. He gave his reasons for falling out of love with the Democrats. But you have made up your mind before even viewing the video. That's called prejudice. You should be exposing your students to a variety of points of view to see issues from different angles. That's what teachers should do.

No answer.

**Average Anomaly** - You claim to be inclusive and celebrate diversity, yet you are so closed minded that you refuse - even in private - to watch a video and read an article, both of which I sent you during this conversation. You are an utter fraud and a complete hypocrite.

I waited, checked for a response, and saw one word.

BLOCKED!

# 18
# Cookton Follies

Now I knew what I was up against, the thought of quitting did arise. School teaching - who needs it? Apart from the long hours and battle to control the class, now there was this political element. Irvine was clearly a zealot with whom I would never agree. Hall had warned me the education system was heavily biased towards leftist 'progressive' ideas. Until coming face to face with it, it hadn't seemed that big a deal.

The strange thing was, I still thought of myself as a left wing progressive too, as I used to understand the term. I believed in fairness and equality. Naturally, I thought girls and boys should have the same opportunities in life, and be free to pursue any path they wanted. Yet what I saw in Irvine had little to do with justice. It was a barely disguised vindictiveness towards boys and 'masculinity' as she conceived it.

At school, it seemed girls were seen as intrinsically wonderful merely for being girls, while boys were thought to be flawed and potentially dangerous. At the same time, boys were said to be automatically privileged and advantaged. As I looked around my classes, I saw little evidence for this. It was the girls who were doing much better.

The different way boys and girls were treated was comically shown by the workshops put on in my second week at Plumston Park. The girls' workshop was about leadership, while the boys' was on 'Remaking Masculinity.' It turned out the workshop was not about celebrating masculinity, but treating it as some kind of mental disorder to be cured or controlled.

On my way there, I walked past a classroom where one of the leadership workshops was already in session. An energetic looking women was standing up the front, wearing a *The Future is Female* t-shirt. A minute's observation was enough to pick up the whole you-go-girl vibe of the class - then I hurried off to the boys' workshop.

About forty or fifty boys were crowded into a classroom, mainly Year Nine and Tens. It looked like they hadn't kicked off yet. I snuck inside and took a seat up the back.

Standing at the front was a goofy looking guy in his forties. He had a ponytail and wore a Hawaiian shirt. He looked around the room with a big smile and began to speak.

'Hello boys. My name's Craig Cookton and I'm a facilitator with RMM. That means *Remaking Masculinity*. You see, we've noticed boys have been having a lot of problems lately. What's worse, they've been causing a lot of problems for girls. And look boys, that's not cool, alright?

So what we do at RMM is travel around schools and talk to boys. Because one of the biggest problems is boys don't talk about their feelings. That's why I'm here, to tell you that feelings are cool. If you want girls to like you, you have show them you're not afraid to cry or talk about relationship issues and stuff like that.'

It was an odd opening, as if Mr Cookton didn't know how to structure a talk. Instead of building up to his conclusion, he just seemed to blurt it out straight away. Still, after my own ludicrous effort in Year Eleven history, I was in no position to preach.

'Now, I can guess what you boys are thinking,' said Cookton. 'You're like: *who is this lame old dude, Craig? He looks like my dad. What would he know?* Well, boys, prepare yourself for a shock, because I want to let you in on a little secret. A long time ago, I used to be a boy too.'

Craig Cookton seemed to intend this as a joke. He stopped for the laugh... which didn't come. There was a dead silence. It was only broken when a lad up the back called out, 'Does that mean you're a girl now, Sir?'

Then the laughter came. I felt a bit sorry for Craig, but he took it in good spirits.

'Gee, I guess I walked into that one. To be honest, you've sort of stolen my thunder. For a start, some boys do turn into girls, even physically, and that's fine. If that's the sort of path you're on, there's a phone number you can call. It's on the website. But secondly, you know, I kind of have changed into a girl. Not physically but mentally - and that's a *good* thing. Girls are cool, right? The whole idea of gender is what we call a *social construct* anyway' - Craig made air quotes with his fingers - 'but girls have been constructed better than boys. That's why we're trying to change the way you boys see yourselves.'

I looked around the crowded room. The boys were staring at Cookton with little enthusiasm. Suddenly, his face took on a serious look.

'I tell you what, boys, I have to admit I was a bit of a bad apple back in the day. I'm going to tell you a story I'm not proud of. One day, when I was about your age, I went down behind the science blocks at school. I smoked a cigarette with some tough boys to show I was tough too. Five minutes later, I was in the boys' toilets spewing my guts out. Well, you know what? It was a terrible experience but I'm kind of thankful, because maybe the next day it could have been heroin or LSD. Gosh, it kind of makes me shiver when I think about it.

But boys, why did I even smoke that cigarette? Peer group pressure. Now look, I'm going to say a really bad word now, but it's for educational reasons, so don't report me. OK? You see, one of the tough kids - Louie Peters, his name was - he called out to me, 'Want to smoke a fag, fag?' In case you don't know, fag is slang for a cigarette, but it's also a demeaning, homophobic term for a male homosexual. In other words, Louie Peters, was trying to shame me into trying drugs by calling me gay.'

'Are you gay, Sir?' said a boy near the front. I recognised him as one of the Lebanese boys from my Year Ten class. He and his mates stifled giggles as Craig Cookton turned to face him.

'It's not really appropriate for me to comment on my private life, but I guess if I'm trying to get you guys to talk about your feelings, OK. Being gay is perfectly fine, and if any of you boys have those sort of feelings that's very cool. As for myself, I'm not here to talk about my past. Let's just say I'm married to a wonderful woman named Suzanne. We're best friends, ever since I found my feminine side.

Getting back to that cigarette, I gave in to peer group pressure because, even at the age of fourteen, I felt the need to conform to ideas about masculinity. I wanted to be hard and tough like Louie Peters. That's what I thought being a man was. So I want to ask you boys: what are some of the things masculinity means to you? Is it fighting? Being violent and cruel? Hiding your feelings? Is it objectifying women?'

A polite, studious Chinese boy from my Year Nine class raised his hand.

'What does that mean, Sir? Objectifying women?'

'Good question. What's your name?'

'Tim.'

Craig Cookton looked around at the roomful of adolescent boys. At the age of fifteen or sixteen, no doubt most of them were struggling with their sexual feelings, one way or another. I wondered if Cookton's feminist theories were going to help them.

'Can anyone answer Tim's question?' he said. 'What do we do when we objectify women?'

A hesitant hand went up next to me. One of the nerdy white kids.

'Is it when you object to girls? Like, complain about them and stuff?'

Cookton smiled.

'Good try. I can assure you that complaining about women is pretty uncool. It's misogyny, actually. When you think about everything women have to put up with from men, they're the ones who should be complaining about us blokes. But no, that's not the answer. Anyone else?'

A confident hand went up from a boy in my Year Ten class.

'Looking, Sir? Looking at girls?'

Craig turned to face him.

'Correct. When you look at girls, you objectify them. Looking at girls is pretty uncool. In fact, it's harassment, and you know what, boys? You can get in a lot of trouble for it these days.'

Tim raised his hand again.

'What if a girl talks to us, Sir? Can we look at her then?'

'Yes, but only in the face. Understand? There's different kinds of looking. When you look in a girl's face, you can see her personality. Certain other parts of the body are off limits. I guess you know what I'm talking about, right?'

'What about her arms, Sir?'

'Arms are OK, but no lower. Definitely not the legs. You can't see a girl's personality in her legs, can you?'

'What if she's a female football player?' said another lad, a blond surfie type from Year Ten.

'No, boys, that's no excuse. Now look, we're getting a bit sidetracked here. I don't want to get too technical, but there's a feminist concept called the 'male gaze.' Putting it in laymen's terms, so to speak - layperson's terms - the male gaze is when a boy looks at a girl in a way that objectifies her. That's really uncool guys. Girls aren't there to be stared at.'

'What about her arse, Sir? Can we gaze at that?'

Craig Cookton had been pacing the front of the room. He stopped in his tracks. Slowly he turned and surveyed the crowd.

'I want the boy who said that to own up now.'

A hand went up on the far side of the room, from a shaggy haired lad I'd crossed paths with before. A known troublemaker from my Year Ten class. He had the habit of twisting his long black hair around to cover his face so you couldn't see his eyes.

'What's your name, son?' said Craig, trying to look stern.

'Randy.'

'Are you trying to be funny?'

The boy next to him, a pimply fellow thug, spoke up. 'That's his name, Sir. Randall Wright.'

Craig tried to look the kid in the eye, which was hard with his hair in the way. Sooner him than me.

'Righto, Randall, I'm going to use some pretty harsh language with you, man to man. You're being a real dickhead, OK? I'm going to call you out on it, because what you said is super uncool. An arse is not a person, it's an object. I just told you about the male gaze. I want you to try to summon some female empathy. That's a really neat thing women know how to do, which is to pretend you're someone else and imagine how they feel. We're going to workshop this with a little role playing. What I'm going to do is direct the male gaze at you and stare at *your* arse. How does that make you feel?'

'It makes me feel like you're a fag, Sir.'

The room burst into laughter. Cookton looked panicked, like he was on the point of losing control of the class. At that moment, I empathised with him.

'Now look, Randall, that's pretty rude. I'd send you out of class, but if anyone needs a workshop on remaking masculinity, it's boys like you. In fact, I've a good mind to keep you in after the bell goes.'

'So you can stare at my arse, Sir?'

The class erupted again. Craig lost his cool.

'Right, that's it. Get out!'

'Sir! What for?'

'For being a dickhead. Out!'

Randle Wright stood up noisily, flicked back his long black hair, and walked out without looking back. I could see Cookton trying to compose himself.

'OK boys, I guess we've covered that topic - and the take home message is?'

'Don't look at girls, Sir?' said Tim.

'The face is OK. Any other part of the body, you need consent.'

A hand went up at the back. Another dodgy character from Year Ten.

'Is it OK to imagine them?'

I remembered the boy from last week. A red headed kid who, for the benefit of the tougher boys, tried to hide his intelligence behind jokes and overtly rude remarks. Craig Cookton took off his glasses again, and peered at the boy with justified suspicion.

'What do you mean?'

'Is it OK to look at girls in your imagination? You know, like, in masturbation and that?'

Craig stood up straight.

'Goodness, boys. I really think we're getting off topic. But I guess if we're creating a safe male space here, and that's an issue you want to workshop, fair enough. To answer your question, if you need to masturbate, I wouldn't suggest you imagine a girl's body. You should be trying to visualise her personality.'

'But what about, you know... at the climax, Sir? Know what I mean? Can I visualise her body then?'

'At the point of climax, you should be focusing on her face.'

'Climax on her face! That's disgusting, Sir! You're a pervert.'

There were some gasps around the room. As for Craig Cookton's face, it turned white with rage.

'Oh for Heaven's sake, you can join your juvenile mate outside. I must say it's been quite a while since I came upon such a silly, puerile group of young men. Be warned, boys - if you're going to disrespect women like this, you can jolly well get into a lot of trouble these days. So I suggest you start taking this workshop seriously.'

With a visible effort, Cookton managed to compose himself and resume control of the class. He walked over to the desk and found a file on his laptop.

'OK kids, let's do a little masculinity detox. It's probably a good time to watch this. There's a really neat ad made by Gillette. They're a shaving company, if you don't know, and they used to do these silly macho ads brainwashing men into being boofheads. The wonderful thing is they've finally made it out of the Stone Age. They've hired a feminist to design their latest campaign.'

Cookton projected his laptop onto the whiteboard.

The Gillette ad ran for about ninety seconds. It began with four men studying themselves in a shaving mirror with looks of shame. Meanwhile, we heard audio snippets: 'Bullying... the Me Too movement against sexual harassment... toxic masculinity.' Then came the ad's male voiceover asking, 'Is this the best a man can get?'

We then saw a montage of images of 'toxic masculinity.' A group of boys bullying a frightened kid. Two young boys play-fighting at a backyard barbeque. Men lusting after women. A sitcom scene with a middle aged white man ogling a black female maid (this, presumably, to show racial inequality as well). A company manager talking down to a female board member.

The sombre voiceover said 'we can't go on making the same old excuses,' which segued into a bunch of men saying 'boys will be boys' over and over.

'But something finally changed,' said the voiceover. We saw a snippet of smug leftist host, Ana Kasparian, talking about sexual harassment, and a group of media heads joining in. The voiceover then claimed there would be 'no going back, because we believe in the best in men.'

To the strains of heroic backing music, the ad segued into its second half, which was mainly men shaming each other. The ad's feminist creator had a weird intersectional fantasy going on where she imagined men of colour leading the charge for gender equality. In two separate scenes, heroic African-American men stepped in to prevent white men harassing women. Gosh. I suppose every white man does need a role model.

Another such man-of-colour made his young daughter repeat the phrase 'I am strong.' It is well known this demographic is leading the way to bring back the nuclear family. Inspired by these heroic examples, two white men joined the party. A father stopped the two young boys fighting at the barbeque. Another consoled his teenage son. The inspiring music came to its conclusion as the voiceover proclaimed, 'Because the boys watching today... will be the men of tomorrow.'

I looked over at Craig Cookton. Tomorrow's man. I made a mental note that as soon as I got home, my Gillette razor would be going straight in the bin. My reaction was a visceral, emotional one. It was only later, when thinking it through, that I pondered why it was so.

Maybe it was the demonisation of men's sexuality, and the shaming of men's natural attraction to women. Perhaps it was the wholly negative portrayal of men, tied to the slogan 'the best a man can get.' The ad contained nothing about men's heroism, their decency, or their struggles. It was all about their alleged propensities to violence and sexual assault - yet another salvo fired in the current Me Too craze.

Or perhaps I was just sick of the one-sidedness of the gender war between men and women. This shaming campaign was all one way traffic. As if young girls didn't bully each another. As if women didn't lust after men. As if women didn't treat men terribly at times. Yet the ad was all about scolding men. No wonder Craig Cookton liked it.

Feminist doctrine seemed to have got into everything - even Gillette razors, for God's sake, a supposedly pro-male company. They had paid some preachy, sanctimonious feminist to hijack their product and lecture their clients about 'toxic masculinity.'

They had even bastardised the phrase 'boys will be boys.' It used to be an affectionate phrase acknowledging young lads' love of boisterous outdoor games, which often led to cuts or bruises, which were a small price to pay for the joy of it all. Now the phrase had been stolen, twisted to mean something ugly - rapes, assaults, and God knows what else.

Gillette wanted to browbeat men about masculinity, did they? For the sake of comparison, imagine the biggest tampon brand running a campaign about 'toxic femininity.' Suppose such an ad was made by a man, who saw fit to chastise women about, say, nagging, gossiping, or paternity fraud, to say nothing of various other behaviours one might mention. Now tack on the mocking slogan 'girls will be girls' and the challenge, 'is this the best a woman can get?'

Just imagine the seismic howls of outrage such an ad would draw from women - both feminist and non-feminist - and the furious cries about misogyny, women-shaming, and patriarchal control.

There is no doubting the rage such an ad would draw. Yet here we were watching the Gillette ad. Its feminist creator felt entitled to scold and chastise men for their supposed misdeeds - and Gillette had turned full-cuck in allowing it.

I came out of my red mist, and refocused on the class. Craig Cookton was trying to kick off a Q and A. He was looking around the group with that goofy Cookton smile.

'Well, boys, that was pretty awesome, wasn't it? Let's workshop it. Any questions?'

There was dead silence for about twenty seconds. Then a lad from my Year Ten class raised his hand. I'd formed the impression he was one of the smarter boys, but not the type to be bullied - either by teachers or fellow students. He'd asked me a couple of pointed questions last week, and I felt nervous on Cookton's behalf. His question this time was simple and to the point.

'Why don't you like boys?' he said.

Craig Cookton was briefly stumped.

'What makes you think I don't like boys?

The lad pointed to the whiteboard, which Cookton had paused on the last frame of the Gillette ad.

'I do like boys,' said Cookton. 'I love them. I just hate what they do.'

It was the old Christian line. Love the sinner; hate the sin.

Cookton's youthful inquisitor seemed quite worked up. Who could blame him?

'Boys... men do heaps of great stuff. Inventing things, exploring, fighting bushfires. Why don't you talk about that?'

'What's your name?'

'Martin.'

'Right, Martin, nice to meet you. You make a good point. Gillette did used to make ads like that. They wanted to do something different this time so they brought in a feminist to talk about all the bad things men do.'

'Well, it sucks.'

'Now come on, Martin. That's pretty rude. The woman who made this ad is just trying to help boys like you. How about you show her a little respect?'

A couple of boys in the far corner began booing. It caught on, then spread like wildfire, and a few second later the whole room was booing Cookton and Gillette.

Cookton held up his hands. I wondered if he'd been given this reception at other schools.

'I'm really disappointed in you boys. Gillette is just trying to get you all to be better men.'

Martin wasn't having it. He sat back in his chair, folding his arms.

'Do the girls have to watch stuff like this,' he said, 'about being better women?'

'Yes,' said Cookton, in a snooty tone of voice, exactly like the one Ange used when she was wrong and trying to pretend she wasn't. 'Right now, the girls are doing a workshop about being better women. About being leaders, in fact.'

I recognised this sneaky species of lie, the type that took a quarter truth and pretended it was a whole one. I had little doubt the girls were being praised, lauded, and encouraged right now, rather than mocked and shamed.

'Why should girls be the leaders?' said Martin. 'What's so great about them?'

'Why shouldn't they lead?' said Cookton petulantly. '*You* ruled for all of history. Why shouldn't they have a turn?'

There it was. A ridiculous over-simplification of the past, and the attempt to equate Martin with the entire masculine gender since the dawn of time. Again, Martin wasn't buying it.

'I ruled for all of history? I wasn't even born. You're an idiot, Craig.'

'Is that right? Well I'm going to deconstruct the rubbish you said earlier - then let's see who's the idiot. You think men are so great for being inventors and explorers? If men hadn't invented all those things, we wouldn't have climate change.'

'Right, Craig. And you wouldn't have that laptop to show us your silly little ad.'

'And as for explorers,' said Cookton, 'they're exactly the sort of toxic males who started colonialism and white supremacy and racism against people of colour. Ha! So much for your macho explorers. Gillette is no longer promoting those harmful ideas about masculinity. They're leading the way to a better world.'

'It's good that they make razors,' said Martin. 'You can use them to cut off your balls.'

Surprisingly, Cookton took this as a victory. He surveyed the class with a smug smile.

'There you have it, boys. We've flushed out the bigot. That's exactly the sort of homophobic and misogynistic remark I would expect from a dinosaur like Martin. And you,' he thrust out an arm at the lad, 'can go and join the toxic masculinity party with the other two cavemen. Out!'

'Good!' said Martin, standing up and leaving.

He paused at the door and looked back.

'You fucking suck, Craig. You know that?'

'Toodle-oo,' said Cookton, with a wave. 'Run along now.'

Craig Cookton sighed. It was difficult work. No doubt he meant well, but he was way down the wrong path.

'Look boys,' he said. 'We're just trying to help you. Boys have been having a lot of problems lately, and doing a lot of bad things. There's school shootings in America. There's domestic violence and online misogyny. There's far-right extremism and sexual assault.'

Cookton looked at his watch.

'Like it says in the Gillette ad,' he said, 'the same old excuses aren't good enough. Boys will be boys? Well, no. Not if I can help it. Not if *Remaking Masculinity* can stop it. We want you to be more like the girls. Boys will be boys? No. Boys will be girls. So that's my take home message to you. Be a girl.'

The school bell rang. The boys stood up and got out of the room as fast as they could. I thought about staying behind to chat with Craig Cookton, maybe even offering him a kindly word. Then I stopped, and wondered if I might end up saying exactly the same thing as Martin. I shook my head and walked out of the room.

# 19

# Gulag

After sitting through the *Remaking Masculinity* workshop, I was soon thinking about remaking my career choices. While the workshop itself was little more than a joke, it was one more sign of the anti-male slant in the system overall. If the girls were seen as leaders-in-waiting, it seemed the boys were rapists-in-waiting. Masculinity itself was considered flawed, a toxic force needing to be controlled.

At the same time, the sight of the hapless Craig Cookton was a reminder of my own aversion to teaching. Although Cookton was pretty much a clown, my own teaching efforts had been less than stellar so far. Maybe I should just pack it in. But how could I quit now, three years into my teacher training? I'd be a failure, letting down not only myself but Ange, her parents, and the future I had imagined. I'd have to find some other way to earn a living, and at age thirty-five it would mean starting all over again.

A chat with a friendly teacher helped me get back on the horse. There was a period off before lunch, and Beck Irvine was away somewhere. Susan Jordan, a veteran of twenty years teaching English, was the only other person in the staffroom. A curvy blonde with a kindly manner, she was Irvine's opposite, and with her for a mentor my life may have taken a different path. When she asked about my prac, I hesitated, then decided to come clean.

'I've got to admit, the job's a lot harder than I thought it would be.'

Mrs Jordan smiled.

'Did you think it would be easy?'

'People don't realise how much goes into it.'

'Of course,' said Jordan. 'They think the job starts at nine and ends at three.'

I sighed.

'More like starts at 3am, finishes 9pm. For me, anyhow. Planning lessons, getting resources, trying to fix whatever I did wrong the day before. It never ends.'

'It gets easier,' said Mrs Jordan. 'You've just got to slog through until it does.'

'I'm not sure I've got it in me.'

She gave me an appraising look.

'I think you do,' she said at last. 'As long as you're in it for the right reasons.'

'I need to earn a living for a start.'

'If you're here for the money, you've got the wrong gig. The pay's nothing to write home about.'

'Whatever you guys are on, they should double it.'

'Preach!'

'I meant to say, I need to earn a living doing something meaningful.'

Mrs Jordan nodded.

'Teaching's a vocation, really. You've got to love it, and you've got to like the kids.'

'I'm not sure I do. Not when they're teenagers.'

'One day they'll be human beings too. It's our job to help them get there.'

I thought about voicing my views on the school's treatment of boys, but dismissed it as too risky.

'I'm just wondering, Mrs Jordan...'

'Susan.'

'Thanks. I'm wondering, Susan, how long 'til the job gets easier. I'm really stretched. It's hard enough learning the course content, let alone managing the kids.'

'That's only the start. You'll have to deal with parents, staff, endless paperwork...'

'And pledge allegiance to equity, diversity, and inclusion. The political stuff.'

'That's all part of it now,' said Mrs Jordan. 'I won't lie to you, John. This is not a job you can do half-hearted. You've got to really want it.'

'I don't mind putting my heart into the job. I'm just worried it wants my soul.'

'What do you mean?'

'It's just that... oh never mind.'

Mrs Jordan sighed, then gave me a pep talk.

'I don't know you, John, but I've got a feeling you can do this. Teaching's a tough job and plenty can't hack it. It's got the highest attrition rate of any profession these days. Even if you get through your prac, it will take five years to establish yourself as a teacher, 'til you really feel on top of it all. But if you stick it out, you can help make the world a better place. You can make a positive difference to these kids, and some of them really need that. I think you can do it.'

'Thanks, Susan. To be honest, those are the first encouraging words I've heard since I got here.'

Mrs Jordan smiled.

'Who's your mentor?'

'Miss Irvine.'

'Oh.'

Mrs Jordan's expression flickered. She turned to her desk for a moment, then back to me.

'Look at it this way,' she said. 'You only have to put up with her for three more weeks, then you'll never have to see her again. I wish I could say the same. Don't repeat that. Good luck, John.'

I left the staffroom and walked out into the bright sunshine. It would be another ten minutes before the kids came out for lunch. I walked down to the leafy part of the school grounds and stopped to reflect.

No, I wouldn't quit. I'd just have to grit my teeth and get through it. It's a pity Irvine was such a little fascist, but as Sue Jordan said, it was only another three weeks. It was rotten luck to have landed Irvine as a mentor - or perhaps I'd 'attracted ' her, as those New Age types put it. Anyway, it was short term pain for long term gainful employment.

Presumably, not all teachers were rabid leftists. Of course, most of my life I had been a leftist myself, in a fairly mindless way. But the left had changed into some sort of cult, filled with zealots like Irvine. She was entitled to her views, of course, but the tinge of fanaticism had begun to grate. Like so many of her type, she had the smug conviction that anyone who disagreed with her was stupid or evil.

Perhaps Hall was right after all. Sure, we disagreed on refugees, but you can't agree on everything. Perhaps he was even right that mass immigration wasn't that great for social cohesion. There was plenty of 'diversity' on show in this school, and what did it do for unity? During my playground duty, I'd seen what looked more like 'Balkanisation,' in so much as the various ethnic types tended to form small enclaves to hang out in their own groups.

Unity had once been considered a strength. National unity. For most of those on the left, the idea was heavily out of favour. In their minds, it equated to fascism, racism, and xenophobia. But while a sense of national unity may have driven Nazi Germany, it had also united England to oppose them.

What sort of unity did we have now? I'd recently read a novel by a Lebanese-Australian author. It seemed to be autobiographical, about his time at a Sydney school with a large Muslim student base in the early 2000s. There was one scene where the students openly cheered news of the September 11 terror attack. The author was a Muslim himself, so there was little reason to doubt the story was true. So much for unity. At least back in the 'bad old days' of the 1940s, no one at that school would have been cheering for the Nazis to bomb Britain.

There *was* still a sort of unity leftists were striving for, and that was unity of belief. There seemed to be this constant push to force a given ideology onto people. That may have been alright if it was one I agreed with. Yet along with the anti-male stuff, there seemed to be an anti-Anglo, anti-European tone to it all. Globalist propaganda, Hall would have called it.

Nowhere was this more obvious than in the course material. The heavily feminist *Women in History* course pushed the simplistic view that men were the villains of history and women the victims. Irvine's Year Nine class, *Empire and Consequence* was about the evils of colonialism, and the unique wickedness of whites and Western civilisation. It was Helda McGovern all over, although McGovern-lite at this level.

The resources, to use the term loosely, seemed to have come largely from the propaganda unit at the BBC, England's... ahem... 'national broadcaster.' The BBC had changed a lot in fifty years. It had once been stuffy and conservative, to the extent that groundbreaking shows like *Monty Python* and *Doctor Who* had been lucky to get past the gatekeepers and be made at all. These days, *Monty Python* wouldn't be made, but for different reasons - because the Python guys were a bunch of white males who would never meet today's diversity standards. As for *Doctor Who*, it was unrecognisable now, little more than a propaganda vehicle for 'woke' politics.

As far as I could tell, the BBC had been taken over by radical leftists. The rabid anti-Brexit campaign was one sign of it; the diversity quotas in casting were another. To some degree such casting was understandable, as Britain had changed. More disturbing was the BBC's Orwellian depiction of the past. There was a *Doctor Who* episode set in 1820 where half of those in a crowd scene were 'people of colour.' Some of its history shows used similar tactics, if not quite as blatantly. It was part of a bizarre push to persuade people that Britain, rather than having been populated mainly by Anglo-Celtic types, had always been a heavily diverse multicultural country.

This was almost comical at times, yet some of this material was used in the school's coursework to teach ignorant children, who had no reason to doubt it. This was all part of the push for a leftist 'progressive' outlook. Apparently the future was going to be some kind of globalist, multicultural paradise - and not forgetting it would be female too - and all driven by the lofty sounding DIE principles - diversity, inclusion, and equity.

As I began to see the farce being played out, I became less and less inclined to be a part of it. In an odd way, this helped with the teaching. I was happy to fail, which removed all the pressure. I could observe class from a place of detachment, almost amusement, and if I ended up failing the prac, well, hip-hip hooray.

Still, I thought I may as well get the teaching degree, for the sake of earning a living. So I gave lip service to what I was supposed to teach, even if half of it was bullshit. I did such a good job that even Irvine was satisfied, to the extent that she left me to run the show on my own for a couple of days. She went off on a two day professional development workshop. This at the end of the third week of my five weeks at Plumston Park. With Irvine away, I'd be flying solo for the Thursday and Friday.

Without Irvine's scrutiny, I took the opportunity to change the tone of the class. Having settled in by now, the manic energy of my first class had gone, and I was able to relax and speak more conversationally. On the Friday of week three, I took Year Eleven's *Women in History* once more, and set class a discussion question.

'When Justin Trudeau became prime minister of Canada in 2015, he appointed his first cabinet with half women and half men. Why do you think he did this, and was it fair? Take it up in your groups.'

After each group had reported back, there was an open discussion. Class's leading light, Bianca, raised her hand.

'Trudeau led the way and took a big step towards gender equality.' Her face took on a coy look. 'He's also kind of hot.'

Some of the girls giggled. I couldn't help remembering Craig Cookton's words about the evils of objectifying women.

'So a fifty-fifty split in Justin's cabinet means gender equality, does it?' I said. 'But do we agree that girls and boys are equal in ability?'

'Yes,' said Bianca.

'If men and women are equal, why do we need quotas for those sort of jobs?'

'To make sure it's fair.'

'What if sixty percent of women are the best candidates? Is it still right to have a fifty percent quota?'

'That would be unfair, Sir.'

'Why?'

'Because ten percent of women who deserved to be there would miss out.'

'Then what if sixty percent of the men were the best? Should we give them the jobs?'

'That's discrimination.'

'I see. Let's take an example closer to home. Suppose that of all the high school kids who go on to university, sixty percent are girls and forty percent boys. Is that unfair to the boys?'

A girl named Celia shot up her hand.

'If girls study harder, they deserve it. If the boys don't study, that's their fault.'

I glanced at Hunter. He was looking down at his desk, but seemed to be paying attention.

'I think you've hit on the right answer, Celia. We need to forget about all these silly quotas and just let people get on with it and do their best. I mean, we're supposed to be equal, right? We will never achieve real equality if we constantly focus on people's gender.

We do need to give everyone the chance to compete. That's our job as teachers, to help everyone start from where they are and join in. There's where feminism did a lot of good for women. If you'd gone to high school fifty years ago, your career choices would have been much more restricted. Now, you can pretty much do whatever you want.

So yes, I agree with you that if sixty percent of girls are the best students, they should be the ones going to uni. Really, it's the boys we should be worried about now that they're so far behind. If we want equality, don't you think we should be helping them catch up?'

Bianca's hand went up again.

'They've got male privilege, Sir.'

'If it was 1970, Bianca, I may have agreed with you. But as I said, boys are doing far worse in education now and most uni graduates are girls. Apart from that, men on average die younger, go to jail more, and have loads of other problems. I'm not sure how much male privilege there really is these days.'

'You're wrong, Sir. Or why is there a gender pay gap and more male chief executives?'

'I don't know what you've been told about the gender pay gap, but... look, I'd better not go there. Let me just say this: if you want to be on the right side of the pay gap, be very careful what you choose to study at uni. Don't do an arts degree for one. Avoid low paid jobs like social work or, God forbid, teaching. Get into IT or engineering. If you want to be a CEO, study business or something else that will take you down that path.'

I had been pacing the front of the room. I paused mid-pace, and turned to the class.

'But you know what, girls? What I just said is all bullsh… ah, nonsense. There's more to life than money. You should choose a career that interests you. When you come to the end of your life, you'll look back on whether it had meaning, not the size of your bank balance. OK, your life might be a bit *shorter* - but you can't have everything.'

I sat down at the desk.

'Let's not pretend that all your dreams are going to come true, even if you work hard. I speak from experience. I had a dream once - to become an actor. I thought if I just worked hard and kept trying, I might not necessarily crack it in Hollywood but at least I'd be an indie film star. And look at me now. Here I am teaching Year Eleven history at Plumston Park High School.'

'You, Sir? An actor? Were you in any movies? Anything on Netflix?'

I shook my head.

'Just a few bit parts, I'm afraid. I'm sorry to say there are no guarantees that life is going to be fair to you. Just remember, you and your group aren't the only ones it's unfair to. It's unfair to everyone, one way or another.'

'That's a bit of a downer, Sir,' said Celia. 'Aren't you supposed to empower us?'

'I don't mean it like that. Fact is, life is a gift and an opportunity. What I notice is there's an awful lot of complaining these days. It's like an Olympic sport. I'm getting pretty bored with it, to be honest. If someone tells you girls you're oppressed, don't believe them. You're freer than any women in living memory. Do something with your lives as well as you can. There's no guarantee you'll succeed, but don't complain. Just get on with it.'

Jonathan, the class sycophant, raised his hand.

'Excuse me, Sir. How can you say girls are free, when there's the constant threat of rape?'

I paused for a few seconds, surprised by the *non sequitur*.

'What on Earth has rape got to do with the topic under discussion?'

When the boy replied, I had the sense he was doing some kind of audition.

'We will never have equality,' he said, 'as long as there's rape and toxic masculinity.'

'I appreciate your concern, Jonathan, but you're confusing two different things. There's equality, and then there's a small minority of humans who do terrible things. But if you're going to suspend equality while we wait for people to stop doing terrible things, you're going to be waiting a long, long time.'

I took a sip of water.

'That other term you used, toxic masculinity, is one we should file under G for Garbage. Whatever masculinity is, some of the so called 'male' qualities are for better and some are for worse. The idea there's something wrong with masculinity itself? Anyone who tells you that, take a long, hard look at them.'

I paused.

'And if equality's your thing, we'd better include 'toxic femininity' as well. Let's not pretend girls aren't just as capable of bad behaviour as boys. I mean, we all know about bullying, don't we? Boys' bullying tends to be direct and physical. Girls' bullying is more social - gossip, exclusion, or put-downs. I'll bet some of you girls know what I'm talking about, right? I don't know which kind is worse. Maybe we should call it toxic humanity, instead of trying to pretend one gender's got a monopoly on being awful.'

The school bell rang. As I returned to the staffroom and packed up my briefcase, I felt for the first time I'd found myself as a teacher. I had been myself, spoken my mind, and thought I had gotten through to at least some of the kids. *I can do this*, I thought to myself. *I can be a teacher after all, and make a difference.* I caught the train home, knowing I would enjoy my weekend, for the first time in at least a month.

On the Sunday morning, there was an email from Miss Irvine.

> Dear Mr Gilbert,
>
> You are relieved of teaching duties for Monday, pending a performance review at 3.30pm.
>
> Your attendance at school is not required until the review.
>
> J. Irvine.

It hit me like a slap in the face. Hopefully this was just a routine, mid-prac review. Somehow I knew it wasn't.

At 1.30pm on the Monday, I began my long journey to Plumston Park.

Two nervous hours later, I walked into an empty classroom to be met by three inquisitors. There was Helen Franklin, the head of department, Jim Brown, a senior English teacher, and Irvine herself. As it turned out, Franklin did most of the talking. The other two were there to observe and decide my fate.

Franklin was a tough old battleaxe. She'd probably seen it all and more. She gave me a weary look, as if this was just one more task in a very long day.

'Sit down, Mr Gilbert.'

I obeyed, taking my spot in front of the panel.

'I didn't realise I had a mid-prac review,' I said.

'Your performance is always under review,' said Franklin. 'It will be for the rest of your *practicum*. It will be again when you start your first job, and will continue until the day you retire, if you ever get that far.'

Franklin took off her glasses. Irvine seemed to be enjoying herself. Jim Brown just sat there like a shag on a rock.

'I'll get straight to the point, Mr Gilbert,' said Franklin. 'We've had a complaint.'

'What for?'

'Your Year Eleven history class on Friday.'

I adopted an innocent look. After all, I *was* innocent.

'I see it as part of my teaching brief to challenge the girls. It will empower them to think critically. It wasn't my intention to upset them.'

'The complaint wasn't made by a girl. It was one of the boys.'

My thoughts flew to the horrible little sycophant, Jonathan. Franklin put on her glasses and glanced at a piece of paper on the table in front of her.

'According to the complainant, you made several misogynistic remarks.'

'I assure you that's not true.'

'Apparently your whole demeanour was extremely negative. You disempowered the girls by telling them their dreams might not come true.'

'Well, of course they mightn't. Plenty of mine haven't. Some of my nightmares, sure...'

'It may have been defensible if you'd put this in a framework of educating the girls about structural inequality.'

'I never even raised the topic.'

'Indeed. Apparently, for reasons best known to yourself, you also saw fit to discuss the gender wage gap...'

'I was just telling the girls how to avoid it.'

'... and toxic femininity. Pray tell, Mr Gilbert, what is that?'

'Look, Ms. Franklin, this has been taken way out of context. If only you could have heard the class overall.'

'Any more classes you give will be closely monitored. To be honest, we're wondering if it's best to let you go.'

'What for? I've done nothing wrong.'

At this point, Beck Irvine joined in.

'You're not really a team player, are you, Sir? You don't want to stay on message.'

'I've made every effort to comply with the course outlines.'

'You've made a token effort, but you seem determined to impose your own ideas whenever it suits you.'

'That's not the case. In fact, I've been extremely cautious in what I've said in class?'

'Is that so, Sir? What have you been hiding?'

'I didn't mean it like that. Look, I've done nothing wrong. I did my level best last Friday to empower the girls. I stand by everything I said.'

'Even when you trivialised the topic of rape?'

'I did no such thing. I was telling the girls how to empower themselves to achieve equality, and that silly little boy, Jonathan, brought up the topic of rape, right out of the blue. It had nothing to do with the discussion, and I slapped the boy down. Maybe I was too harsh on him, but I assure you his complaint is entirely frivolous.'

Franklin held up her hand, indicating to Irvine that she'd heard enough.

'Mr Gilbert,' she said. 'I'm going to ask you to step outside for a few minutes while we confer.'

I stood up and departed the room. When I returned, Irvine had a strange, sulky look on her face. Franklin regarded me sternly, then delivered her judgment.

'Mr Gilbert, I'm going to give you the benefit of the doubt, but you need to understand you're on pretty thin ice. Both my colleagues voted to terminate your *practicum*. As head of this department, I overruled them. Rest assured, however, your teaching will be closely monitored for your final two weeks. You'll need to give your lesson plans to Miss Irvine twenty-four hours in advance. We'll take a dim view of any inappropriate content or tone in your lessons. You may resume teaching on Wednesday, as long as Miss Irvine approves your lesson plans.'

Franklin began sorting her papers, ready to leave.

'You may go, Mr Gilbert.'

I stood up.

'Thank you, Ms Franklin for giving me another chance.'

'You'd better make the most of it.'

'I will. I've really learned from this incident. Thank you.'

I gave a small, respectful bow to Ms Franklin, then left the room without looking at Irvine or the other disgusting little Nazi.

I caught the train home and avoided everyone for the rest of the day. I barely said a word to Ange and went to bed, pleading a headache.

I lay awake for hours, tossing and turning. Why was I trying to become a school teacher in the first place? The friend who'd sold me the idea three years ago had given me a sales pitch. Mind you, she wasn't really a teacher, just someone starting out on the same path as myself. It's easy, she said. All you have to do is show up, breeze through your lessons, then waltz out with a fat pay cheque.

Easy? What a load of bull. The job is a vampire that sucks you dry. When you're not teaching, you spend all your time planning lessons or grading papers. When you *are* onstage, it's a constant fight to maintain the illusion you're in control, knowing there's a pack of hyenas ready to rip you apart if you lose it.

Maybe if you're a confident extrovert, you can breeze in and bang out a lesson without raising a sweat - but that's not me. The reality is I was an introvert who liked learning a lot more than I liked teaching. Oh, I could do it one on one, or to small groups. Put me in front of mob of annoying kids just there to muck up, and there's the risk I might blow my top and throw one of them out the window.

All my time on prac - this one and the others - I felt that my life just disappeared. This was not an easy job. It's not one you could do half-arsed to collect a pay packet. To do it properly would require full commitment and a passion I didn't have. I'd have to work extremely hard just to get by. Why squander my life energy on becoming a mediocre school teacher?

Then there were the politics, which had become more and more intrusive. Clearly, there was a heavy ideological slant to modern education. They might clothe it in buzzwords like diversity and inclusion, but they hid something much darker. It was Hall's Trojan horse all over again.

I could have gone along with it, prior to Hall's influence. But now? Bowing down to the feminist regime would mean a betrayal of my own gender, while accepting the anti-white, anti-European spiel would be deserting the culture I'd grown up in, for the sake of some naive, poorly thought out globalist Utopia.

As was also clear, any serious departure from The Message would see me sent to the re-education Gulag, or erased altogether.

I opened my email and sent Edward Hall a message.

> Hey Edward,
>
> Sorry about how we parted. I didn't mean to be a jackass. I want to catch up with you for a chat, if you'll accept my apology.

I'm thinking of chucking in my teacher job. You were right about the indoctrination. I don't know if I want to be a part of it anymore.

The next morning there was a brief reply in my inbox.

No offence taken, John. As for your school teaching, it boils down to this: are you prepared to be a professional liar for the rest of your career, just to earn a living? Or have you got something better to do with your life?

Hall's words stayed with me for the rest of the day. They were with me on the long train journey to Plumston Park. They were with me when I walked into the staffroom and heard the same old blue pill banter from the staff. They were with me when I watched Irvine teach, and when I went through the motions myself.

In the end, though, the last straw was Angie's ukulele song.

# 20

# Ukulele Smash

Yes, it was Ange who broke me. I arrived home from school that day - the Tuesday - drained and fuming. Barely had I got in the door than Ange walked up with a strange smile on her face.

'Hey babe, check this out.'

'Give me a minute. I'm half dead.'

'This will perk you up.'

She made me sit down on the couch, then she opened an Instagram video on her phone. There she was onscreen, prettier than ever, strumming her ukulele, and singing a song packing every feminist cliché in the book.

**'Easy With a Peeny' - by Angie Gardiner.**

Equal pay, there's a long way to go

Eighty cents in the dollar is pretty damn low

Only five percent of girls become CEOs

Oh yeah


Making jokes with your big dumb mates

One day it's sexist jokes, the next it's rape

Rape culture, there's no escape

Oh yeah

You say female comedians ain't funny

Your failed sense of humour is misogyny

But don't laugh just to condescend to me

Oh no


We're not winning awards, maybe we just suck

When you're born with a peeny, you get all the
luck

Peeny privilege brings in the big bucks

Oh yeah


Life's easy with a peeny,

Breezy when you've got a weeny

The days are super dreamy

For the 'good ole boys'


Jacinda and Merkel are kicking some arse

Trump and Putin should be given a class

When will the future be female? It's what I want
to ask

Oh yeah

Emotional labour is slavery

Better pay reparations babe, my EL ain't free

No I won't marry you, get off your knees

Oh no


There's one thing I believe is true

John Lennon got it right in '72

Women's lives matter, spread the good news

Oh yeah


Life's easy with a peeny,

Breezy when you've got a weeny

The days are super dreamy

For the 'good ole boys.'


The song ended. I just stared at her.

'What's a peeny?' I asked, knowing the answer but not wanting to believe it.

Ange looked down at my crotch. 'What do you think?'

'So if you're born with a penis, life's a breeze.'

'Awesome, hey?' said Ange, with the same cheeky smile she'd had in the video. 'Look how many views it's had.'

I peered at the video's view count. Fifty-thousand already.

'Wow,' I fumbled. 'I'm speechless.'

I had to get away before I said something cruel in the heat of the moment. She was looking at me with those big brown eyes, eager for my approval. I hugged her, then let go.

'Well done, Ange. It's terrific. But despite my peeny, I haven't had a very easy day. I'm just going to have a lie down to recover. Er... why don't you send me the video so I can watch it again?'

Angie hugged me once more. I absorbed it passively feeling an odd mix of love, rage, and sorrow. It was like tasting a custard tart with Hot English mustard on top.

I showered, then after resting for a while in the privacy of my room, steeled myself to watch the video again. Yes, Ange had managed to drag nearly every feminist cliché into one little song. A song with the basic premise that life's a breeze if you're born a man.

Life's easy with a peeny, is it? I had never found it so. Indeed, as I looked at the view count on Angie's video - it was now past seventy-thousand - I could not help recalling my own past struggles in the music business more than a decade ago. The years learning to play an instrument, finding band members, rehearsing, chasing down gigs, writing songs, paying to record them, then trying in vain to get anyone to listen to them. My songs had been good, damn good. Whether you liked them or not, they were a hell of a lot better than Angie's silly little four chord song.

Yes, that's what it was. A 'four chord song.' Not just any four chords - *those* four chords - the most hackneyed, flogged-to-death combination in all popular music. C-G-Am-F. Those letters may as well stand for Couldn't Give A Fuck. The same old silly chords, but played on a ukulele. Life's easy with a peeny, is it? Not as easy as when you're a cute twenty-five year old girl with minor talent, and your audience is dumber than a sackful of hammers.

First the day I'd had at school, now this - something inside me was about to snap. I got up and locked the bedroom door. If she walked in here now, this relationship would be over. It was all I could do to stop myself walking out of the room and telling her we were through. Yet as I pictured the imaginary scene - her face falling as I told her I hated her song enough to break up with her - my rage drained away, leaving a hole filled only by sorrow.

I sank onto the bed and lay down in the dark, hands behind my head. When it came to the crunch, did I really love Ange? Or was I merely pole-axed by her beauty and youthful intensity? I saw that if I continued down the path I'd been going, my whole life might be a lie. I'd have to pay lip service to the lunacy taught at school, and go along with Angie's belief system as well, always tempering my words, self censoring to ensure they were acceptably PC.

If I didn't want to go down that path, the only choice would be to leave her, a prospect that terrified me. Even with my hatred for her ukulele song, I couldn't do it.

But I *could* quit teaching.

Yes, that was the answer. I couldn't handle both teaching *and* Ange. The 24/7 lying would be just too much. If I at least escaped the teaching, Angie's foolishness would be tolerable, or at least manageable. Where I went from here, career wise, God only knew. I'd just have to figure that out. Something totally devoid of politics, that's for sure.

Oh yeah, I'd quit - but I wouldn't go quietly. Why not give them something to remember me by? A plan began to form. I sat down at my desk and sketched it out.

I played it straight on the Wednesday and Thursday. Irvine had put herself in the odd position of simultaneously trying to ignore me - her natural disposition - and put me under Stasi-like scrutiny. I conjured an especially fawning persona for those two days, being sure to empower the girls at every opportunity and scorn men, whites, and Western civilisation. I didn't lay it on *too* thick, just enough to make her think I'd buckled under to the performance review and her threat to fail me as a prac teacher.

In plotting my revenge, I considered a dramatic public scene telling the class what I really thought of what they were learning. No, that would be too confrontational, and needlessly unpleasant. Mine would be a quiet protest. Formal and dignified, I would put it in writing.

It would take the form of a weekend homework assignment, for Year Eleven's *Women in History* class, and for Year Nine's *Empire and Consequence*.

I played it straight until the Friday afternoon, so Irvine would not suspect. I told class they had an assignment for the weekend, which I would be collecting and marking the following Monday. The assignments would be sent to each student's email address. Technically, I would be expected to forward it to Irvine too, but that email might just get lost in transition.

For Year Eleven's *Women in History*, the homework was to watch four short videos, by Janice Fiamengo and Karen Straughan. They were two of the smartest female critics of feminism, and had dissected the movement's false beliefs with ruthless precision. Any prolonged exposure to their work would help counter the doctrine the students had been taught.

1. 'Feminism, a Victim Mentality Disorder' - Janice Fiamengo.

2. 'Feminism Wants Your Soul' - Janice Fiamengo.

3. 'The Dangers of an Ideological Approach' - Karen Straughan.

4. 'Is Feminism Hate?' - Karen Straughan.

As for Year Nine, studying *Empire and Consequence*, I set them a quiz with the following multiple choice questions. Some of the answers were a little flippant, and some of it may have gone over their heads, but I hoped it would make them think.

## Year Nine Quiz

1. Many people believe racism is one of today's biggest social problems. The best way to solve it is to:

a) Follow Martin Luther King's advice and judge people by their actions and character, not by the colour of their skin.
b) Think obsessively about race all the time and encourage others to do the same.
c) Empower minorities by telling them their dreams will inevitably be crushed by racism and white supremacy.
d) Shut up about it. It's boring.

2. Which people are racist?

a) Whites
b) Blacks
c) Asians
d) Arabs
e) Everyone else
f) All of the above

3. Multiculturalism is a fantastic idea in theory, as it promotes cultural exchange and brotherhood. What are the biggest obstacles in the way of its success?

a) Purposely denigrating the culture and people of the 'host nation.'
b) Constantly banging on about racism, and fighting over racial quotas for everything.
c) The pretence that all cultures are equal and compatible.
d) All the other problems too.

4. Multiculturalism is globalism on a small scale. What are the best aspects of it?

a) We can visit other cultures without paying expensive airfares and accommodation costs.
b) All the world's cities will end up being pretty much the same, so we won't have to waste money flying overseas anymore. This will help climate change.
c) Awesome choice of cuisine.
d) Humanity living in harmony as one people. World peace is now almost here, thanks to the success of the multicultural experiment.

5. Japan has a strong and unique national culture, renowned the world over. It is also close to an ethnostate and allows very limited immigration. If the UN forced Japan to become 2% English, French, Turkish, and twenty-two other foreign nationalities, Japan could become 50% multicultural. Would Japan be:

a) Much better. It would finally be a diverse modern country.
b) Just another boring globalist country like all the others.
c) No longer Japan.
d) None of your business. Let Japan decide what it wants to be.

6. Western Civilisation began in Europe a few thousand years ago and spread around the world. It is:

a) The most evil civilisation ever.
b) The greatest civilisation ever.
c) A mix of good and bad like any other civilisation.
d) Known for its outstanding achievements in art, science, and other areas, and largely responsible for inventing the modern world, so cut it some slack.

7. White Western academics and school teachers who spend their careers denigrating Western Civilisation and trying to undermine it should be:

a) Applauded as the noble heroes they are.
b) Given jobs and awards.
c) Scorned as traitors and fools.
d) Sacked from their jobs, as unworthy heirs to Western Civilisation.

8. Identity Politics is a system which tries to force collective identity on people based on narrow characteristics like race, gender, sexual orientation, and other traits. In your opinion, is identity politics:

a) An idea which had some merit at first, but has grown into a never-ending whine of irrational complaints.
b) A rort where conmen and opportunists try to extort money and jobs from the system.
c) A crude and simplistic way of viewing the world.
d) All of the above.

9. 'White wimpiness' is a phrase used to describe white people's attitude to the topic of racism. Which of the following two states of mind best reflects white wimpiness?

a) Cringing apology and guilty self-loathing.
b) Pride in your ethnic, national, and cultural character, and disdain for race hustlers.

10. Compare media coverage of the last two US presidents, Obama and Trump. Obama's coverage was heavily favourable and Trump's has been overwhelmingly negative. Is this because:

a) Obama was a messiah and Trump is worse than Hitler. The media simply reported those facts fairly and objectively.
b) The media was already heavily biased, and Trump's election made them completely unhinged.
c) Does anyone even care anymore?

11. Fifty years ago your grandfather was a student at this school and stole another kid's lunch. The victim's grandchild is a student here now. Should you let him steal your lunch?

a) Yes, every day.
b) Yes, and breakfast too.
c) No, what's it got to do with me?
d) No, but I'll try to make friends with him.

12. Feminists seem to believe that the greatest impediments to their happiness and success are men, masculinity, male privilege, and patriarchy. The logical solution is to form an all-female country, as all these impediments would then be removed. This has not been done yet because:

a) Then there would be no one to blame.
b) Complaining is easier.
c) They'll get around to it one day.
d) The patriarchy has forbidden it.

13. Everyone who questions progressive left wing values and thinks differently to me is:

a) A Nazi
b) A fascist
c) A white supremacist
d) Sane

14. The biggest cause of misery and failure in the world today is:

a) The Patriarchy
b) White Supremacy
c) Structural Racism
d) The fools who teach this stuff in schools and universities.

I emailed this quiz to Year Nine, and that was that. I caught the train home from Plumston Park with a sense of liberation. I would certainly be sacked. To steal their thunder, I composed the following email, which would go to both Helen Franklin, the department head, and Beck Irvine, my mentor-tormentor. It read as follows:

> To Helen Franklin and Beck Irvine,
>
> This is my formal resignation from my prac placement, and from school teaching itself. I will give you my reasons.
>
> First, thank you for allowing me to work at your school. To be fair, I have gained a newfound respect for the teaching profession. It is a very difficult job requiring skill, courage, and dedication.
>
> In trying to meet the high demands of the profession, I was certainly tested. I can't claim to be a great teacher, or even a good one. I think I *could* have been good with continued effort. I would have put my heart into that quest if not for the politics which have infested the education system like termites.
>
> The agenda against men and boys is misguided. You, Beck, have accepted a feminist view of history which is partial at best. Based on a sense of grievance, you want to empower the girls and make a better world. That would be fine if you did not also treat the boys in your care with indifference bordering on contempt. Whatever the rights and wrongs of the past, the boys in your class had nothing to do with it. Neither did the girls. Let them live their lives.

I'm awarding you a fail as a history teacher. Your performance needs a thorough review. You need to examine your motivations and ask whether they're in keeping with justice, with being a good teacher, or simply an expression of your personal vendetta against imaginary enemies.

The education system today should also lose the silly anti-Western bias. Guilt isn't good, at least not when taken to ridiculous excess. While it would be stupid to teach only the achievements of Western Civilisation, it's far stupider to teach only the mistakes.

More to the point, if there's any hope of reaching the wished for social Utopia in Australia, we're going about it the wrong way.

I feel sorry for you. Multiculturalism is a grand social experiment in which theory makes its optimistic journey into real life. It's not easy to manage this disjointed, incoherent society with its hundreds of demographics, and you're expected to make it work through the magic of Diversity, Equity, and Inclusion. Politicians, do-gooders, and naive Utopians handed you this mess, and now you have to run it. Good luck.

By the way, Beck, give my regards to Virginia Fox.

Regards,

John Gilbert

I pressed send on the email. Then I packed a suitcase and printed out the airline ticket I would use to fly to Melbourne and hang out with Hall for a few days.

Angie was out, teaching her English as a Second Language course. I opened the door of her room and left a note telling her I'd be away.

I walked through the front door and saw she'd left her ukulele on a chair on the front porch. She must have been practicing, or perhaps composing a new masterpiece.

The sight of this childish toy guitar brought back all the frustration of the past week. Life's easy with a peeny, is it? With an oath, I dropped my suitcase and picked up the ukulele. I seized it by the neck, raised it above my head, then brought it crashing down towards the porch railing with the intention of smashing it to smithereens.

Then stopped. The ukulele was childish, sweet, and innocent, and did not deserve such a fate. I placed the ukulele gently back on the chair, and went on my way.

# 21

# Oh FOC, the Backlash

I slept through the short flight to Melbourne. It seemed only minutes between the 6pm Sydney takeoff and 7.30 arrival in Melbourne. From there, it was a short taxi ride to Hall's place in the inner city suburb of Brunswick. The cab pulled up in a side street outside a small, one storey house. As I rang the buzzer, it occurred to me the roles had reversed. Just a couple of months before, it had been Hall at *my* door.

I heard footsteps from within, and the door was flung open.

'If it ain't me old mate, Johnny Gilbert!' said Hall, feigning surprise. 'What brings you to these Godforsaken parts?'

Hall had been expecting me, of course, since I emailed him on Wednesday. I went inside and followed him down a short passage. He stopped halfway along it and opened an internal door.

'Dump your kit in there, old boy.'

The room was a kind of office. It reminded me of Frank Gardiner's study. Angie's dad, that is. Hall's was smaller, but much the same. Papers, drawers, and a shelf full of books.

'Are you hungry?' said Hall. 'Or would you rather a drink?'

'I had something at the airport. How about a beer?'

In a matter of minutes we were walking up Brunswick's main street. Brunswick had a grungy, inner city vibe, rather like Newtown in Sydney. We entered a local pub and made for the back bar, where I was surprised by a familiar face. He recognised me first.

'Hey, it's the geezer we met in Sydney. The one with the Antifa girlfriend.'

It was Davo, Hall's travelling companion from the night of the Stefan Molyneux show. With some embarrassment, I recalled my prior assumption that he was a Nazi. Mind you, he did look the part with his blond, Aryan looks and muscled physique. A scene flashed through my mind, from the night of our first meeting. The two 'Nazis,' Davo and Hall, sitting at that hotel room table, my dash for the exit, and Davo tripping me up so I landed flat on the floor. I'd honestly thought they were going to kill me.

As if reading my mind, Davo, in the present, raised his arms in a bogey-man gesture. He looked towards the door of the hotel and laughed, as if expecting me to make another run for it.

'What happened, Antifa? Did she throw you out?'

'More like the other way round,' I said. 'What do you think I'm doing here?'

'You've come to protest us having a drink in public? Where's the rest of your gang?'

Hall stepped in.

'Easy, Davo. Johnny's not the man he was. Fair play to him for admitting he was wrong. Takes a big man to do that.'

He turned to me.

'Is it true though - you've left Ange?'

'I don't really know.'

I sat down at a table with Hall and filled him in on recent events. A couple of beers later and we were up to date.

'So what now?' said Hall.

'No idea. I just wanted to get away and clear my head.'

'You can stay with me. I don't have much on next week.'

'That's decent of you, Hall. What do you actually do? I've never really asked.'

Hall smiled.

'Same as every day you've known me. I'm a teacher like you. A freelancer, though - and excommunicated, again, just like you. An escapee from the system.'

'A schoolteacher?'

'Not schools. I was an academic for a while, before I was drummed out.'

'You were sacked?'

'Not exactly, but it was only a matter of time.'

'What did you teach? The humanities, I suppose.'

Hall nodded.

'I got out just in time. When I was a student, they still allowed some free and critical thought. They taught you *how* to think, not *what* to think. An arts degree was worth doing then. Today, I wouldn't bother.'

'But how do you earn a living?'

'There's more than one way to get paid, old boy.'

Clearly Hall was going to remain cagey for the time being. I felt suddenly tired, as if the week's events had caught up with me.

'How about we call it a night? I'm done in.'

'Right you are, Johnny. Now, as for tomorrow, I'm out all day. Why don't you head into town and come back by sundown? We'll make a proper night of it.'

I couldn't blame Hall for not wanting to leave me alone in his place all day. He had no reason to trust me to that extent.

I woke late the next morning. It was a fine, clear Saturday as I caught the tram into central Melbourne. I left the phone off as I browsed cafes and bookshops and parks. I felt free, almost too free. Rudderless. There was no direction, no plan. Everything was unformed and uncertain. It was exactly what I wanted.

The one noteworthy event that day was the Aztec exhibition at The Melbourne Museum. The Aztecs were a relatively short lived civilisation - just a few hundred years - yet at its height, the Aztecs must have thought they would last forever. Turns out they were brought down by two external factors: the invading

Spanish, and an epidemic which the Europeans may also have brought. Between the two, much of the Aztec population was wiped out. All that was left of them now was this travelling exhibition. What a comedown for a once mighty people.

I caught the tram back to Brunswick by 5pm, then Hall and I adjourned to the same pub as the night before. We were well into our third beer when the conversation turned to Ange.

'Has she changed at all?' asked Hall. 'Have you ever tried to chip away at her ideas?'

'I don't bother. Last time I tried, it led to Mateo.'

'That was a while ago. You mean to say you've not challenged her since?'

'It's pointless. Her mind is set.'

'You never know. It took a couple of shocking events to give *you* the red pill.'

I shook my head.

'I was never hardcore like her.'

Hall looked doubtful.

'Are you sure you want to stick around for another twenty years of that? Sure, she's gorgeous, but think of what you'll have to put up with. You'll never be able to speak your mind.'

'It's hard. The social justice stuff is hell, of course, but underneath all that she's got a good heart.'

'I don't envy you.'

'Maybe we'd better change the subject. I came here to get away from her.'

'Right you are, Johnny, and I reckon it's my round. Same again?'

When Hall went to the bar, I took out my phone, which had been turned off since Sydney. Almost without thinking, I turned it on. By the time Hall returned, the phone had come on... showing eighteen new text messages and twelve missed calls.

Instantly regretting my decision, I realised Ange was probably about to unleash some new drama on me. Sure enough, most of the messages were from her. I was about to turn the wretched phone off again when it began to ring.

To my surprise, caller ID showed it wasn't Ange on the phone, but her father, Frank. This was a first. I'd given him my number as a courtesy, but he'd never actually rung it. With a sick feeling, I realised he must have found out about my resignation from the teaching gig at Plumston Park, and the outrageous manner in which I'd done it. Still, if he was going to give me a dressing down, I might as well cop it while I was cushioned by a few drinks.

'Frank. Er... this is a surprise. How are you? And Norma?'

'Never mind all that, John. Where are you?'

'Melbourne,' I said. 'Is something wrong?'

'There certainly is. What do you mean by deserting your post like that?'

'Look, Frank, I tried. I really did - but I won't be a party to the ridiculous rewriting of history and the abuse of innocent young minds. That's not why I set out to become a teacher.'

'What teaching got to do with it? For God's sake, John, have you spoken to Ange?'

'My phone was out of battery. I've only just charged it. What's the matter?'

'She terribly upset. I don't know the full story but apparently she's under heavy attack online.'

'What for?'

'Her feminist song.'

'Easy With a Peeny?' I said. 'Oh no.'

'I thought it was charming, myself, but it looks like she's under fire from far-right trolls. I don't do social media, of course. Ridiculous waste of time. Do you have a Twitter account?'

'No,' I lied.

'Well, for God's sake start one and go and see what's happening. This is your job, John. Ange needs you. What do you mean by leaving town at a time like this?'

'This is the first I've heard of it. Put Ange on the phone.'

'She's at your place. Give her a call at once.'

'Of course, Frank. I'm on the case.'

I hung up. Hall was scrutinising me. I filled him in on the conversation, then we logged on to Twitter on Hall's phone. Frank was right about one thing - Ange was under heavy attack - but he was wrong about the attackers. It wasn't the far-right. Oh no. Ange was getting absolutely smashed by her comrades on the left.

I rang Ange.

'John! Where are you?'

'I've just popped down to Melbourne for a bit.'

'Come back. I need you.'

'I've only just got here.'

I glanced at Hall, who was pretending not to listen.

'Look, Ange, why don't you come down here for a bit?'

'I'm not going to bloody Melbourne. Don't you know what's happening?'

'Frank said there's some kind of stink over the peeny song. Said you're copping it from the far-right.'

'It's not them. Do you think I'd care? It's our lot.'

'You mean the political left?'

'Yeah, they're bullying me.'

'I don't understand. Aren't they all feminists?'

'They're calling me a racist, John.'

'What for?'

'Nothing!'

'Well, you are white. For some of those nut jobs, that automatically makes you one.'

'It's bullshit, John. I'm the least racist person in the world.'

'I know. It must have been something you said. Some micro-aggression they've blown out of all proportion.'

'Just because I said EL was slavery.'

'What's EL again?'

'Emotional Labour!'

'Oh yeah. Sounds like clash of the titans in Crazy-Town. And the moral of the story is, lay down with mad dogs, wake up with rabid fleas.'

'What's wrong with you, John? You might be a bit more sympathetic.'

'You know, Ange, I'm getting pretty sick of these people and their constant offense-taking. It's enough to turn a guy to the right.'

'Stop joking around. I'm getting bullied. It's awful.'

'Don't worry, it'll soon blow over - and next week it'll be someone else's turn. No one's going to remember in a few days.'

'Don't be so naive. My reputation's totally trashed. I won't even be able to get a job. As soon as an employer Googles my name, they'll think I'm a racist.'

'Just for that stupid emotional labour line? I don't think so.'

'There was something else, something worse. I should never have mentioned that John Lennon song. Oh my God, why did you have to tell me about it? I'm getting killed!'

Ah yes, the Lennon song. Way back in the ancient past of 1972, former Beatle, John Lennon - no doubt aided and abetted by his wife Yoko - wrote and released a rather infamous song. It was a feminist song, but I'm not going to mention it by name because the song title contains a word that simply cannot be said. It is a word so terrible that if a white person says it out loud, it can cause people of colour to instantly drop dead around the world. It's a six letter word starting with N and rhyming with bigger.

Times sure do change. Back in 1972, John Lennon used the word not just in the lyrics of the song, but its title - 'Woman is the N..... of the World.' In the wake of early seventies feminism and the civil rights movement, Lennon merely sought to draw an analogy between the plight of women and blacks at the time. This in terms of their being, in some respects, second class citizens. If you look at it through a feminist lens, you can see Lennon's point.

Some months ago, in the attempt to suck up to Ange, I'd mentioned the song to her in casual conversation. Unfortunately, she'd remembered, and referred to it in a line from her ukulele song. 'John Lennon got it right in '72.' That was all she said - and didn't she regret it now? She hadn't even said the word or the song title. Merely referring to it and saying that Lennon 'got it right' was apparently enough to prove she was a paid up member of the KKK.

'Look, Ange, I reckon this will all blow over pretty fast, but that doesn't help when they're all laying into you. Is there anyone with you tonight? What about Nina?'

'She won't return my calls. I'm blacklisted.'

'No pun intended. So much for the great friendship. You see what these people are like?'

'What am I going to do, John? Help me.'

'There's not much I can do tonight. I've had a few beers and I can't think straight. First thing in the morning, we'll sort this out. Why not have a drink yourself and go to bed?'

'Yeah, I might do that.'

'One thing, Ange. You're not on social media now, are you? I strongly advise you not to engage with these people - and especially not after a couple of drinks. Just turn off your laptop and your phone. Clear?'

'OK, John. Thanks.'

To my dismay, I heard sobbing on the other end of the line.

'I love you, John.'

This was rare. Taken aback, I fumbled for a response.

'I'm crazy about you too, Ange. Always have been. Don't worry, we'll sort this out. Now get some sleep.'

I hung up.

'You won't believe the mess she's in,' I said to Hall. 'We'd better have one more drink and pack it in. Sort it out first thing tomorrow.'

'Right you are, Johnny. Consider me at your service.'

The next morning, I picked up some takeaway coffees and headed back to Hall's for a dose of crisis management. Hall logged onto Twitter from his laptop and we surveyed the torrent of vitriol aimed at poor old Ange.

'Oh FOC, the backlash,' said Hall. 'Look at all the Feminists-Of-Colour piling on. That's the trouble with making allies of people who hate you. It can all fall apart so fast.'

At this point I must make a confession. While it was awful to see my beloved under so much heavy fire, part of me was looking on with a sliver of satisfaction. *You see, Ange? These are your people. These are the ones you admire.*

The attacks were of several kinds. There were the straight out nasty ones, which did little more than dish out abuse. *WTF do you know about slavery, bitch?* Or, *Take a knee, you fuckin fake feminist Klan ho.* There were loads of those.

Then there were the smarter feminists-of-colour, less overtly vicious, but still relishing the chance to put the boot in. *Yass!! We've found a winner for the whitest woman in the world award!* Or, *When Karens turn white supremacist...* Or, *The early suffragettes were racist too. Ain't nothing changed!* There was also a nasty meme where someone had freeze framed a shot of Angie's face with the caption, *Sings crap songs about justice... secretly voted for Trump.* That was bound to piss her off.

The other main category was comments from white leftist women. For some of them, Angie's fate was a warning of the thin ice on which they stood. Subconsciously aware of this, they joined in at the vicious end of the scale, or re-tweeted the more violent comments.

There were also the kinder ones who took the tack that *We know you didn't mean it, but see it as a learning opportunity.* The 'opportunity,' it seemed, was for Ange to grovel in front of random feminists-of-colour and let them berate and chastise her endlessly about race. For some reason, it was this group that irked me the most.

'What's your plan, Johnny?' said Hall.

'I suppose I'll have to fly back. It's a drag. I've only been here five minutes.'

'Is she worth it? She's had it coming a long time. Let her stew awhile.'

'She needs me.'

Hall stared at me for a bit, and seemed to be making a rapid assessment. At last he replied.

'Alright, Johnny. Loyalty's the mark of a man, long as it goes both ways. You should see this as an opportunity. Here's a chance to get your girl out of the cult that's ensnared her.' He glanced at the Twitter feed on his laptop. 'If this ain't enough to turn her off the far-left, I don't know what is.'

'You think?'

'For sure. It's make or break for you two, so here's how it is. If you can leverage the crisis to make her see sense, you've got a future. If you still can't red pill her, give her up as a lost cause. You can save twenty years of wasted time.'

'Are you sure?'

'I'm so sure I'll get on the goddamn plane and come with you. We'll tag team her back into sanity.'

'You don't have to do that.'

'It's no bother. Truth is, I'm an old romantic at heart, and you and Ange have got something. I've only met her once, but it was plain to see. Besides, saving sanity is my job, as I hinted last night.'

'It's good of you to offer, Hall. I don't know if...'

My phone rang. I answered at once.

'Ange, how you doing?'

'I'm still in bed.'

'It's pretty late. You'll feel better if you get up. Go for a run around the coast.'

'I can't face anyone, John. What if I meet someone we know?'

'So what? You've done nothing wrong.'

'I must have. Everyone hates me.'

'Come on, Ange, you're letting these people get inside your head. They're trying to shame you and it's working. You're tougher than that.'

'I'm tough against the enemy. Not against my friends.'

'Did you ever think maybe these people *aren't* your friends?'

'I've made up my mind. I'm going to make a public apology.'

'An apology? I'm not sure that's a good idea.'

A look came over Hall's face. With a furious gesture, he demanded the phone. I handed it over.

'Angie,' he said. 'This is Edward Hall. We met at the whiteness workshop. I heard about what happened and it's lousy, but I've got three words for you: Do not apologise.'

I could not hear Angie's reply, but it only made Hall more emphatic.

'It's the worst thing you could possibly do. They *want* you to apologise. They want you to grovel, and if you've got any dignity you won't give them the pleasure.'

Hall listened to her reply.

'It won't help,' he said. 'They'll only come at you harder. You've got a school of sharks on your tail now. If you want the whole university, your apology will bring 'em. Now, I'm gonna hand you back to Johnny.'

Hall held his hand over the mouthpiece.

'Tell her you'll be on the first plane home tomorrow.'

He gave me the phone.

'He's right, Ange,' I said. 'Lay low for a bit. Soon as I hang up, I'll arrange to come home.'

'Can you come back today?'

'Tomorrow, I reckon. Should be back by lunchtime. Now remember, stay off your social media, and don't do anything public - at least, not 'til we talk it over in person.'

I hung up, sighed, and got ready to book a flight.

# 22

# John, You're a Nazi

As we loitered at Melbourne airport the next morning, I repeated a point I'd made the night before.

'It's decent of you to come, Hall, but you can't stay with us.'

'Don't mind me, old boy, I'll make my own arrangements. You take care of Ange and consider me on standby.'

We said little during the flight, then parted at Sydney airport. I took a bus to Tamarama and spent the twenty minute trip wondering how to handle the scene ahead. While I was all set to play white knight for Ange against the online hordes, I agreed with Hall that the crisis might work to our advantage. There might never be a better chance to prise Ange away from the far-left.

I opened the front door and walked down the hallway. There was no sound from Mateo's room. When I opened Angie's door, her room was empty. No one in the living room either. Perhaps she'd gone to her parents' house. However, when I opened my own door, there she was sitting on the bed. Her posture was slumped in defeat, such that I felt a surge of anger at what the cruel mob had done to her. I dumped my luggage and was about to go to her when she spoke.

'Why didn't you tell me?'

'I only decided to go to Melbourne at the last minute. It was a crazy week. Sorry, Ange.'

'I know about you, John. I know all about it.'

I paused. There was something odd about her tone.

'I didn't *want* to quit teaching,' I said. 'They gave me no choice. As I told your dad...'

'Not that.'

She turned to look at me. It was like the scene from that horror film, *The Ring,* when the ghost girl looks out of the TV screen and turns her deathly gaze on the viewer.

'John, you're a Nazi.'

I saw that my desktop computer was on. I'd unplugged it at the wall socket before Melbourne. Clearly, Ange had plugged it back in. The monitor was now displaying my Twitter account with all its recent posts. She'd also printed out my questionnaire for the Year Nine kids at Plumston Park. It was right there sitting on the desk. I made a weak attempt to go on the offensive.

'Who said you could use my computer? This is a serious betrayal of trust.'

'A *betrayal*!' Angie's voice rose to a shriek.

'Well, explain yourself,' I demanded.

'*You're* the one needs to explain, John. It was yesterday after you rang. I was going crazy after everything that happened, and I got the paranoid idea you were cheating on me.'

'I would never do that.'

'So I checked your emails to see if you'd hooked up with some bitch in Melbourne. Turns out it was this Edward Hall guy. So I read the rest of his emails to you, and guess what? He's a full on Nazi.'

'That's not true. Not unless you call anyone outside the far-left a Nazi.'

'I saw some of the videos he sent you. Turns out you've got a whole list of them, you dirty dog. MRA stuff, nationalism, pro-white.'

'Well gee, it's not like you found a stash of porn.'

'I would much rather find a bunch of porn than this. I mean, you're such a liar. If you believe in all this right wing stuff, why not just be honest about it?'

I laughed out loud. Literally.

'You mean in the free and tolerant land of Antifa, where the slightest impure thought means expulsion? Maybe you've got a taste of that too, now they've turned on you.'

Angie's face fell. I saw that her eyes were full of tears.

'How can you do this to me, at a time like this? *This* is the betrayal.'

'It ain't me, babe,' I said. 'It's your leftist pals sticking the knife in. And unlike them, I'll stand by you, no matter what. Alright - if you really want to know, I'll tell you the whole story.'

Angie turned her face of misery on me. I gazed into the distance.

'It all started when I went to the Bronte Buddhist Centre one night. Meditation made me a Nazi.'

'Don't talk rubbish, John. I can't take any more.'

'Dipak, the head Buddhist rang me the next day. Some mad bitch had accused me of 'exposing myself' during the meditation.'

'Huh?'

'Yeah, some nut job.' I shook my head, still in disbelief. 'She said I'd exposed myself while everyone was sitting round meditating. All I did was loosen my pants a notch cos they were too tight. She was so sure of it she had Dipak believing it too. It could've ruined my reputation, my whole teaching career.'

'Why didn't you tell me?'

'It was at the height of Me Too. All that *believe women* stuff. Remember the hearings with Kavanaugh and Blasey Ford? I found out how Kavanaugh felt - and I wasn't sure you'd believe *me*.'

Angie didn't reply.

'It was the day before the rally with Stefan Molyneux and Lauren Southern. I wouldn't even have gone but I was still shook up. Then, in the fight during the show, it was Antifa knocked me out, not the other mob. The 'Nazis' didn't kidnap me, they rescued me. Edward Hall was one of them.'

'So you went to their hotel on purpose?'

'I woke up there - in more ways than one. They never forced me. They never stopped me leaving.'

'Then why didn't you?'

'It was Hall. He got in my ear and made me think. I started to see everything in a new light.'

'Why'd you listen to him? He's a fucking Nazi!'

'Is he?'

It was my turn to play Ghost Girl. I turned on the death stare.

'You know what, Ange? Hall ain't the Nazi. It's you.'

Angie recoiled.

'How can you say that after what I've been through this week? I've been called a racist. A white supremacist.'

'I know. I flew all the way back here to play white knight, but you blindsided me before I could get a word in. Well, if that's how it goes, so be it. For once, I'm going to speak my mind.'

I faced her, and months of repressed anger came out in a rush.

'I'm sick of your attitude. I'm sick of your moral grandstanding, calling everyone a fascist who doesn't bow down to your far-left ideas. I'm sick of you telling me what to think, especially when half of it's bullshit - your white fragility and male privilege and the rest of it. You think it's easy with a fucking peeny? Try it and see how you go.'

Angie's face was white, like I'd slapped her. I was just warming up.

'I'm sick of your arrogance. I'm sick of your little Antifa revolution, your reckless destruction of our countries. I'm sick of you stirring up racial hate, then complaining we're in a state of racial uproar. I'm sick of your whining and complaining, and your endless negativity. And most of all I'm sick of your hypocrisy. You say yours is the side of love and tolerance. You leftists are far more intolerant than any fascist I've ever met.'

Angie made no reply.

'You wanna know why Hillary lost the 2016 election?' I said. 'People didn't vote for Trump because they love Trump. They did it cos they can't stand people like you.'

There was a long pause. Eventually, Angie spoke in a small, hurt voice.

'I had no idea... no idea you hated me so much.'

'I don't hate you. I fell in love with you the first second I ever saw you.'

'But not anymore. Or what was *that* all about?'

'I still love you. It's just your politics get on my nerves. My view of the world's changed.'

Angie slapped her hand down hard on my mattress. It made a muffled thud, like a gunshot through a silencer.

'That bloody Hall. We would have been fine without him.'

I shrugged.

'Maybe - but what's seen can't be unseen. It's true I didn't mind your views, before Hall. Not that there was much *mind* involved. I just went along with it like every other blue pill normie. I didn't really care. Unfortunately, I suppose, now I do.'

Angie turned her face upon me again. It wasn't a death stare this time but a look of fear, or resignation.

'So that's it for us, is it? I've lost my friends and reputation. Now I'm going to lose you too.'

'I don't know, Ange. Maybe we can start afresh.'

'How's that going to work? Me in love with a Nazi. That's crazy.'

'Stop calling me a Nazi - and stop acting like one yourself. Let's see if you can put some of that famous leftist tolerance into practice. See if you can get on with someone who thinks differently to you. I've been doing it all year.'

'This is all too much, John. It's too much!'

I felt an unfamiliar sense of power. For the first time in our relationship, I felt I was holding the aces. Or was it simply the liberation of being finally able to speak my mind? Having been outed, there was no longer any point lying. I would speak the truth and she could take it or leave it - and if she left *me*, so be it.

'Since we're laying all our cards on the table, Ange, here goes. I think you're in a cult. You've been hypnotised into believing a lot of things that aren't true. This isn't me trying to one-up you, because I was brainwashed too - for years. Look at it this way, here's our chance to escape.'

'I can't handle this now. I've been getting mocked and humiliated all week. The one thing I thought I could count on is you.'

'You can. It's only in a crisis you find out who you real friends are - and it's not your so called allies on the left, is it?'

Angie moaned.

'I've been getting bullied for days. People are calling me a white supremacist. They're ringing the language college trying to get me sacked. They're even harassing Daddy, telling him he raised a KKK daughter. I want to kill myself!'

She turned her teary face towards me but could barely look me in the eye.

'I want to ask you, John, and please be honest. You've heard my song. Do you think I'm a racist?'

I felt a surge of anger, mixed with pity - and the overwhelming desire to wake her from her enchantment.

'Of course not. The only racism in you is towards your own kind - but let's leave Helda McGovern's mental illness out of it for now.'

I paused, trying to choose my words carefully - and failing.

'On the other hand,' I said. 'I've got to be honest. Your song did annoy me. All that stuff about male privilege. You've been fed this garbage all your life. It's a lie - and I'm sick of it. Did you get attacked on Twitter by anti-feminists too?'

'Yeah, but I just blocked them.'

'But you didn't block the idiot leftists who called you a white supremacist?'

'They're on my team, John. They're my allies.'

I raised my voice.

'No they're not - get it through your head! These people are insane. I mean, what's all this fuss about anyway? You said emotional labour is slavery, and you mentioned some song John Lennon wrote in the early seventies. Big, big deal. Who gives a damn if John Lennon said the N-word in 1972? I certainly don't - and any pea-brained zealot who does, you need to put 'em in the rear view mirror and move on.'

I took a few steps towards the bed and put my arms around her, lifting her to stand. She was limp, unresisting. I held her for a minute, then let her sit back on the bed. I sat back in the chair opposite.

'Why not walk away from them? I did.'

'I can't, John. This is who I am.'

I sighed. Maybe she was a lost cause after all.

'Did you ever think,' I said, 'what you've been taught to believe might be wrong?'

She made no reply.

'Did you ever wonder,' I continued, 'about all these big bogeymen you and your Antifa pals think you're fighting? Patriarchy, white supremacy, capitalism. What do those concepts really mean? If they even exist and you do destroy them, what are you going to put in their place?'

'Something better,' said Ange.

'I'm not sure what,' I replied. 'A genderless world? A post-racial Utopia? One world socialism? We're not remotely close to any of those things.'

'It's because of all you damned right wingers,' she said, with a flash of venom. 'If you'd all just get out of the way, there'd be nothing to stop us.'

'That's what you expect, isn't it? Years of targeting white males and what we created. You really think we're just going to roll over. Plenty have, and I used to be one of them. Not anymore.'

I paused and looked out the window into the back garden.

'Maybe the best cure is to let you lot succeed. If I had to define Hell, it's a world full of the idiots attacking you on Twitter this week. You want all the right wingers out of the way? Fine - let's get divorced. Your group can go somewhere new and make your Marxist Utopia. Everyone else can stay here. See how it pans out from there.'

'Why should *we* have to leave? Why don't *your* lot go and start again? We'll take over here and do it right.'

'We built this society. Why should we leave? But there you go - that's the essentially parasitical nature of your enterprise. You want to wait until everything's up and running, then claim it for yourself and take over.'

'Well, hello? That's how a revolution works.'

I stared at her.

'Fuck your revolution.'

I adopted a condescending tone, wilfully provocative.

'These rebellions rarely work out, you know. Besides, you'll be one of the first sent to Gulag, thanks to your peeny song. You might be better off giving your leftist Heaven a miss. Stay here with the right wingers. Stay with the tolerant side.'

'You guys aren't tolerant. You're a bunch of rednecks.'

I raised an eyebrow.

'Can you be a bit more specific, Ange? What is it you object to?'

'You're homophobic.'

'Wrong.'

'Racist.'

'No more than anyone else.'

'You want to put women back in the kitchen.'

'That's a lie.'

'But you're anti-feminist.'

'With good reason. Go watch a few Karen Straughan videos and get back to me.'

'You're authoritarian.'

'No more than you idiots. Look, Ange, I reckon your head's full of straw enemies. This idea you have that everyone outside the far-left is a hillbilly, wife-beating, homophobe... it's not true. Sure, you'll get some of that sort, I won't deny it, but I'd bet a lot of 'right wing' people are far more tolerant than your team. More easygoing too. See, if you make some little *faux pas*, like with the Peeny song, we might not necessarily like it, but we won't try to *destroy* you over it.'

I paused before continuing.

'I'm not the only former leftist who can't stand them anymore. Have you heard of the Walkaway movement? This guy, Brandon Straka - he's gay, by the way - started it because he realised how intolerant the left has become. Then again, I don't suppose you *have* heard of him, right? Because the press certainly haven't mentioned him.'

I shook my head in disgust.

'That's been one of the biggest red pills for me. Seeing the blatant leftist bias in the mainstream media. Once you've seen it, you can't un-see it.'

'But *why* don't you like us, John? What's your problem?'

'Your beliefs are wrong for a start. All this anti-Western

stuff, white wimpiness, the warped feminist view of history I had to teach at school. All this so called righting of historical wrongs - which in practice just means people like Beck Irvine bullying young boys. It's not just factually wrong, it's harmful.'

'We're trying to make a fairer world.'

'You think you can just overturn everything from the past and make it all better?'

'We can try.'

'I don't think your revolution can work. See, you're not starting from a place of honesty. You believe things because you want them to be true, not because they *are* true. As a result, you ban scientific research you don't approve of, rewrite history, and cancel people whose opinions you don't like.'

'Maybe we've gone too far at times, but we'll get it right.'

'I don't see how your new society can ever work when you think of all the mental pathologies you're taking with you. Blame, lack of accountability, celebration of victims. Daddy issues, self-hate, pathological altruism, emotion over reason. Intolerance, purity spirals, envy and resentment. What a witch's brew of bad habits. All these terrible traits have been not just condoned but encouraged. I'll give your Marxist paradise three months before it bursts into flames, and you'll be screaming to get back to what you knew and ought to have taken good care of.'

There was a long silence.

'So, am I getting through to you, Ange? Is any part of this connecting?'

She didn't look at me.

'Alright,' she said at last. 'If you really want to know, I've been having doubts for a while now.'

This was a surprise.

'Is that right?' I said.

'Like a few weeks ago, we had to go and protest one of Daddy's work colleagues over something he said.'

'What was it?'

'Let's not get into it. It was nothing. Anyway, I didn't want to join in, but they made me.'

'Really? And what else?'

'Oh, just little things. The bullying. The… fanaticism.'

'Even so,' she continued, with a trace of defiance. 'If this had happened last week' – she pointed at my computer with its damning evidence – 'I would have walked.'

'But now you've found out the true nature of your so called allies, maybe you'll walk away from *them*.'

'Not so fast, John. There might be a few… issues with our side, but nothing we can't fix. No one's perfect.'

Angie looked at me.

'What happens now,' she said, 'for us?'

'We could break up,' I said. 'There's no point butting heads every day.'

'I don't want that.'

'If we stay together, we'll just have to agree to disagree without killing each other. A novel experience for you, I know.'

'Get off my case, John. It's not my fault you were too wimpy to stand up for yourself and disagree with me.'

'You're right. I was a wimp. I didn't want to lose you, so I went along with it all to keep the peace.'

'What else can we do?' said Ange.

'We could stay together,' I said, 'and you could loosen up a bit. Listen to some different opinions. Take the red pill, dammit!'

'Then I wouldn't be me.'

'You would. Just a different version.'

'I don't know, John. This is all too weird.'

'Maybe you're right, but before we call it quits, will you grant me one last request?'

She turned her dark eyes upon me.

'Depends what it is.'

'Talk to Edward Hall. He came back with me from Melbourne.'

'The Nazi? Why would I talk to him?'

'The man has a way about him. The silver tongued devil. Then again, maybe he's not a devil, but something else altogether.'

'You're pushing it.'

'Let's make a deal - have a one on one with Hall and let him do his worst. If he can't change your mind, that might be it for us. But if he can somehow make an impression on you, maybe we can find common ground, instead of grounds for divorce.'

I sighed, and thought of the hopes I'd once had for us.

'What have we got to lose?'

# 23
# RPA

I'm not sure Angie would have agreed to see Hall, but a stroke of good timing was on our side. That night, the language college where she taught bowed to activist pressure and suspended her from work. If Ange had been in a state of hurt disbelief before, it was replaced by a growing sense of outrage.

'Two years helping immigrants learn English and this is how they repay me!'

I saw my chance.

'Why not speak to Hall? He can advise you on what to do.'

When she reluctantly agreed, I told Hall to drop by. At 11am the next day, there was a knock on the front door. I opened it to find Hall leaning up against the porch wall once more. As he entered the house, Mateo came out of his room.

'Morning, Comrade,' said Hall jauntily.

Mateo did not reply, merely glared at him before closing his door. Hall raised his eyebrows, then followed me through the living room.

'How's Ange?' he asked.

'Pissed,' I replied. 'They've suspended her from work.'

'What - over *this*?' said Hall. 'Then she's ready to listen. You going to sit in?'

'Better not gang up on her. I'll wait outside.'

Unknown to Hall and Ange, I had set my computer to record the meeting. I didn't want to miss a minute of Hall's intervention. Telling them could have made them self conscious - so I didn't. A tad unethical, but so be it.

I knocked on the door. Angie was sitting at my desk. Hall made a small bow, then took the arm chair opposite her.

'Sorry to hear what happened,' he said. 'It's no fun when the mob comes for you.'

Ange didn't reply, just sat there looking guardedly at Hall. I went out to make them a coffee. As I later heard on the recording, Hall got straight to the point.

'John's asked me to have a word with you,' he said. 'There's no point me sugar coating it or tiptoeing round the issues. I've got one shot at getting through to you, and the only road to that's a little straight talk. So I'm gonna say my piece and at the end of it you can curse me, or blacklist me, or kick me out the door. But hear me out.'

There was a pause before Hall continued.

'The first point is the true nature of your so called allegiances. Pro tip, Ange: leftist women of colour are not your friends. Sure, they'll make an ally of you, but it's strictly temporary. See, in their eyes, you're sitting pretty on the second rung of the privilege ladder. You're one rung below the white men - looking down on the people of colour, gays, trans, disabled, and the rest of the usual parade of victims.'

'You can *fool* yourself feminists-of-colour are on your side,' Hall continued, a little louder. 'But they hate your whiteness far more than they love your femaleness. So put away any delusions about fighting a common enemy. You *are* the enemy, and the sooner you get it through your head, the better.'

'Some of my friends are women of colour,' said Angie. 'They don't hate me.'

'I don't mean all of them,' said Hall, 'but the sort who've been abusing you on Twitter all week. They don't hate you in a trivial way, like you hate spinach or you hate Mondays. They hate you with a depth and intensity you can't currently conceive. For a point of reference, think of your feminism and all the pot shots you've aimed at men over the years. Every grievance you've harboured, every complaint you've ever made - you'll get it all back, but race instead of gender. You'll be asked to kneel and say sorry and make amends. They might call you an ally now, but they're calling you a Becky or a Karen behind your back. Be saying it to your face, soon enough.'

'But I helped them,' said Angie. 'I did everything right.'

'It don't make a scrap of difference!' said Hall. 'They've been *taught* to hate you, by the same debased education system you've been through. Just look at you - pretty, white, born into some level of affluence. You won't be first up against the wall come the revolution, but you won't be too far back in the queue. So forget your so called allegiances. They don't mean a thing.'

'Wait a minute,' said Angie. 'All we want to do is bring everyone together. We want to empower people of colour, to make up for what white people did in the past.'

'Empower them all you like,' said Hall, 'as long as you realise some of them want to *disempower* you. Is that wise? If every other group is self-biased it's folly not to do it yourself. When you're under attack, siding with the attackers is, shall we say, a *losing* strategy.'

'Don't you feel guilty,' said Ange, 'for all the terrible things we did? The slavery and empires and invasions.'

'If you're asking,' Hall replied, 'about my own part in it, let me put it in statistical terms. When it comes to white guilt, last time I tested it came out zero.'

'What do you mean?'

'Zero percent. That was the reading last time I ran my conscience through the guilt-ometer.'

'How can you say that?'

'Wake up, Ange! White guilt's a scam peddled by the mentally and morally lazy, fallen for by dupes and cowards. I'm responsible for my own actions, that's all. It don't matter a damn what anyone else did five years ago, or five hundred years ago. As the great man, Thomas Sowell, said, 'Have we reached the ultimate stage of absurdity where some people are held responsible for things that happened before they were born, while other people are not held responsible for what they themselves are doing today?' And Sowell a black American himself.'

There was a pause.

'When you realise white guilt's a rort, Ange, you see the absurdity of it all. It's the usual collectivist tactic the left employs to do its evil work. Putting individuals into classes, treating them all the same, and trying to dictate terms on that spurious basis. If they really want to play that game, I'll indulge them. How far back do you know your lineage? Three, four generations?'

'Something like that.'

'For the sake of argument, let's say you're descended from Governor Phillip himself, first ruler of this colony. Does that mean *you*, Ange, are liable for whatever imperial sins he may have committed?'

'Maybe I am.'

'Speak for yourself, but no one else - and certainly not for me. See, I *do* know how far I go back. Wish I could claim Ben Hall as one of mine. The bushranger - ever heard of him? Sadly, that ain't my line - but I do come from criminal stock, as it happens. Fella named James Hall, my great grandad and then some, a convict who came out with one of the early fleets. Fourteen years hard labour he did, for some trifling offence. A slave, in other words, for the new colony. Now, there's some who'd want to hold him accountable for his part in white privilege or some such rot, though I'd like to see those fools get through fourteen *days* of his life, never mind years.'

Angie made no reply.

'Then there's me,' Hall continued, 'a distant relative, and those same fools want to tar me with guilt for James' part in displacing the Aborigines. I'm going to draw a parallel with our American cousins. White America's sin was displacing the Indians, and they also took black slaves from Africa. Now, if I'm guilty of James' offence, these race hustlers may as well take a modern black man descended from slaves and make him share the blame for what happened to the Indians. Might as well, if they're going to hang me for what my great granddad did two hundred years ago.'

'What about the system of racial inequality they created? The one you benefit from now.'

'Even if that were true - which is another debate in itself - why would I be such a fool as to oppose it? I'm not bamboozled enough to start a revolution against myself. It's all a scam. Stop falling for it.'

Angie started to say something, then broke off.

'Now, take what happened to you last week,' said Hall. 'You've been bashed from pillar to post over nothing. Maybe that's enough to wake you up from the illusion you're fighting patriarchy, or capitalism, or whatever else you've been told. We've been dragged into in a race war. We never wanted it but as your leftist pals are hell bent on it, they've left us little choice.'

'Mind you,' he continued. 'that's only a symptom of the *real* war. The one waged by those who want to tear our society in two and remake it. They're dealers in chaos, and racial tensions are the easiest to stoke. Still, if the race war is contrived, it's a reality we have to contend with. Stop fooling yourself which side you're on. Remember what Yasmine Chemali said at the Whiteness workshop? If that wasn't a statement of intent, I don't know what was. And remember her 'white ally,' poor deluded Helda?'

'What about her?'

'Don't take it personally, Ange, but there's nothing more pathetic than self-hating, do-gooder white progressives like her. They think it's noble to hate their own country and tribe. Well, it ain't! They think there's virtue in moral self flagellation. There's not! They think treason to their own kind will spare them the pent up revenge of those who've been taught to hate them as a class. It won't!'

'But they're making a stand again racism.'

'Calling out racism today doesn't take any moral courage. It might have in 1820 or 1920. Today, it's the ultimate act of banality.'

There was a silence before Hall resumed.

'When it comes to moral courage, I look at a man like Jared Taylor. He was onto this anti-white stuff years ago. When the likes of you and me would have been marching down the street with the hippies, Taylor was pointing out the real agenda of diversity, the racial double standards, and the long term effects of it all. He said it despite the cost to his wallet and reputation, simply because it was the right thing to do. Taylor's worth a thousand moral conformists. He pointed out all the lies and the folly. Tell you what, Ange, a man who lets lies and folly stand unopposed, just for the sake of a quiet life, well, he ain't a man at all.'

'OK, Edward, if you're going to make such a big deal out of race...'

'It wasn't me. I was living in the colour blind, post-racial age until you leftists *forced* everyone to make a big deal of it.'

'If you're going to criticise multiracial societies, then tell me straight. Are you a white nationalist?'

'No. I'm not saying that. Although when you see how it's all panned out, some countries would turn back time if they could. It's a bit late for that now.'

'Multiculturalism is a success in Australia.'

There was a pause.

'Australia's one of the better examples,' said Hall, 'but is it a success in Europe or America? I doubt it.'

'Wait,' said Ange. 'Think of all the families that came here after the war and made new lives. They added to this country. Made it better.'

'I'll grant you,' said Hall, 'that many brave and decent people came here. They worked hard and established themselves. My problem's not with them, but the race hustlers and complainers. When you look at how things are now with all the tensions and the resentment, and ask if we have a cohesive, unified society, then it's a no from me. Diversity is our stress, not our strength. I'd say that on balance, the great Western experiment with multiculturalism is a failure.'

'That's your fault,' said Ange.

'No, it's yours,' Hall replied. 'The idiot leftists ruined it for everyone. Like I told Johnny, I used to believe in the great One World social experiment too. Racial harmony, brotherhood, all of that. That was before I realised the far-left academics are teaching everyone to hate us, if they didn't already, with their war on so called 'whiteness.' That's what doomed it.'

'I don't object to the multicultural ideal in principle,' Hall continued, 'but to all the things which have corrupted it.'

'Like what?'

'If only we could get a big sack and fill it with all the rot your side's been peddling the last few decades. Toss in your race obsession and identity politics. Throw in your victim and blame mentality. Leave room for your censorship, fake 'hate speech' laws, and your lies about crime stats. And not forgetting your corrupt media and education system. Put all that in the sack and fire it into outer space so aliens can make a study of how to ruin a civilisation.'

'Give me an actual plan.'

'An amicable divorce. Society has never been more divided;

let's make it official. Divide our countries in half. Call your half Woketopia, and everyone - and I mean whites and non-whites alike - everyone who believes in diversity quotas, whiteness, and systemic racism, can go live in Woketopia. Everyone who's bored with all that - again, I mean whites and non-whites - can stay in our half.'

'Come on, that's never going to happen. Do you have a Plan B?'

'Plan B is what I'm doing now, which is to wake a few people up. Get them to stand up for themselves and stop being stood over by conmen. That's what I'm trying to do with you now, Ange. When your so called allies hate you, helping them just makes you a useful idiot.'

'I'm not an idiot,' said Angie.

'Not an idiot,' said Hall. 'A *useful idiot*. As in, you don't really know what you're fighting for, or against, for that matter. You're being played for a fool. You and the thousands of other leftist students in the West led astray by your Marxist professors. Most of them are just higher up the useful idiot chain themselves.'

'There's a guy called Yuri Bezmenov,' Hall continued. 'He was a Soviet defector, claimed to be ex-KGB. When he escaped to America in the 1980s, he gave his views on how the KGB waged war on the West.

According to Yuri, the Cold War had very little to do with spying or weapons. It was more about what he called 'ideological subversion.' This was a kind of psychological warfare, and it was done by filling the heads of students with Marxist-Leninist ideology to the extent that it changed their perception of reality. Once they reached that point, they could no longer make sensible judgments about what was best for themselves, their families, or their country.

You might say the Cold War is over and the Soviet Union long gone, but the effects of ideological subversion continue to this day. Look at all your leftist academics, and the armies of SJW zombies they've created. Look at the results. Thousands of people trained to oppose their own society and believe in some vaguely conceived Marxist alternative.

Yuri Bezmenov spoke about people in the grip of ideological subversion. They were programmed to react critically to their own countries, while at the same time holding highly unrealistic ideas about the 'beautiful Soviet system of equality.'

As Yuri said, these people were so indoctrinated they could even be shown Russian concentration camps and still refuse to believe it. Not until they felt the military boot in the arse would they finally realise what the great system of equality means in practice. In the free West, these people might be lauded for their social justice crusades. Under the Soviet system, they would simply be 'squashed like cockroaches.'

All of this, Yuri said decades ago. Go watch his videos on YouTube and hear for yourself. He does have his critics too, those who doubt his credentials. But take a look around at how things are now and I reckon he's got it bang on.

Just look at your colleagues and their noble rebellion. You're like the Red Guards in Mao's Cultural Revolution, trying to smash the 'four olds.' Old ideas, old traditions, and so on. The trouble is, you're partly succeeding, to the extent Western countries are a divided mess these days. The process of ideological subversion has succeeded brilliantly. If Yuri Bezmenov were here to see it now, he'd be amazed how far it's gone.'

There was a pause before Angie responded.

'Surely you're not trying to say all of the great social reforms of the last fifty years are just some kind of *subversion?*'

'Of course not,' Hall replied. 'But the crazier ones, yes, without a doubt. I'm sorry, Angie, but you and thousands like you have been recruited into a cult. It's hard to see because our social institutions are infected as well - the press, showbiz, and the education system. It's all part of the *long march through the institutions*. The far-left cult is in control.'

'So now you want me to join your far-right cult. Is that it?'

'What you do is up to you. All I want is to make you question what you've been told. My job, as I see it, is to deprogram a few people. To show them that their precious beliefs are neither noble, practical, or true. They're not creating a better world, but a far worse one - and they're being played for fools.

You might think your revolution points to something better. I'd say it leads only to social collapse. Rebellion for its own sake, taken to the point of pathology, is worthless.

And that brings us to your comrades in Antifa.'

# 24
# You Ain't the Good Guys

I opened the door of my room.

'Are you finished?'

'We've finished part one,' said Hall. 'Now, I want to say a few words about Antifa.'

'You're an expert on that too, right?' Ange said, with a touch of sarcasm.

'Not at all,' Hall replied, 'but at least I've read Comrade Bray's book.'

'Huh?'

'Mark Bray. Author of *Antifa: The Antifascist Handbook*. As close to a manifesto as I can find. Bray's a university professor, and no fool. His book's well written and shows how Antifa thinks. There's also Comrade Ollie on YouTube, who's made a video on the topic. So, on the basis of these, I'll give my impressions of the Antifa mindset. Have you read Bray's book yourself?'

Angie looked a little sheepish. 'Not yet.'

Hall raised his eyebrows, as if to say *Why am I not surprised?* If that was his thought, it came out in his next remark.

'I'll make a distinction between the core and the casuals. Never mind the casual Antifa types. They're followers, not leaders. There's thousands of SJWs been made into foot soldiers for the revolution, but how many have really thought it through is hard to say. I'll focus on the hardcore types, the ones who've studied it and take it seriously.'

Hall began rummaging round in his bag.

'It's a long and complicated topic, and I've found it best to put my thoughts into writing. That'll save me losing my train of thought, and you interrupting with questions. We can leave questions til the end.'

Hall handed Angie a typed essay. She took it and frowned.

'How long is it?' she said, as if being assigned an extra reading for university.

'Not long enough,' said Hall. 'Then again, it's long *enough*. At least for now.'

# Impressions of Antifa

## Fascism and Anti-Fascism

Who are Antifa? They're a loosely organised bunch of revolutionaries. They define themselves by what they're against, as much as what they're for. For Antifa, there are three types of people in the world: fascists, anti-fascists, and everyone else. The first two groups are locked in mortal combat for the souls of the third.

'So, what is 'fascism' as they see it? It's based around the big three bogeymen - capitalism, patriarchy, and white supremacy. Throw in nationalism as well. You could add something like 'heteronormativity,' but let's leave the silly academic terms out of it for now. Or maybe I'll invent one myself: Cappatnatsup. Sounds like an Aztec god, but it's really a Western devil. Capitalism, patriarchy, nationalism, and white supremacy. Cappatnatsup for short. This is the four sided devil Antifa want to overthrow.

Antifa is essentially an *oppositional* force. On the surface, and in their PR material, they're opposed to swastikas and concentration camps. Dig a little deeper, and they're against far more than that. To put it simply, anything considered normal before 1960 is the enemy. The hardcore Antifa types want nothing less than a revolution, and a radical reshaping of human society.

## Pathological Revolution

In discussing Antifa's mindset, it is useful to construct a profile of *the Antifa*. This does not refer to any one individual, but to the traits and beliefs of the intelligent Antifa member. This profile will include generalisations, from which individuals may differ. For ease of language, I will make *the Antifa* a 'he' - though there are also plenty of female radicals.

The Antifa is a Marxist who wants to reform the entire social system. He takes rebellion to the point of pathology. He has the profound desire to dissolve structure, to erase ideas of identity that have been around for centuries. He thinks these structures have caused the world's inequality.

He sees the world as a series of oppressor-oppressed relationships. Male: female, white: black, rich: poor, Western: non-Western, for example. The Antifa sees all such opposites as socially created rather than natural. He is a fanatical egalitarian, and thinks erasing these concepts will lead to equality. He thinks erasing the idea of gender will create gender equality, eliminating the idea of race will produce racial equality, and removing national borders will lead to one united world instead of the current one of rich and poor nations.

The Antifa wants to erase social structures, just as Mao's Red Guards wanted to smash the 'four olds' during the Chinese Cultural Revolution. That is: Old Customs, Old Culture, Old Habits, and Old Ideas. The Antifa has a blind faith that once the old structures are dissolved, new and better ones will automatically arise, or will do so under his enlightened social engineering.

The Antifa is an extreme 'social constructionist.' That is, he believes there's no such thing as human nature. He thinks everything is malleable and up for grabs. Everything can be remade by a progressive reformer like himself.

Who are the 'fascists' the Antifa sees as the enemy? Put simply, a 'fascist' is anyone who stands in the way of the Antifa's revolution. Anyone who holds to traditional ideas of race, gender, nations, or other old social structures. Especially those who actively want to preserve those things, or criticise the left's campaign against them.

Essentially, the 'fascist' wants to hold on to and take pride in the past, while the Antifa wants to destroy it in pursuit of a better future.

The Antifa sees life as a battle between fascism and anti-fascism. He divides the world into two groups. Group A lives under the protection of Cappatnatsup – capitalism, patriarchy, nationalism, and white supremacy - and is largely comprised of straight white males and their associates. Group B is everyone else, the *coalition of victims*. The supposed victims of Cappatnatsup are the women, gays, people of colour, immigrants and refugees, trans, disabled, and the rest of the so called marginalised.

It's worth noting there are many who qualify for Group B who want no part of it. Plenty of women, gays, people of colour, and so on refuse to identify as victims, and do not support the Antifa's revolution. These people are a nuisance to Antifa, who ignore or try to discredit them.

Apart from those people, the Antifa compulsively supports anyone in Group B and undermines anything to do with Group A. This is all part of his war on fascism. So, the Antifa will side with the 'undocumented' immigrant, or the squatters under attack in 'their' buildings. For the really hardcore Antifa, law itself is a manifestation of fascism. He wants to undo concepts like property ownership and citizenship.

The Antifa believes all social problems stem from the existing order, from Group A and the systems of Cappatnatsup. He believes that by overthrowing them, Group B will take their place, or else Groups A and B will merge into one equal group and a new world order will begin.

## Antifa the Creator, and the Golden Future

The Antifa has a pathological need to rebel, but he will deny he is a purely destructive force only wanting to dissolve what exists. No, he is a creator. He is going to *create* a new world.

It will be a Utopian world without hierarchy, borders, or oppression. A Marxist world of equality. There will be no more social classes, no more rich or poor, and the old concept of race will be seen as a historical fiction - a scientific relic like flat Earth theory, or phrenology, or blood-letting by leeches.

It's been said that fascism looks to the past to some mythical Golden Age. That may be true, but the Antifa projects the Golden Age into the future. He is an idealist, but thinks his glorious future is reached by destroying the past. The past's only value is to provide negative examples of imperfect worlds. Its only use is to show us the flaws that won't be allowed in the Antifa's paradise. There's no end to the beauty of this imaginary future world. Education will be free, leisure time abundant, and liberty everywhere. War and poverty will no longer exist. They, and all other social problems, will disappear into the inferior past.

The hardcore Antifa is a fanatic. He believes so strongly in this future world he feels entitled to force everyone else to pursue it too. He will actually silence people he doesn't approve of. Anyone who doesn't share the Antifa's values automatically becomes a 'fascist.' The fanatical Antifa forces his values on others. In order words, he acts like a fascist. As it's all in a good cause - indeed a Holy cause - the hypocrisy doesn't matter to him.

The end goal of the Antifa's quest is to him so noble, so desirable, that anyone who stands in its way can only appear wicked to him. The Antifa holds the almost religious conviction he is fighting for Good against Evil. He is a crusader against unbelievers.

When it comes to silencing fascists, as he calls them, the Antifa believes he has the right - even the duty - to disrupt their meetings, ban them from social media, harass them into silence, get them sacked from their jobs, and completely erase them from public life.

## The New Fascist

But what is a fascist as the Antifa sees it? It's not as if the streets are overrun with neo-Nazis or the KKK. I will write fascist as 'fascist' from now on, for we are dealing with a creation of the Antifa's own mind, rather than anything close to actual Nazis. In reality, the new 'fascist' is simply a normal, rational human being. The Antifa complains that far-right ideas are 'entering the mainstream.' But it is far-left ideas that entered the mainstream. The so called far-right is simply a response to them.

The Antifa likes to demonise his enemy, a standard leftist tactic. He has created a straw fascist which many leftists believe is real. The straw fascist is the white supremacist, homophobic, sexist, wife beater, who makes fun of disabled people in his spare time. The straw fascist wants to put gays, immigrants, and non-whites into concentration camps.

The real 'fascist' - as opposed to the straw one - is simply someone who refuses to bow down to the Antifa's revolution. The real 'fascist' has become aware of the far-left's 'long march through the institutions,' that is, the acceptance of formerly extreme ideas into government, the media, and the education system.

It is now normal, for example, for patriotism to be seen as a vice, and anti-Western or anti-American attitudes a virtue. It is now normal to be obsessed with race or gender, or to always think of oneself as a victim of external forces.

More radical ideas have entered the conversation to some degree - like abolishing the police or national borders. Even the traditional nuclear family is something to be overthrown. The Antifa may not say it directly. He'll say he wants to *dismantle heteronormativity*. You can call a knife a culinary manipulative cutting implement, if you like. It still does the same job.

These ideas and many more have entered the mainstream. They are examples of what Yuri Bezmenov called 'ideological subversion,' which is about inverting normal, healthy values. We are in an upside down world, for example, when you have mass riots and looting in major cities, and large corporations come out in support of the rioters and donate money to their cause.

So, who is the new 'fascist' really? He - or she - is a counter revolutionary. He is a rebel against the revolution. He may once have been a leftist himself, but now rejects them. The new 'fascist' rejects the excesses of leftist beliefs. He believes in nations and borders. He is pro-Western, pro-European. He rejects white guilt and 'whiteness studies.' None of this makes him into the Antifa's straw fascist. It just makes him sane.

The new 'fascist' loves his country and wants to preserve its culture. He grants all other peoples the same rights to love their own countries and culture. He accepts a certain amount of multiculturalism into his own country as adding to it, but does not want to see his own culture displaced or diminished.

The new 'fascist' does not see masculinity as a disease, something to be controlled or cured. He grants that feminism has some validity, but he - or she - is quite prepared to also point out its flaws and falsehoods.

The new 'fascist' dislikes the leftist dominance in universities, and its divisive identity politics. He rejects the promotion of victim mentality, with its endless blaming and complaining. He is appalled by the rise of group think, and the push for censorship of those who reject far-left ideas. He opposes the mental thuggery that exists both inside and outside the university - as with the 'cancel culture' mob, and Antifa's efforts to harass those they disagree with.

The new 'fascist' is even more appalled by Big Tech's evident bias, as seen in the expulsion from Twitter, Facebook, and YouTube of dissident voices. He is disturbed by this creeping authoritarianism. The new 'fascist,' often against his or her will, has become a counter revolutionary.

This was not a war of his making. It was the radical leftist who started waging war on white males and Western nations, on reason, on history, on freedom of thought and speech. The new 'fascist' was slow to react, but eventually made the logical response. He began to play the game the far-left insisted on. He adopted his own form of identity politics and became - against his will - racially conscious. He began to resist the erosion of his own country and culture, and the intrusion of far-left ideas into its social institutions.

The new 'fascist' noted the howls of outrage from those who want to play the game of identity politics with only one set of goalposts, at one end of the field, and who want to referee it too. The new 'fascist' put a set of goalposts at the other end of the field, and told the leftist he wasn't refereeing the game anymore.

So, the new 'fascist' is not the sieg heiling Nazi, or the 'deplorable' the Antifa wants you to see. He is a rational being who has decided to play the game the leftist forced upon him while also forbidding him to play it.

It is true there are some right wing types who fit the Antifa's profile of a fascist. There *are* those who may be homophobic, favour traditional sex roles, and prefer to associate with members of their own race and culture. Some of those people are Antifa's own allies, but as they happen to be non-white, the Antifa ignores them. This is a pointer to the Antifa's fanatical obsession with whiteness, as well as his pathological need to rebel against his own society.

There are also plenty of white conservatives who fit that psychological profile to some degree. There is no denying that. But there are also many whites the Antifa would call 'right wing' who have no problem with homosexuality, who favour equal rights for women, and have no animosity towards people of colour.

At the same time, there are many members of the so called victim groups - women, gays, non-whites, and so on - who reject the victim status the far-left tries to impose upon them. They see far-left ideas as tedious or destructive. They have no need for the Antifa's revolution.

## Debate and the Authoritarian

So, why not just let people believe what they want to, and where ideas are in competition, let them fight it out?

You might think the Antifa is in favour of debate and the battle of ideas. This is not the case. The Antifa wants to stop the 'fascist' speaking at all. *The Antifa Handbook* includes a quote at the front stating that fascists are not there to be debated, but destroyed.

One might suppose they mean the literal fascists and Nazis from World War Two, but we must remember the term fascism now includes anyone who merely refuses to accept the Antifa's far-left ideas.

The Antifa has little or no interest in debate. This may seem odd. If the leftist's ideas are so inherently good, it should be easy to persuade others. That some people remain unconvinced is a great affront to the Antifa and his future Utopia. So, he is not going to bother debating people. He is going to win the debate by simply declaring himself the winner. The 'fascist' will not be allowed to speak at all.

You may wonder how this authoritarian behaviour squares with the supposed anti-authoritarian nature of Antifa. We must remember they have the almost religious conviction they are fighting a war of Good against Evil. They are happy to proclaim the 'righteousness' of their cause. Antifa believe they are acting from a higher moral authority, which gives them the right to 'nip in the bud' any trace of fascism.

It is easy to expose the hollowness of this claim.

## The Claim to Higher Moral Authority

The Antifa believes his moral authority comes from two main sources, one in the past and one in the future. From the past is the Nazis and the Holocaust. The Antifa believes, or at least pretends to believe, that the next Holocaust is always only just around the corner. If tiny sprigs of fascism are not stamped out immediately, Nazis and concentration camps will soon reappear. So, the Antifa flatters himself that his act of silencing right wing speakers is not an act of thuggery, but a heroic act of stopping the next Hitler.

The Antifa's other source of moral authority comes from the future. It is that ideal Marxist Utopia in which he believes, a place so wonderful only the evil could stand in its way.

This is the Antifa's scam: to point to the worst possible outcome of his opponents' belief system - the Holocaust - and the best possible outcome of his own - the future imagined paradise. *See*, he says, I'm *creating Heaven and resisting Hell, at the same time*. This is his justification for silencing his political enemies.

The Antifa's claim to a higher moral authority is hollow. For a start, his future Utopia is hypothetical only and we're asked to take it on faith. But why should we believe today's fanatical leftist authoritarians are capable of creating any kind of paradise?

More seriously, by invoking Holocaust-prevention as his source of moral authority, the Antifa is ignoring his own side's catastrophes. If Antifa aligns with communism - as it does - and 'fascism' with Nazism, you only have to point out that far more people were killed by communism than ever were by the Nazis. Stalin, Mao, and Pol Pot between them are responsible for many millions of deaths. Yet the Antifa wants to claim some kind of high moral ground as the basis of his actions.

The Antifa says his justification for stamping out right wing ideas is preventing the next Holocaust. The right winger may as well say he's entitled to stamp out the slightest trace of Marxism in order to prevent the next Cultural Revolution, or 'Gulag Archipelago,' to quote the title of Solzhenitsyn's book about the Russian prison camps.

The Antifa might try to disavow communism. *I know about the Gulags, but we want socialism, not communism.* But as the Antifa's scam is guilt by association, that excuse won't do. As soon as there's the slightest whiff of what he sees as right wing ideas, the Antifa wants to stamp out the next Hitler. If he is so concerned for the future, why not apply the same vigilance to stopping the next Stalin?

Here you have the usual leftist double standards. On one hand, they've got a hair-trigger, hyper-vigilance about 'fascism,' so the merest hint of it and they go into panic mode and spring into action. At the same time, they've got this cavalier, reckless approach to their own vaguely perceived future world which couldn't possibly go wrong. They'll ignore all past communist atrocities as mere 'mistakes' and move forward with I'm-better-than-you righteousness and the blind optimism it's all going to work out just fine.

If we're going to play the 'Never Again' game on the basis of past atrocities, both sides could easily play it. But look which side is *actually* doing it - censoring and 'cancelling' people - to see which side are the real authoritarians.

The Antifa's mindset is *After Hitler, Never Again*. The right winger could claim the same bogus moral authority by saying: *After Stalin, never again*. But the 'fascist' does not do that because, unlike the Antifa, he is not a fascist. He knows it is absurd to claim that the slightest hint of a given idea automatically ensures the worst possible outcome of that idea.

You could make the case that conservative values have led to countries that were stronger and more cohesive than most Western countries are now. You could also propose a new version of that sort of society which retains fair recent progressive reforms - more freedom for women, acceptance of homosexuality, and so on - but rejects far-left extremist ideas. It's no Utopia, but at least it's attainable.

## The Fanatic's Guide to Free Speech

The Antifa is fully entitled to pursue his ideal world and no one should prevent him. The problem is, the Antifa does not give his opponents the same right. The hardcore Antifa is not a fool, but he is a fanatic who feels entitled to control the speech of others. He claims the moral right to prevent people expressing views he doesn't like.

When you point out that this violation of free speech seems hypocritical, the Antifa says he's not against free speech *per se*, only against those who use it in the service of fascism. He's actually in *favour* of free speech. You see, when we get to the Antifa's new perfect world, everyone will be just *swimming* in free speech. But in order to get to that beautiful place, we have to go through a brief reign of terror when every trace of right wing thought is smashed and stamped out. So if you'll forgive this temporary period of fanatical leftist oppression, very soon the Golden Age of freedom will be here.

In other words, the Antifa is one hundred percent in favour of free speech as long as whatever is said is approved by the Antifa. Everything else will be banned.

## Antifa: No Accountability, No Self Criticism

The Antifa will rarely practice any self criticism, or admit that the policies he supports have caused major social problems. He'll support multiculturalism as part of his globalist vision, for instance, but also push ideas like white privilege and 'whiteness studies.' Having supported a risky social experiment and also done his best to sabotage it, the leftist will never blame himself when it doesn't work out. He'll just point to *all those white racists*.

The Antifa will never admit his policies have failed, or had negative effects. He won't admit that the victim and blame mindset, and the whole oppressor-oppressed framework, have been disastrous. He won't see that setting various groups against each other is a bad idea, or that the so called far-right is a reasonable response to the far-left. None of this is ever the leftist's fault. It is all the *fascist's* fault for not accepting the leftist's divine vision, for not believing in his ideal future world.

The Antifa will rarely consider that his core assumptions may be wrong. The idea of equality, that all humans are interchangeable, that gender and race are 'social constructs,' that diversity is a strength. The Antifa believes these ideas not because they are true, but because he *wants* them to be true.

The hardcore Antifa won't accept that his false assumptions may lead to poor results. He may even see social problems and upheaval as a good sign, as part of his ongoing revolution. He may revel in the chaos. It's all part of the rebellious joy of destroying old social structures. And once 'old' society is in turmoil and finally collapses, the Antifa thinks he'll be there to create something better.

The Antifa has a blind faith in his future world. He believes everything is 'socially constructed' anyway, so why not start from scratch and build it all up again from ground zero? There's no such thing as nature, to the hardcore leftist. Everything is malleable. So all that tribalism, those inbuilt 'irrational biases' - they can all be overcome by the power of education. All those millennia of biology and culture will fall away once the Antifa puts the correct *education* in place.

It's no coincidence these academics have such faith in education. That's their own domain. They believe the academics should be put in charge. They think all social ills can be cured with the right training. There's no end to their ambitions when it comes to social engineering.

The Antifa is, therefore, an optimist. But his rejection of the idea of nature may be one of those false premises that gets his enterprise off on the wrong foot to begin with. That, along with his fanatical, authoritarian behaviour, means that plenty of others don't share the Antifa's optimism about his ability to create a better world.

## Finding Utopia

There's little doubt the Antifa acts from good intentions. Any reasonable person knows this, and does not stop the Antifa expressing himself or pursuing his dreams. Yet the Antifa does not return the favour. He believes the 'fascist' is evil, and wants to control him.

The Antifa's belief he has the right to silence others is based on the false idea that his own cause aligns with moral good and his opponent's with evil. It is justified by spurious claims to higher moral authority, and by pointing to the worst possible outcome of his enemy's values and the best possible outcome of his own.

The Antifa often fails to understand his enemy's character or to look at the enemy's ideas objectively. The Antifa also fails to examine his own character and ideas, especially the false premises he may have accepted. The Antifa is too quick to condemn his enemy's failures and excuse his own. He is too attached to ideas that he wants to be true, even if they aren't.

Still, the Antifa should be allowed to pursue his Utopian world. Ideally, the Antifa should be given a state or a city. All who want to take part in the experiment should be allowed to live there. The inhabitants should be given free rein to run their society with progressive leftist ideals. It would be instructive to all of us to see how it worked out.

As for the Antifa's influence in the rest of the world, his views should be seen as just one opinion among many. The Antifa does not have any moral authority to silence his perceived opponents. As soon as he tries, he has lost all credibility and should be treated as just one more religious fanatic.

# 25

# The Hall Gang

I left Angie alone for the rest of the day. She was away all the next day as well, and the one after that. I assumed Hall's intervention had failed and Ange had decided to sever ties. But on the third day, Friday, she came back. She walked into my room and sat down.

'I went to class yesterday,' she said. 'For the first time since... what happened.'

There was a silence. Finally I had to break it with a prompt. 'Was everything OK?'

Her words came out in a rush.

'I felt like a leper. No one would look at me. I'd feel them taking little sneaky glances. As soon as I looked up, they'd turn away.'

'What about Nina?'

'She's ghosted me.'

'That's pretty lousy.'

'Yeah. Then again, I used to be like that too. A bully, I mean.'

I let that slide.

'It'll blow over,' I said. 'Give it time.'

'I don't really care anymore,' said Ange. 'I'm thinking of dropping the course.'

'That's a bit drastic.'

'Look who's talking. Teacher.'

She had me there.

'Why don't you take a term off?'

'That's what Daddy said too.' She winced. 'I hate to think how much embarrassment I've caused him.'

'It's not your fault everyone's insane. You realise they're all mad, don't you?'

'I'm starting to *get it*.'

She laughed. 'Maybe I should become a fascist like you.'

I couldn't tell if she was joking.

'How'd you go with Hall?' I said cautiously. 'Have your views changed at all?'

'I'm not sure. That's why I need some time off. I've got to have a rethink. Change a few things.'

'Including me?'

She looked at me and smiled.

'John, you're one thing I *don't* want to change.'

I felt a rush of emotion - hope, relief, and a dash of terror all at once. I felt lightheaded, and turned away to compose myself. Ange didn't seem to notice.

'The future's all cloudy,' she said. 'Right now, I've just got to look after the basics - like paying the rent. That's why Mateo's got to go. He's three months behind.'

'Why didn't you say?'

Angie shrugged. 'Couldn't admit I was wrong,' she said. 'Anyhow, I can't cover for him anymore. Let's go give him notice.'

'Now?'

'Should have been weeks ago.'

We walked through the living room and up the hallway, then Angie knocked on the door of what used to be her room. After a few seconds, Mateo opened the door a crack and showed his face.

'Can you come out please?' said Ange. 'We need to talk.'

There was a pause. Mateo stared at us for a bit. We could hear the baby crying inside the room.

'It's not a convenient time,' he said. 'Come back tomorrow.'

'It won't take a minute,' said Ange politely.

'Later,' said Mateo. 'Busy now.'

He closed the door. Angie and I turned to each other. I took the door handle, pushed the door open, and stepped into the room. It was surprisingly neat. With the three of them sharing, I'd assumed it would be a chaotic mess, but everything was orderly and in place. Liana was sitting on the bed rocking the baby. It was enough to trigger an automatic sense of guilt - which I squashed.

'Step outside, please,' I said to Mateo.

With a sulky look, Mateo came out into the hallway. The three of us walked to the living room. Ange and I sat on the sofa; Mateo took a chair opposite. Ange got straight to the point.

'Do you have the rent?'

'Sorry,' he replied. 'Not much work this month.' This was at the restaurant where he was employed.

'I'm sorry about that,' said Ange. 'But you're way behind. You need to pay now or we'll all be evicted.'

Mateo flared up.

'They cut my shifts. That's not my fault.'

Angie remained calm.

'It's not my fault either - and I don't see why it has to be my problem. They've cut my shifts too. At the college. You know, where I used to be your teacher. So, I need your rent.'

Mateo shrugged.

'I'll give it to you when I give it to you.'

'That's not good enough,' said Angie.

'I've got a baby to feed.' said Mateo.

It was Angie's turn to shrug.

'That won't work on me anymore. It's time you found somewhere else to live.'

A petulant look came over Mateo's face. Petulant and sly.

'So you *are* a racist.'

The dirty bugger. Clearly, he knew about Angie's recent scandal. I wondered if she would cave. This was her kryptonite, after all - but there was a new steel about her.

'You know what, Mateo? That's not going to work on me anymore either. Besides, if you think I'm a racist, why do you want to live here?'

I could see his brain ticking over, trying to work out the best response to that. Angie continued before he could find it.

'I'm giving you two weeks' notice to move out.'

Mateo hadn't expected that. His face was like an emoji of surprise, his hairy eyebrows adding to the effect. He tried to backpedal fast.

'Hey, give me another week. I'll get your rent.'

'Too late,' said Angie. 'I took you in and gave you a home. Now you've got the nerve to call me a racist. You prick. I want you out of here.'

'What about Liana and Alonso? said Mateo, his face turning all sad-emoji. 'Where are we going to go?'

'That's your problem,' said Ange, standing up, 'and I've got enough of my own.'

I stood up as well. Mateo kept his seat.

'I'd give you notice in writing,' said Ange, 'but you don't actually live here. You're a squatter. Go squat somewhere else.'

Later in the pub, we recounted the incident to Hall over a beer. Hall nodded his approval.

'Well, if that ain't a pivotal moment, I don't know what is,' he said. 'Antifa-Ange would never have done it. Squatter's rights are a big thing for you anarchists, aren't they? And now you've gone all fascist landlord on Mateo's arse. I'd never have believed it.'

Angie sipped her beer and smiled.

'Squatter's rights are good in theory, until you're the one who has to actually pay the bills. I feel like an idiot putting up with it so long.'

'Let's hope he goes quietly,' I said. 'We don't want any trouble.'

'Should have thought of that before, old boy,' said Hall. 'No good deed goes unpunished. You were asking for trouble soon as you let him in the front door.'

'That was my fault,' said Ange. 'I didn't even ask.'

Ange looked sheepish.

'Sorry, John. I look back at myself and cringe.'

I placed my hand on her arm.

'We've all been there,' said Hall. 'At least you had the sense to grow out of it. Some never do. Does this mean you've walked away from the left?'

She stared at him.

'I've walked away from *them*. Doesn't mean I've gone right wing, ok?'

Hall smiled.

'Turn to the dark side, Ange,' he said. 'You won't have to walks on eggshells anymore, tiptoeing round thousands of invisible micro aggressions.'

'Because you're racist and sexist anyway?'

'Because we're not a bunch of moral puritans who take themselves way too seriously. Try it. You'll like it.'

'I'll drink to that,' I said. The three of us raised glasses and clinked them together.

I hoped this would be a turning point in our affairs. The online abuse against Angie had died down. The absurd furore over the Peeny song was last week's news and the vultures had moved on to fresh prey. We spent the weekend in a state of cautious optimism about the future, although we didn't discuss it in detail. On the Sunday, however, we woke to a new wave of online attacks. The source was soon clear. Several of the hostile tweeters linked back to a short item on a minor left wing news site.

**Racist Evicts Family of Colour**

Infamous right wing folk singer, Angie Gardiner, is well known for her collection of racist songs that mock people of colour. But words are not enough for this budding white supremacist - she's gone to the next stage and put words into action. Gardiner is now trying to evict a family of colour from her home in Sydney's affluent Eastern suburbs.

Asylum seeker, Mateo Caceres, moved into a spare room in Gardiner's twelve bedroom mansion. When his young wife arrived with their infant son, Gardiner reportedly tripled the rent, then gave the young refugee family an eviction notice when they were unable to pay. She then threatened to enlist far-right extremists to throw the Caceres family onto the streets.

I stopped reading.
'I've heard of fake news,' I said, 'but this is ridiculous.'
   'I'm not right wing!' said Ange.
   'You're not even a folk singer,' I added.
   'Where's this twelve bedroom home I'm supposed to own? I'm only twenty-five!'
   'They're just making it up - but people seem to believe it.'
   I pointed at Angie's Twitter feed, which was full of leftist attack dogs abusing her.
   'That's it,' said Ange. 'I'm going off Twitter for good.'
   There was also an email from her employer, the Language College of Sydney.

Dear Angie,

Due to breaches of contract, we are unable to continue our partnership. First, as a language provider, we liaise closely with international bodies and have a commitment to diversity and inclusion. You recently performed a song online which violates our policy on hate speech. The song has traumatised our clientele. Some students no longer feel safe to continue their studies with you on our staff.

Second, we have been made aware that you gave lodgings to a former student of this college. Inappropriate relationships between teachers and students are a breach of your employment contract. Should this become a legal matter, understand that you will be fully liable for any consequences.

In light of these contract breaches, your employment is terminated, with immediate effect. Thank you for your services to the Language College of Sydney, and we wish you every success in your future career.

Warm regards,
J.Z. Robson.


Ange passed me the message. I had just finished reading it when her phone rang. When she saw who the caller was, she put it on speaker phone.

'Angie, are you alright?'

'I'm fine, Dad.'

'Look, what's this rubbish about you being a white supremacist? I'm getting abusive emails at uni. Is this some kind of right wing prank?'

'No, it's the idiots from Antifa.'

'What are you talking about? They're the good guys.'

Angie sighed.

'No, Dad. They're not.'

She glanced at me.

'I haven't got time to talk about it now. I'll come over later and explain.'

'Please do - and bring John.'

'Sure. Look, Dad. Whatever these people are telling you, ignore it. I've made a mistake, but don't worry. I'm going to clear up the mess - and then some.'

She hung up, and sat down on the bed.

'I. Am. Done. These people are nuts.'

'Walk away, Ange. You won't look back.'

She nodded.

'You don't have to talk me into it anymore. I don't know where I'm going - but anywhere will do as long as it's away from them.'

I put my hand on her shoulder, and fancied I could feel her heartbeat racing nineteen to the dozen.

'I'm done too,' I said. 'Done being nice. There's only one way that website found out about the eviction.'

I turned on my heel.

'John, what are you doing?'

I faced Angie.

'Something I should have done a long time ago.'

I left the room and strode up to the other end of the house, Ange following. I knocked on Mateo's door. There was no answer, so I knocked again. Finally, the door opened a crack.

'What do you want?' came a voice from inside.

'Get out here now.'

The door shut again. I pushed it open, hard, and it slammed into Mateo's head. I grabbed him by the shirtfront and pulled him out into the hallway. I shoved him against the wall, feeling a fury that surprised me.

'You're leaving,' I said. 'Now.'

'Hey, I've got two weeks' notice.'

'I'm giving you two minutes notice. Pack your things and leave.'

'I've got a wife and baby. Where we gonna go?'

'You should have thought of that before you sicked your mob of leftist thugs on *my* wife, last night.'

It was only later I realised what I had called Angie. I turned to her now.

'Ange, go and get our suitcases. We'll gift them to Mateo and Liana and help them pack.'

'You bastard,' said Mateo. 'Everyone's going to hear about this. Everyone's going to know what a big racist you are, you white Aussie dog.'

'I don't give a fuck. Come back here and I'll kill you.'

Liana, came out of the room, holding the baby, and started to cry. My mood changed. I flashed back to the night of the refugee film. Maybe I *was* a bastard. I held up my hand in a half apology.

'I'm sorry, Liana. Look, guys, I don't wish you any harm, but you were only supposed to stay a few days. Let's do this the easy way. We'll help you pack your stuff, then I'm going to hire a truck. You're on your own from there. Just like the rest of us.'

I felt through the pockets of my pants, found my wallet, and pulled out couple of fifty dollar notes.

'I'll add another hundred to this to get you a few nights in a hostel. But that's it.'

Mateo looked sulky, but Liana whispered something to him. Ange was watching all the while but didn't interrupt.

'Do you want us to help you pack?' I said.

'That's alright, Johnny,' said Liana. 'We'll be OK.'

I nodded, relieved at the peaceful resolution. 'It's ten o'clock. I'll hire a truck for twelve.'

I held out my hand to Mateo. He threw me a surly look, but Liana gave him a nudge. Slowly, he raised his hand and we shook.

'Sorry, guys,' I said. 'I know it's not easy. Best of luck to you all.'

Later that evening, Hall dropped over once more. He was going to stay a couple of nights, then fly back to Melbourne.

The three of us sat around the kitchen table with a bottle of wine.

'So what's all this now?' said Angie. 'We're a gang of Nazis - is that it?'

'In the eyes of Antifa,' I said, 'I suppose we are. Really, we're just normal people. Westerners in the Wild West.'

'We're not going to turn back the clock, are we?' Ange continued. 'Back to the days of racism and sexism and all that from the 1950s.'

'No,' said Hall. 'We'll keep what was right about the sixties revolution. All the decent reforms. We don't want to go back to the fifties. But we'll dump the rubbish from today too, and bring back the best of the past. Make something new.'

'A new revolution?' said Ange.

'Only against what really deserves it. No more censorship. No more falling for the white guilt con job, or teaching kids to hate their own society. Tell the far-left they don't own universities any more. Tell 'em we're not going to bow down to identity politics, or their precious feelings. It's on for young and old, and they'd better get used to being offended.'

'What if they don't like it?' I said. 'What if the censorship and control gets even worse? They might make all that illegal.'

'Well then, said Hall, 'That'll make us outlaws.'

'The Hall gang,' said Ange.

'If you say so,' said Hall. 'Like three bushrangers that came before, in the early years of this colony. Ben Hall, Frank Gardiner, and Johnny Gilbert. Wild colonial boys - and the way of the outlaw may not be easy. Hall and Gilbert died with their boots on, and Gardiner's fate is unknown, lost in the mists of time. Still, it's better to die on your feet than live on your knees.'

We raised our glasses in a toast. I looked at Angie, and remembered the rabid leftist she'd once been. Her politics had been no act of rebellion, but submission. The real revolutionary act was her escape.

As for Edward Hall, his past was a mystery. Where had he come from? Perhaps one day he'd tell us his own story.

So ends the tale of how I changed from mild mannered John Gilbert into the kind of man I would once have feared and despised. I was still a stranger to myself. Yet, to my new mind, not as strange as the man I once was.

If you want to conquer evil, you have to understand it. To understand it, you may need to become it. When you become it, you may learn that evil was something different all along. If I was evil now, it was because being good no longer made any sense. Good, as we were once taught to define it.

You should never look a gift horse in the mouth. If it's a wooden horse, however, you should check it for termites. Especially if that horse takes the form of beautiful ideas of love and justice. Wars are fought in the mind as well as on the battlefield. It's conquest by concept - with an emphasis on the con.

We have been deceived for too long, and always by those who tell us they are the most moral, the most honest, or the most wise. It could be a newsreader, a teacher, a foul mouthed youth in a black mask, or the most well spoken politician in the world. From now on, all bets are off, for these people have lost our trust. It will be a long time before it's ever regained.

In the meantime, I'll throw in my lot with Hall and Ange. Where this path leads is anyone's guess. I'll follow it to the end, and there may be further tales from the culture war along the way.

This war may one day come to an end. Or perhaps it'll just roll on until Doomsday. I like to think some greater reality will finally emerge, beyond the fictional realities that currently keep us enthralled. We will wake from our trance, rub our eyes, and look back in wonder at all the follies we used to believe.

# Author's Note

I have written on controversial topics before, but never thought I would write a book dealing with the topic of racism so directly.

It was already a touchy subject, but exploded in 2020, with all the race riots and protests in America. Various activists are demanding that we do not ignore the issue of race and racism, but confront it. That is what I have done in this book, although perhaps not in the way they would like.

I respect all races and wish them well, but refuse to have my own singled out for attack.

Some of the incidents in this story are made up, some are based on real events. I did attend that speaking tour by Stefan Molyneux and Lauren Southern in 2018. It should go without saying that these two are not 'Nazis' despite what those who protested their tour would have you believe.

This book is dedicated to free speech and free thought, and all who protect them.

**If you liked this book, *Conquest By Concept*, help spread the word. Tell a friend… or five friends. You support is important, and much appreciated.**

**Website - www.vortexwinder.com**


**Books By Duncan Smith**

The Vortex Winder
The Maelstrom Ascendant
Cultown
The Vast and the Spurious
The Tightarse Tuesday Book Club


**Albums By Lighthouse XIII**

Waves Upon Waves
Vortex Winder
The Maelstrom Ascendant
Cultown


**Contact**

Alfadex Books can be contacted on matthew.alfadex@gmail.com.

'oppression porn for feminists' and says it's only a matter of time before a black American writes a novel where slavery is restored.

Jones' crooked agent tells him to delete the review and write the slavery book himself. Jones does so, putting it out under the pen name, 'Marla Okadigbo,' supposedly a black American woman. The book is a hit until the author's true identity is revealed. It then becomes a scandal, and perception of the book changes from a story of the struggle for black liberation to one of oppression by white supremacists.

Meanwhile, Jones is haunted by the spirit of the real Marla, a black slave from the early 1800s, and feuds with his girlfriend, Sonia, a white English teacher struggling to help school students in the poor neighbourhood where she works.

**The Vortex Winder**

When fading rocker, Jimmy Brandt, saves the life of an insect, his own life is forever changed. The insect turns out to be an advanced being who gives him the 'Vortex Winder,' a device which grants a different special power each week. Each power leads to unexpected results.

Jimmy makes a comeback to rock music and records his album. Yet his comeback is a quest within a quest. Driven by the Vortex Winder, Jimmy makes an amazing journey. From a simple job interview, to a love affair in Germany, or a harrowing stint in a foreign prison, the adventures of Jimmy Brandt are always a surprise. Trailed by his mentor, Iolango, and his tormentor, Elijinx, Jimmy follows the events of his life to a stunning conclusion.

**The Maelstrom Ascendant**

Rocker Jimmy Brandt has given up on his dreams. He's settled down in the suburbs with his girlfriend and cat... until strange forces tempt him back to his former life. Soon he faces a choice between good and evil - and life is so rewarding when you turn to the dark side.

Flying high again, Jimmy battles divas, despots, and most of all, himself. Yet the higher you fly, the further you can fall. Only an old, forgotten friend can save him. But does he want to be saved?


**Cultown**

Thomas Swan forms the Milinish, a cult with an odd mix of scientific and religious beliefs.

From humble beginnings in Sydney, the Milinish moves overseas to become the fastest growing cult in America. Yet Swan's mad reign spirals out of control. Finally, on the brink of disaster, he decides to tell all.

Here, in the ultimate inside story, Thomas Swan reveals the secrets and scandals inside the Milinish, the greatest cult of the 21st century.

*'Exposes not just the cultishness of religion, but of science too. This is the best novel yet written on the trouble between science and religion.'*
J. Williams, Fuse.

# Lighthouse XIII Albums

**Waves Upon Waves**
Mountain Gods, SMS: Save My Sanity, Between the Stairway and the Highway, Reaper Bones, Leuchtturm, LHXIII, Temporary Kingdom, Retro Stereo, Waves Upon Waves, New World Alchemy.

**Vortex Winder**
Vortex Winder, Road Rage, Trade Winds, Black Art, Life Line, Spark, Z Club, Epitaph, Elijinx, Oceanus.

**The Maelstrom Ascendant**
Black Phoenix, High and Mighty, The Price of Dominion, Moonlight Tiger, I for an Eye, Haunted, Death Bed Regrets, Extinction.Net, Quitter, The Maelstrom Ascendant, The Ephemeral and the Eternal.

**Cultown**
Amnesia, Skeptic Eclectic, Evil But Not Vile, In Nihilum, Cultown, Helix Eternal, Doom Pipers, Fallen to a Higher Place, The Scythe and the Scalpel, Triangle of Fire, Transcendence, The Cultimate Culminates.